"VIDAL POSSESSES SUCH OBVIOUS WIT AND INTELLIGENCE...

DULUTH

is a book so radical in approach (even for Vidal) that it is certain to delight and surprise some readers while boring and disgusting others. Imagine... a mixture of *Dallas*, *Close Encounters of the Third Kind*, and *Mary Hartman, Mary Hartman* penned by a schizophrenic creator who imagines himself to be part Barbara Cartland and part Vladimir Nabokov, and you'll find a rough idea of what Vidal has concocted... Vidal demonstrates a keen eye for the trivialities and absurdities on which Americans spend so much of their emotional (and literal) currency. In particular, his portrait of the upper class— forever fussing over tax shelters, face lifts, nose jobs and the latest chic fashions—is wonderfully nasty."

Los Angeles Times

"MAKES YOU LAUGH OUT LOUD...VIDAL MANAGES TO INFUSE MOST OF THE NOVEL WITH AN OUTRAGEOUS ABANDON EQUAL TO THE BEST OF *SATURDAY NIGHT LIVE*."

The Miami Herald

"If S. J. Perelman and Max Shulman had collaborated on an X-rated film for the Marx Brothers, it might have been the basis for DULUTH. Add to this the insanity of the Mad Hatter's tea party, provided the title was changed to *Malice in Wonderland*, and you have some faint idea of what goes on in this book...outrageously, hysterically funny...if you like burlesque at its wildest and rowdiest form, this is for you."

San Diego Union

DULUTH

GORE VIDAL

BALLANTINE BOOKS • NEW YORK

Library of Congress Catalog Card Number: 82-40126

ISBN 0-345-31220-1

This edition published by arrangement with Random House, Inc.

Manufactured in the United States of America

First Ballantine Books Edition: December 1984

for Richard Poirier

1

Duluth! Love it or loathe it, you can never leave it or lose it.
Those words—in bright multicolored neon-blaze from atop
the McKinley Communications Center Tower, the highest
point in busy downtown present-day Duluth.

If, as it has been so often said, every society gets the Duluth that it deserves, the United States of America in the last
but one decade of the twentieth century has come up with a
knockout.

From the rows of palm trees on Duluth's languorous lake
front to the elegantly better homes and gardens on Garfield
Heights to the tall obsidian towers of McKinley Center, two
million human beings have their being in a dynamo of city
where their nonbeing is provided for in a superbly landscaped cemetery, known as Lincoln Groves.

All appetites are catered for in Duluth. From casual lake-
front sex to warm meaningful relationships in the ethnic barrios at the glittering desert's edge, there is something—if not
someone—for everyone. There is also gambling at The
Dude Ranch at the end of brothel-lined Gilder Road as well
as social climbing and contract bridge at any number of private clubs of which the most exclusive is The Eucalyptus,
set on a high hill overlooking the Duluth Woods, at whose
verdant heart there is a swamp known to insect-lovers the
world over as a unique macrocosm of insect life, vermiforous and otherwise. Duluth's proud claim to be the bug capital of the world is no idle boast.

Small wonder then that Tulsa-born and -bred Beryl

1

Hoover has a sense of being home at last as she plumps herself, dolphinlike, beside Edna Herridge in Edna's reliable old station wagon with the legend "Herridge Realtor" on its dusty door.

"Mrs. Hoover . . ." Edna begins, starting up her jalopy.

"Beryl . . ."

"Beryl . . . Edna."

"Edna?"

"I am Ms. *Edna* Herridge."

"So you are. My mind was elsewhere." Beryl's mind is indeed elsewhere. She has just observed through the frosted glass of the car window—the month is chill February and though it is only noon, the lights of the aurora borealis fill the entire southern sky like the long cold fingers of some great metaphor—a number of white men slowly hoist from the frozen ground a black man with a rope that has been slung over the branch of a tree. As the white men all pull together, the black man slowly leaves the ground for whatever afterlife the Supreme Author may be writing for him.

"I believe, Edna, that a Negro is being lynched."

"You'll love Duluth. I can tell." Edna revs up her jalopy's motor. "We have excellent race relations here, as you can see. And numerous *nouvelle cuisine* restaurants." Edna swings into Main Street, glittering from the recent snowfall that has turned Duluth into a winter wonderland where cars skid, pelvises and femurs snap on the ice-slick pavements, and Edna's brother, the Mayor, appeals, yet again, for all-around good humor as opposed to the more expensive snow-removal units that City Hall cannot afford. Good humor he gets, certainly.

"You are from Tulsa, of course." Edna races through her third red light; then skids on two wheels at the corner of Garfield and Main. "This is Garfield Avenue. The promenade of Duluth's elite. Houses range from one hundred Gs to the chill mill. Bitter—that is, better—homes cost more."

"For me, the sky's *not* the limit," says Beryl, with a laugh. But, of course, it is. Beryl is a divorcée *cum* widow

2

with money. A lot of it. The result of having taken oil-rich Mr. Hoover to the cleaners. At least that is the story that she has seen fit to bruit about Duluth, where face value is the universal currency and the one thing at which everything is taken.

A figure of some allure, Beryl is addicted to basic black, even when she goes to her Tulsa office where she personally keeps the books. From time to time, Pink Lady in hand, she can be seen at one or another of Tulsa's clandestine gambling casinos. She is something of a woman of mystery to the croupiers because she never bets.

Beryl is free—except for Clive, her son, whom she adores despite the fact that he has a nose like a flattened baked potato. Beryl is guilty about that nose because Clive inherited it from her even though a year *before* Clive's birth, the greatest of all rhino plasticeurs in Century City, Los Angeles, replaced Beryl's baked potato with a tiny *pomme soufflée* of a nose that took by storm all Tulsa—and will do the same in Duluth *if* Clive does not show up in town, wearing her former nose, thereby giving the game away. He must undergo surgery first, she thinks. "This is no place for Clive," she murmurs, as the station wagon skids along a wide avenue lined with gracious oaks whose frozen Spanish moss resembles . . .

"What was that, Beryl dear?"

"What was . . . ? Oh, I said that this is really the place to be alive! To live it up!" Beryl looks down at the glittering downtown area. On top of the McKinley Communications Center Tower the huge neon sign proclaims: "Duluth! Love it or loathe it, you can never leave it or lose it." Beryl frowns. "Just what does that sign mean? About not being able to leave or lose Duluth?"

"I don't really know," says Edna, evasively. "It's always been there," she adds.

"Is it true, do you think?" Like so many practical people, Beryl likes to ask questions.

"You must ask my brother. He's the mayor of Duluth.

3

And a real rotter.'' Edna turns off Garfield Avenue. ''Here's gracious home number one!'' The station wagon hurtles between a pair of Palladian plinths and into a huge snowdrift, where it comes to an abrupt halt.

''We are buried alive,'' says Beryl, grasping the point. ''In a snowdrift.''

'' 'Spring,' '' sings Edna, always the good sport, '' 'will be a little late this year.' ''

Right then and there, both girls know that they are going to become great chums in the days ahead, as they wait for the spring thaw.

''Rumor has it,'' says Edna, making conversation, ''that you were seen at The Dude Ranch last night.''

''Yes,'' says Beryl. ''It is one of the finest gambling casinos that I have ever sipped a Pink Lady in. Personally, I don't gamble but I love the sense of drama that you get when a fortune rises or falls on the mere turn of a card or a throw of the dice.''

''I suppose you know that no one knows who actually owns The Dude Ranch,'' says Edna, opening her window and poking the snow with a finger. The snow is packed absolutely solid. ''But The Dude—as he is universally known—is numero uno behind the scenes here in Duluth.''

''He is known as 'the will-o'-the-wisp,' '' says Beryl, ''back in Tulsa.''

''Sometimes I think that I know who—if not exactly what—he is,'' says Edna, somewhat kittenishly, under the circumstances.

''Yes?'' asks Beryl, pointedly. ''Then tell me his—or her—name.''

2

Captain Eddie Thurow of the Duluth Police Department—known to everyone as the DPD—is bewildered. He sits at his desk, holding the telephone to his ear with his arthritic shoulder, a painful business but Captain Eddie is into authenticity and since that is the way that the police chief in the new television series "Duluth" does it, that is the way that he is going to do it. Captain Eddie's speech last June on role models to the graduating class of Duluth's Huey Long High was all about role models—and a lot more, too. He is quite a guy, Captain Eddie, everyone agrees. In fact, many people think that he would make a swell mayor. As it happens, he is one of those many people.

Opposite Captain Eddie is a map of Greater Duluth, showing the winding Colorado River that empties into palm-lined Lake Erie as well as the primeval woods and the shimmering mirage-filled desert that begins just to the east of the city. At the point where the Colorado River intersects with the desert, there is a bright red thumbtack. This is where the spaceship landed on Christmas Day. It is now February and the spaceship is still there. To everyone's surprise, no one—or no thing—has ever come out of the spaceship. Worse, no one has been able to get inside the ship or even to make radio contact with the extraterrestrial aliens within. The thing just sits there in the desert, a block or so to the east of ethnic Kennedy Avenue where the barrios begin.

"You say, now I hope I got this straight." Captain Eddie's voice is deep. The police chief in "Duluth" can't pronounce his Rs. Captain Eddie can; and does. "That the FBI will not—repeat, will not—send a crew to determine what to do about this spacecraft filled with illegal aliens?"

As Captain Eddie listens to the voice from Washington, he squints his eyes the way that the well-known actor Ed Asner does on television.'

In the chair opposite Captain Eddie sits Lieutenant "Chico" Jones of Homicide. He is black. A token black, some say. But not "Chico." He prefers the word "colored" to the word "black." "Chico" is old-fashioned. He has not only wife trouble but money trouble, too. He cannot meet his mortgage payments, thanks to the high interest rates. To make ends meet, "Chico," like most of the guys and gals in the DPD, sells key-rings, tourist mementoes of Duluth, and angel dust on the side. But competition is stiff. Ends never do quite meet—except with his buddy, the spectacularly beautiful blue-eyed blond goddess Lieutenant Darlene Ecks, Homicide.

As they drive aimlessly about Duluth, they are, each agrees, good for each other. At least once a week, Darlene handcuffs "Chico" to the steering wheel of their police car and abuses him verbally. He likes this. He also like it when she pounces on illegal Mexican workers in the kitchens of the better Duluth restaurants and strip-searches them, all the while thundering out her own version of "Gimme a pig's foot and a bottle of gin," which is "Gimme a piece of okra and a pair of prunes!" Darlene has great humor. It is her dream one day to open a boutique just across the border from Duluth in Mexico so that "Chico" could visit her on Sundays. They have been lovers for a year. "Chico's" wife suspects the truth. For what it is worth.

Captain Eddie slams the phone down. "No dice!" he snarls at "Chico." "This is our show, they say. Our space-ship."

"In that case, why not just forget about it, Captain Eddie?" "Chico" has a way with him, even Captain Eddie has to admit that.

"You mean . . . ?"

"I mean . . ."

"You mean just . . . ?"

"I mean just . . ."

"*Forget* about it?" Captain Eddie looks very thoughtful indeed. Then he gets up and goes over to the map and with his right thumbnail he pries the red thumbtack out of the map. "Good thinking, 'Chico.' How is Darlene?"

"Chasing wetbacks."

Captain Eddie looks at the red thumbtack that he is holding in his hand. "All we have to fear now," he says slowly and thoughtfully, "is Wayne Alexander of the *Duluth Blade*."

"*Duluth Switch-Blade*," snorts "Chico," scornfully. The DPD does not like the numerous exposés of police brutality that Wayne Alexander has written over the years for the city's one newspaper, which is, admittedly, read only for its want ads and department store sales. But then nobody has read much of anything in Duluth since the day that KDLM-TV broke into the big time as *the* ABC affiliate and flagship for the Great Lakes and Tijuana area. Overnight the *Six O'Clock News* out of the McKinley Communications Tower was able to achieve demographics so colossal that the *Blade* has all but folded.

The news team at *Six O'Clock News* consists of one Oriental female, one Occidental male and one paraplegic Polynesian—a first for the Greater Duluth area, particularly in sports, where Leo Lookaloney is popular not only as an interviewer in the dressing rooms of the Duluth Tigers but as an occasional first base at charity games. These three anchorpersons preside over a program of city fires, conflagrations and holocausts beyond anything known to the rest of the country. That many of the fires are secretly set by the news team is an open secret in Duluth, where not only are grateful landlords able to collect insurance *on prime time* but Captain Eddie Thurow is able to go on the *Morning Show* at least once a month for three minutes to discuss his department's ongoing investigations of the fires.

As Captain Eddie thinks of Wayne Alexander, he loses his nerve. He puts the thumbtack more or less back where it was on the map, originally.

Little do Captain Eddie and "Chico" suspect what extraordinary events have been set in train by Captain Eddie's removal—even for a moment—of the thumbtack representing the craft from outer space from the map of Greater Duluth.

3

Inside the snowbank on Garfield Heights, Beryl and Edna are hitting it off like two houses afire.

"I always knew that one day I'd make it here to Duluth." Beryl daintily mops her face with Kleenex. The air is beginning to get a bit close inside the station wagon due to the intense conversation of the two girls. They have already used up several thousand ccs of oxygen and yet neither has really got much beyond the getting-to-know-you stage.

"I'm sure we'll find you the right mansion, Beryl honey." Edna has figured out that she has latched onto what they call in the realtors' book "a live one."

"Nothing that is not tasteful . . ."

"Tasteful is Edna Herridge's maiden name . . ."

"A view of your glorious lake front . . ."

"Natch."

"Your palm trees, your cherry blossoms on the ridge above the primeval Duluth Woods . . ."

"Not to mention the gorgeous swamp that is a macro-cosm of the higher insect life, the cerise spaceship . . ."

"The *what?*" Beryl has not counted on a spaceship as being part of the view from her manse high on Garfield Heights. She is not sure that she likes the notion. She says as much.

"Oh, it's a rather charming shade of cerise. I'm sure you'll like it, Beryl. We all do around here," Edna white-lies a bit. After all, she is a realtor.

"Well, I hope so." Beryl is dubious. "What does it look like?"

"Well, it's round. And—as I said—sort of red. It looks more like the head of a thumbtack than anything else."

"Maybe a trellis would hide it."

"So far nothing has come out of it."

"What's in it?"

"Aliens, I suppose."

"Mexicans?"

"Haitians. Boat people. Shriners. We're being destroyed from within, Beryl. You *are* a Republican, aren't you, sweetie?"

"There are no lefties in Tulsa, Edna."

"But you're not in Tulsa anymore." Edna is growing sus-picious. It would be just her luck to be trapped in a snowdrift on fashionable Garfield Heights with a Communist from Oklahoma.

Beryl laughs a tinkling laugh. "No. I'm in Duluth. I'm single. I am—if I may say so—attractive."

"Good enough to eat," says Edna, sincerely. Since the death of Mr. Herridge—Edna's tyrannical father—not a day has passed that she has not thought of joining Duluth's Sap-phic circle. But she wants to lose twelve pounds first and, so far, those twelve pounds continue to cling limpetlike to her slight frame. "I love your nose," says Edna.

Beryl flares her nostrils inadvertently, an effect not unlike that of a *pomme soufflée* getting its second wind. "Yes," she says, vaguely. Then she is purposeful. "Edna, I want to level with you. I also want your help. By this time next year I mean to be the social leader of Duluth.''

There is a long moment as the two girls gasp for breath in the now almost airless station wagon. White snow crushes against the windows on every side. Everyone in Duluth knows that since the hedgehog's shadow froze in November, the winter will be a long one. Question: Will the girls last until the first thaw?

''Social leader?'' wheezes Edna.

''*And* arbiter!'' gasps Beryl. ''I mean to replace Mrs. Bellamy Craig II with my own box at the opera. And a Eucalyptus Club lifetime membership.''

''I must put my thinking cap on,'' says Edna. ''You are asking for the moon, you know.'' Then Edna slumps across the wheel.

The air is now all gone save for one tiny cc of oxygen, which Beryl uses to repeat the magic name of the first lady of Duluth. ''Mrs. Bellamy Craig II. Here I come!'' But Beryl is not going anywhere in Duluth because The Supreme Eraser is now erasing her from *Duluth*. Bravely, she has fulfilled her function, which is exposition—something she hates. ''But ours not to choose,'' is her motto, as she goes on to yet another tale. She has prepared the way for Clive— almost. As the eraser expunges the last fragment of her identity, Beryl Hoover realizes that she has been murdered by The Dude, who will try to murder her beloved Clive. She must warn him. But how can she? She is already in a different book, *Rogue Duke* by Rosemary Klein Kantor.

4

Wayne Alexander strides purposefully up the icy steps of the Craig mansion, high on Garfield Heights.

The new English butler ushers Wayne into the palatial living room of the Craig home, where oates-colored drapes are shot through with golden threads and wall-to-wall tufted tourmaline fluffiness covers the floor, making not only for true elegance but for comfiness as well.

"Whom shall I say," asks the new English butler, "is calling she?" Wayne tells him his name and the new English butler goes.

As Wayne stands, looking out the picture window, he can see, just past the black towers of downtown Duluth, the sandy desert where the spaceship, like a cerise mole or beauty mark, is set.

Then Wayne feels two powerful arms embrace him from the back.

"Darling," he says, and turns—lips all puckered for that first kiss. But when he sees who it is, he gives a terrible cry.

Instead of Chloris, he finds, to his aghastment, the bearded face of Bellamy Craig II, whose own lips are puckered, all ready for *his* first kiss. As their eyes open and eye contact is duly made, four lips lose their pucker, four eyes their love-glow.

"Craig!"

"Wayne!"

"For God's sake, Craig, who did you think I was? I

mean, I've got on a man's suit," says Wayne, looking down to make sure that that is what he is wearing, which it is.

"Evelyn, actually. We had a date. I'm sorry, old boy. Carry on. Silly mistake. Could happen to anyone. Chloris won't mind. Ours is an open marriage, as you know. Have a Lark cigarette from this Tiffany box. Here. I'll light it for you with my Dunhill. Some Asti Spumante? Beer? Byrrh? Canada Dry, maybe?" Bellamy is a good host who never overdoes it. But then good taste is sovereign on Garfield Heights. Or as they say in the local French patois, *bon ton*, a phrase that rhymes with a certain delicious Chinese soup.

Wayne puts him at his ease. "That's O.K., Bellamy. I came to have a chat with Chloris."

"I know."

As they have now run out of big talk, they move, effortlessly, to small talk. "How do you think the Dodgers will do?" asks Wayne.

"They've got a good line. But that backfield . . ."

"Yes."

There is a pause. During this pause, a writer like Rosemary Klein Kantor would start hunting and pecking at the console of her word-processor, which is connected with a memory bank containing ten thousand popular novels. Rosemary only uses familiar types. She would take Bellamy, say, from an old best-seller classic like *Anthony Adverse*. Bellamy Craig II has a weak chin, which is entirely hidden by a beard that has been dyed black to take the place of the flaxen gold that mother nature originally intended for him. Bellamy is bald, with a skull full of interesting bumps, particularly over the ears. Bellamy's eyes are powder-blue, while his arms and legs work properly because he is not, as he likes to say, thank God, double-jointed, a condition much feared in Duluth, and for good reason. Bellamy's mother was once a Bohemian innkeeper in Key West, Florida, during the forties and fifties. Later, she started the first dinner theater in Duluth, the basis of the Craig fortune. It was at the dinner theater that she had the stroke that totally paralyzed

her on the opening night of *The Bird Cage* by Arthur
Laurents. She is now upstairs in the Craig mansion. She recognizes everyone who visits her, though no one does, actually.

Wayne Alexander is tall and Giacometti-fat. (Rosemary
also draws on films for her characters: *her* Wayne would be
like the late Dan Duryea in *The Little Foxes*.) The eyes are
hazel, because he has seen a lot. In fact, he has seen it all.
Before he joined the *Duluth Blade*, he was in Nam—or Viet
Nam, as he prefers to call it. He was a grunt, or soldier, as
he always says. He lost his right ear in an obscure engage-
ment. He will tell no one how or when or why.

But the pause has now been broken by Bellamy, making
conversation out of whole cloth. "What do you think is in
the spaceship?"

"Beats me," says Wayne. "It could be empty."

"That would be funny, wouldn't it?"

"I've been doing an exposé of the space program. I think
that they know exactly where it's from but they won't tell
us."

"Why, Wayne?"

During this next pause Mrs. Bellamy Craig II—née Duluth des Bois and a direct descendant of the city's French
founder—enters the room, shouting.

5

Just off ethnic Kennedy Avenue the barrios begin. Mile after
mile of paper and plywood shacks give shelter—if that's the
word—to almost one million illegal and legal Mexican

aliens. Every night the barrios are alive with mariachi music and joyous laughter because illegal aliens are essentially life-enhancing, since their deepest feelings are all on the surface while their shallowest feelings are hidden deep down—unlike the cold Anglos of Garfield Heights who cannot relate to one another without using as an intermediary a wise psychiatrist who will break the ice for them so that Dad can finally kiss Junior. Should there ever be really real people, really warm loving people anywhere on earth, it is those one million or so Chicanos who live in the barrios off ethnic Kennedy Avenue in East Duluth.

But there is also a lot of rage in the barrios, much of it directed specifically against Lieutenant Darlene Ecks. In fact, at this very moment of time, ten of her victims are meeting at the back of a shanty where, in the front room, peasant women with age-old Aztec faces are ironing tacos, folding enchiladas, stitching tortillas by the light of a single kerosene lamp. Sometimes one of the women will break into song—a high eerie birdlike song first sung aeons ago by the ancient Sumacs.

In the back room, the male victims squat in a circle, broad-brimmed sombreros over their eyes. They are all young, vital, sleepy. They are planning their revenge.

"Three times she strip-searches me," says Manuel. "Three times she says . . ."

Together all ten imitate Darlene's bellow: "Gimme a piece of okra and a pair of prunes." They shudder—in unison.

"She must die," says Armando.

"Macho is what macho does," says their quondam leader Manuel, pulling a knife from his belt.

But it is Benito—the youngest—who asks, "Muchachos, what is okra?"

They tell him.

"What is prunes?"

They tell him.

Benito—who had not minded all that much the two-hour

strip-search in the women's room of the Greyhound Bus Terminal—flushes with embarrassment and rage. *"Caramba!* She must die," he says, in Spanish. But then all the men are speaking Spanish to each other, as they are from Mexico.

6

Inside the station wagon, Beryl and Edna have long since breathed their last when Captain Eddie Thurow's Rescue Crew finally rescues them. As luck would have it, Lieutenant "Chico" Jones is in charge of this particular rescue. While the bodies of the two women are removed from the car and placed on stretchers, "Chico" bares his head in the falling snow. The other rescuers naturally follow suit.

"They are gone to a better world," says "Chico."

Actually, Edna has gone into "Duluth," the popular television series that is being filmed at Universal Studios for ABC, where she will play the part of a judge's alcoholic sister, while Beryl has been added to one of Rosemary Klein Kantor's Harlequin-style novels, set in Regency Hyatt England.

But "Chico"—who is all heart as well as all man—could not have known this. Nor can *we* ever know just what might have happened had Beryl Hoover ever confronted Chloris Craig and, *mano a mano*, fought with her for the social mastery of Duluth. That dream is over for Beryl. So, too, is her secret empire, which Clive—who is in mortal danger—will inherit.

Solemnly the rescue crew carry the two bodies, dusted

now with snow like a pair of Mayflower doughnuts, between those two plinths, which are only, as luck yet again would have it, a stone's throw from the mansion of the Bellamy Craig IIs.

7

Like most absolute laws, the fictive law of absolute uniqueness is relative. Although each character in any fiction—as in any life or nonfiction—is absolutely unique (even if you cannot tell one character from another), the actual truth of the matter is more complex.

When a fictive character dies or drops out of a narrative, he will then—promptly—reappear in a new narrative, as there are just so many characters—and plots—available at any given time. Corollary to the relative fictive law of absolute uniqueness is the *simultaneity effect,* which is to fiction what Miriam Heisenberg's law is to physics. It means that any character can appear, simultaneously, in as many fictions as the random may require. This corollary is unsettling and need not concern us other than to note, in passing, that each reader, like each writer, is, from different angles and at different times, in a finite number of different narratives where he is always the same yet always different. We call this *après* post-structuralism. The many studies that are currently being made of the *simultaneity effect* vividly demonstrate, as if demonstration is necessary! that although the English language may decline and dwindle, English studies are more than ever complex and rewarding.

The law of absolute uniqueness requires—except in those

cases where it does not—the total loss of memory on the part of the character who has died or made only a brief appearance in a fictive narrative. Naturally, when the writing of the book is finished all the characters who are alive at the end are available to other writers for reentries, as it were. Sometimes this is called plagiarism but that is a harsh word when one considers how very little there is in the way of character and plot to go around. Ultimately, plagiarism is simply—in the words of Rosemary Klein Kantor herself—*creation by other means*.

The characters that are in any given book—though abandoned by their author when he writes *finis* to his *opus*—will still continue to go through their paces for anyone who happens to read the book. Hence, the proof—or a proof—of the *simultaneity effect*. Once this particular true fiction or fictive truth is concluded by the present author (one able to give, as it were, the worm's-eye view of this Duluth—thus, the reader is warned), the Bellamy Craig IIs, Darlene Ecks, Captain Eddie, the whole vivid living (for now) crew will drift off to new assignments, unknown to them or him. They will forget him. He will not recognize them—except in those cases of Outright Plagiarism when civil law will scrutinize the truth of a fictive text with a thoroughness unknown even at busy Yale.

At this instant—in midcomposition—all the characters are at hand except for the two that have just died. Due to an anomaly in the law of absolute uniqueness, Edna Herridge still remembers, from time to time, that she was once a realtor in quite a different Duluth from the series "Duluth," with a brother who is the mayor. On the other hand, Beryl Hoover has totally forgotten her previous existence in these pages for the excellent reason that the part of *Rogue Duke* in which she first appears was written *before* Beryl's brief appearance and disappearance in our Duluth. Later, as Rosemary pens further installments, Beryl Hoover will then recall *Duluth*—and some very exciting unfinished business that involves Clive. At this point—still in the future—Beryl will try to find a way to warn Clive that The Dude will try to kill him just as The Dude killed her.

8

"Hello, Wayne," shouts Chloris Craig. She is, very simply, beautiful. Then she stops when she sees her husband, Bellamy, standing beside her lover, Wayne. Chloris tries to frown but the plastic surgeons who created her matchless beauty had slyly snipped the frown muscles.

"I was just on my way, Chloris." Bellamy is apologetic.

"I should think so," says Chloris.

The two men shake hands. The husband goes. The lover remains. Thus it has always been in Duluth's higher circles.

Wayne takes Chloris in his toothpick arms. Throws her onto the sofa with the Porthault sheets. They tear at one another's clothes. They make love among the shreds of Valentino's finest gingham. No matter. Chloris is rich.

Finally, lust slaked and sated, they smoke Larks as a new moon rises behind the plate-glass window and the aurora borealis flares in the southern sky over Tijuana.

Gently, Wayne traces a circle where Chloris's navel used to be. When the last team of plastic surgeons took the last tuck in her abdomen, they eliminated, by mistake, her navel. Now whenever Chloris wears a bikini, she must always remember to paint on a navel—using Elizabeth Arden's Pink Dawn. But as Chloris has no secret from Wayne except for the ones that she has, she never puts on a navel for him.

Chloris lets her hand rove, appreciatively, over Wayne's turgid powers. She prefers them tumescent, of course. But turgid is all right, too, because Wayne turgid is better than Bellamy tumescent.

"Did you bring it, Wayne?"

"Yes, Chloris. It's over there. In the Gucci briefcase on that Swedish Knole what-not. Do you want a gander?"

"Later. How much did you bring me this time?"

"The marriage with Henry James. That's all done."

"Good. Can he sue?"

"No. What I've written is in good taste. I've also described *Mother Wore Tights*. The whole picture, every reel. Because that's where she first met Herbert Hoover, on the set . . ."

"And they fell head over heels in love!" Chloris sighs. "God, how I worship that woman! And what a book I am going to make of her star-crossed life!"

As well as being the first hostess of Duluth, Chloris Craig, under the name "Chloris Craig," is known to readers everywhere as a top-selling author. Six of Chloris's books have scored all around the world. In fact, everyone who likes to read sooner or later reads "Chloris Craig." This is because *she gets inside her characters*, according to Virginia Kirkus, the only woman to have read every book ever written and so is seldom seen socially at literary gatherings or even at Frank E. Campbell's regular get-togethers for the old-timers.

But Chloris has a secret. Two secrets, in fact—except that Wayne is on to one of them. The first secret is that Wayne Alexander writes the books for her, a secret that he knows, naturally, as it is hard not to know when you've written a book for someone. The second secret—the one that he does *not* know but is beginning to suspect—is that Chloris has never read a book by "Chloris Craig" or a book by anyone else either. Chloris can only read three-letter words if they are in big enough print. That is why she became a writer. To compensate, as Dr. Mengers, her ears, nose and throat doctor would say—and, in fact, does say.

But Chloris does do a lot of research, if the subject happens to be alive or has known a lot of people who are still alive. She has a tape recorder (Sony) which she works with marvelous precision. KDLM-TV's one-hour special on "Chloris Craig" caused more than one Duluth housewife to rush out and buy a tape recorder and then try to work it the way that Chloris worked it on television. But none has ever succeeded because "Talent is innate. Genius divine," as Chloris herself said at the end of the program when she was able to record, erase, re-rerecord, both forward *and* backward, simultaneously, on the same disk, one thousand Wayne-selected words.

"*Why* was Betty Grable murdered, Wayne?"

This is an old dialogue between the lovers, dating back to their first date on the Persian Paradise Houseboat in the Colorado River that glamorous summer a decade earlier. One look at Wayne and Chloris had felt his turgid powers through corduroy trousers while he had shuddered at the thought of her seething delta beneath the tulle that she wore with an extra fillip over her bikini. She wanted literary fame. He wanted money. She his turgid powers; he her delta. She the name of Betty Grable's assassin; he the motive. Not since Heloise and Abelard Schroeder of Winona has a couple been so exquisitely attuned, one to the other.

"Betty Grable, after she met Herbert Hoover, fell in love with him. But then most women did. He was like that, women tell me."

"I've seen his pictures, Wayne. And I can believe it. That wonderful stiff collar. They don't make them like that anymore."

"Now, as I have been piecing together the events leading up to the murder in 1973, a pattern begins to emerge. In fact, the more that I study this book of yours which I'm writing, the clearer it gets. First, was Betty Grable absolutely positive that Herbert Hoover was really Herbert Hoover?"

"I don't understand you," says Chloris, directly.

"Was the love of her life really Herbert Hoover?"

"But surely, Wayne, the last scrawled message, with the lipstick, on the glass-topped table, those two words— 'Hoover love'—could mean only one thing . . ."

Thanks to Chloris's constant manipulation, Wayne's blood is swiftly being drained from his head to fill that tube which she cannot get enough of. But Wayne is now eager to tell her what he has found out before, as so often happens in their lovemaking, he faints dead away as he bestows—and captures—rapture. Wayne is now in a race with his own blood. Wayne can feel the crimson flood beginning to recede from his brain like the last of the bath water from a Carrara marble sunken tub. As everything starts to go black, he mounts her.

She cries out.

He blurts out, "The Hoover in lipstick was not . . ." Within the blazing magenta of her delta steams and seethes Wayne's purple tumescence. Ecstasy—and unconsciousness—is—or are—near.

"Who . . . ?" Although she is now yelping with esctasy, her steel-trap mind never ceases to try to trap info.

"It was . . . it was . . ."

Wayne comes. Chloris screams. Wayne faints. Chloris sleeps.

Through the picture window, one by one, the shy stars begin to fill up the blue-black sky, always careful to tip-toe 'round the shafts of light from the aurora borealis that makes Duluth by night so unique a wonderland.

9

While the *crème de la crème* disport themselves on Garfield Heights, Lieutenant Darlene Ecks, disguised as a virgin and carrying what look to be all her jewels and accessories in a string bag, is mincing through a mean part of the barrios just off ethnic Kennedy Avenue.

Suddenly a young would-be rapist comes up behind her, puts a wiry arm about her neck and drags her into a deserted hovel on whose walls "Viva Castro" has been painted over and over again by agents of the Federal Bureau of Investigation in order to make it seem as if Castro is behind all the disorder in the barrios when, actually, it is the FBI itself that instigates most of the riots.

"Gringa!" snarls the alien youth from Mexico. He tears the string bag from her nerveless hand. He empties it on the floor. First, the loot. Then the rape. This order of events proves to be his undoing. While he is examining the loot, Darlene tears off her virgin's outfit—a black and white polka-dot dress surmounted by a small band-box hat—to reveal the sexy Ecks body clad in its blue Duluth Police Department uniform, designed years earlier by Mainbocher but never out of fashion as anything in good taste will never be.

Darlene then draws a gun on the unsuspecting rapist, who is now grinning happily at the small color TV that she has packed among the other enticing goodies in the string bag.

"O.K., wetback. Put 'em up. You're under arrest."

The would-be rapist's eyes narrow when he sees what he has taken to be a defenseless virgin transformed before his eyes into a police lieutenant with a gun in her hand. He lets the string bag drop to the floor.

"Oh," he says. He puts up his hands.

Darlene is delighted with her catch. He is her favorite type quarry. Thin macho moustache. Dark Latin Lover eyes. Thick greasy hair. He wears two overcoats. Illegal aliens hate the Duluth winters, which are so unlike the balmy weather of Mexico, a mere ten miles away, across the border.

"O.K., muchacho, this is a strip-search."

"What?" He has not understood her. But then his English is not really up to even Darlene's sort of snuff.

"Off!" Darlene snarls, pointing to the two scuffy highly pointed shoes that all illegal aliens wear.

"What?" Total incomprehension.

Expertly Darlene knocks him down and pulls off one of the pointy shoes. Then she motions for him to complete the job. Crouched on the floor of the hovel, he removes the other shoe and then, reluctantly, four pairs of socks to reveal on each little toe a corn, something that all illegal aliens have as the result of the too-tight shoes that they affect. At the sight of those corns, Darlene starts her ascent to seventh heaven.

10

Wayne has gone. Chloris lies in her round bed, staring at the television set on the ceiling. Idly, she uses her vibrator. Wayne has not really satisfied her. She told him so when he came to. Miffed, he departed without telling her who killed Betty Grable. Chloris thinks he is just stringing her along—taking her for a ride.

As Chloris switches on "Duluth," she wonders just how Wayne lost his right ear. Then she is caught up in "Duluth." An actor whom she has always liked—is it Lorne Greene?—is being warm and confiding as a judge named Claypoole. He is now in judge's chambers, wearing a black robe and holding a gavel. The gavel reminds Chloris that she is still holding the vibrator in her left hand. She puts it on high. This is more like it, she thinks.

A familiar-looking actress appears on the screen. Chloris frowns. I know her, she thinks.

The actress is appealing to the judge to go easy on her son who is also his nephew.

The judge is stern. "I'm sorry, Sis. But you know as well as I do that the law is the law. And if you bend it this way and that—well, there wouldn't be any justice left, now would there?"

Chloris does not like this sort of Communist rant on television—or in real life for that matter. She debates whether or not to switch to something else. But then the camera cuts to the familiar-looking woman's face.

"I know that woman!" says Chloris aloud.

"Of course you do," says the woman, speaking directly to Chloris as she lies on the Porthault sheets of her round bed.

"Of course I do *what?*" says the judge, with the puzzled look of an actor who has been thrown a wrong cue.

"Of course you know me. I'm Edna Herridge, Realtor."

"Edna! My God! I'm sorry I didn't go to the funeral."

"The flowers were nice . . ."

"What flowers?" The judge—it isn't Lorne Greene and Raymond Burr is dead, thinks Chloris, not that that makes any difference on television where just about everyone you see is dead, anyway, including Edna Herridge.

"I was on my way with a client to your house, a Beryl Hoover . . ."

That name, thinks Chloris, that magic name! "Any relation to Herbert?"

"When we got stuck in a snowdrift and died."

"A man died because of your son—in a snowdrift, was it?" The actor playing the judge is doing his best to get the show back on the road where it belongs.

"Then I was assigned to this soap opera. Beryl was really looking forward to getting to know you. You should look her up. Rumor has it that she's in the new novel by *your* Rosemary Klein Kantor. Not ours. 'Bye now." Edna goes back into the plot of "Duluth," very much aware that one more line *not* in the script and she can be had up on charges

24

by Actors Equity. "He's my son," says Edna, weeping. "He's *your* nephew. He's going to be a fine doctor one day . . ."

The actor playing the judge looks relieved, hearing some dialogue from the script. "When I put on this black robe," he says gravely . . .

Chloris settles back to watch. The plot is beginning to thicken nicely. Chloris also makes a mental note to look for Rosemary Klein Kantor's latest novel. She is a little puzzled by the reference to "*your* Rosemary Klein Kantor. Not ours." Surely, there are not two Klein Kantors, she asks herself. But, of course, thanks to the *simultaneity effect*, there is the Klein Kantor creator of the series "Duluth," which is seen in *Duluth* but made in another continuum or alternative fiction, and so its Klein Kantor creatrix is entirely different from our Klein Kantor who has just published an installment of a novel called *Rogue Duke* in the latest issue of *Redbook*, a woman's magazine recently revived by the enemies of the Equal Rights Amendment of whom Chloris is one.

In principle, Chloris likes the idea of Rosemary Klein Kantor's tales of derring-do in Regency Hyatt England, and though she herself cannot read and hates being read to except when the book is her own, she likes nothing better than to be *told* about books. She must get Wayne to tell her about *Rogue Duke*—and Beryl Hoover, who may well be related, in some way, to the dark mystery at the heart of the Betty Grable Story.

11

Meanwhile, in the hovel in the barrio, Darlene has now got to the part of strip-search that she most enjoys. In fact, her jockey shorts are beginning to moisten with excitement. She always wears men's jockey shorts on the job because they make her feel authoritative.

The illegal alien youth is now wearing nothing but a pair of dingy boxer shorts, a size too large for his slender frame. Only one of three original buttons remains at the point of closure in the front and that button hangs by but a thread. In the cold, the youth is beginning to turn blue, a shade that Darlene likes in her illegal aliens. She notes with satisfaction that the surprisingly sturdy legs are shivering while to the west and the east of the hairless chest two dark nipples have shrunk to a size no larger than that of any two bumps of surrounding gooseflesh. The sound of the illegal alien's teeth chattering is music to Darlene's ears.

"Drop those drawers, boy!" she booms.

"What?" This is his only word of English, as he stands, hands to his sides, narrow Aztec eyes wide with terror.

With a forefinger Darlene flicks the button, which detaches itself from the last thread of some long-forgotten Mexican summer. The alien youth gasps. The drawers open but do not fall, held in place by muscular thighs. A thick black bush of pubic hair is totally revealed. With a glad cry, Darlene pulls the drawers all the way down to the alien's corns. He gives a cry. Of shame. She gives a cry. Of surprise. The bush is bare. No okra. No prunes.

Modestly, he tries to cover nothing with his hands. "No you don't, muchacho!" Darlene drags away the hands; stares at the empty black bush. "What are you," she snarls, "some kind of transsexual?"

"What?" he gurgles.

"One of us is missing the whole point to strip-search," says Darlene, testily. "And it is not Lieutenant Ecks of Homicide."

Darlene pulls up a crate and sits on it in such a way that the area of most interest to her is now at eye level. Then, gingerly, she moves her fingers up the quavering and quivering left thigh to the point where the sturdy legs join the thin torso. Victory! Hidden in the wiry thicket are two miniature prunes, removed from view by terror and cold.

"So you had them all along," she says, squeezing the prunes together. She is rewarded with a whimper. Next she removes her comb from her Mainbocher uniform pocket and, carefully, she parts the pubic bush in the middle. As she combs the hair to each side of the central parting, she is rewarded with a highly privileged close-up view of what proves to be easily the smallest and greenest—well, more bluish, she concedes—okra that she has yet found. It sticks straight out, the one eye shut tight with terror.

"For a rapist, boy, you're a nonstarter."

"What?"

On an impulse, Darlene pushed the okra back inside the alien, who screams. "Now you see it!" she shouts. "Now you don't!"

Little does Darlene Ecks dream that at this moment of her greatest triumph to date, she has just created the merciless chief of what will soon be known worldwide as the Aztec Terrorists Society, whose cry "The fire this time!" (in Spanish) will demoralize and destabilize Greater Duluth.

Yet, at heart, paradoxically, Darlene wants to be cherished and protected. If "Chico" were not so heavily married—and so seriously black—he could have been the answer to her prayers. But he is—and he is, seriously.

As compensation, Darlene's day-to-day life is nothing but strip-search, mixed with daydreaming. She is addicted to those glamorous romantic novels in which powerful masterful men, wearing cloaks, save shy heroines from terrible fates. Darlene particularly delights in Klein Kantor novels. In fact, so powerful is Darlene's need for beauty and tenderness that she is able, at the drop of an alien's drawers, to transport herself to the world of Regency Hyatt England and revel in the imaginings of her favorite authoress.

12

Mr. and Mrs. Bellamy Craig II are the cynosure of all eyes as they sit in the royal box—their box—of the Duluth Opera House. It is the first night of the new season. The opera is in Italian, which doesn't help matters. But the Craigs owe it to their social position to preside over the premiere. Bellamy wears special ear-plugs that keep out all sounds. Since like most wealthy Duluthians he was taught at an early age to read lips, he is able to converse with his wife while not hearing one note of the music.

"I do believe," says Chloris, making conversation before the overture, "that *everyone* is here and that we are the cynosure of all eyes."

"That is due to our social position."

"Yes," says Chloris. Between husband and wife small talk often verges on the minuscule—or picayune, as they say in nearby New Orleans—"The Crescent City"—whose favorite daughter at this moment is tapping on the door to the Craig box.

"Who's that?"

"Whose what?" asks Bellamy.

"Oh, you and your stupid ear-flints! Take them out! There's someone at the door to our royal box."

Chloris rises. There is a gasp from the audience. All eyes—some artificially aided with binoculars and lorgnettes—are now trained on Duluth's undisputed social leader, sumptuously gowned in a scarlet velvet creation from Christian Dior which she was able to smuggle past U.S. Customs by sewing a Saks Fifth Avenue label over the Dior label. No fool, Chloris Craig. No flies on her, as the working classes say in East Duluth.

With a gesture not unlike that of the Statue of Liberty lifting high her vibrator—and Chloris on good days (and this is one) resembles the lady at the mouth to New York harbor—Chloris opens the door to the royal box. Standing in the doorway is a small, intense woman with a large parrotlike nose. Although she is not well-groomed, there is a look of intensity about her that Chloris finds disturbing. Next to the small, large-nosed woman is a small but well-formed and well-groomed young man, with a large flat potatolike nose. Never before has Chloris had two such enormous noses in her box at the same time.

"I," says the small woman, "am Rosemary Klein Kantor." She raises her ivory cane as if in benediction. On top of everything else, thinks Chloris, with dismay, she is a gimp.

"Not the novelist?" Chloris's *savior dire* almost never deserts her.

"The same. I reside in New Orleans. Just across the causeway from Duluth. I saw you once when you were signing books at Tess Crager's. You were visiting the Crescent City in your capacity as 'Chloris Craig.' "

"True," says Chloris. "Of course tonight I'm my other self, Mrs. Bellamy Craig II . . ."

"The social arbiter of Duluth. Yes. I would've known

you anywhere from your pictures in *Town and Country* and *Women's Wear Daily*.''

''With me,'' Rosemary turns to the exquisite if over-nosed youth, ''is Clive Hoover . . .''

''Hoover?'' Chloris is suddenly alert. ''I know the name.''

''Mrs. Craig, this is an honor.'' Clive kisses Chloris's powerful hand, made muscular by a decade of vibrator use. ''My mother thought the world of you,'' he says. Plainly a sexual degenerate, Chloris decides. She can always tell. If he is not an interior decorator, he is a computer analyst.

''Your mother, yes . . .'' Chloris's *savoir dire* is sorely tested. ''How is she?''

''She has ridden on ahead.''

''She has *what*?''

''Crossed the shining river.''

''Crossed . . . ?''

''Fallen from the perch.''

''Perch?''

''Beryl Hoover is dead as a mackerel,'' says Rosemary with that sharpness which has made her tongue a byword to be feared in the Crescent City—so unlike the way that she is currently writing, to the delight of Lieutenant Darlene Ecks, her fan.

Rosemary Klein Kantor is queen of romance, Harlequin-style. She is also the acknowledged heiress—as well as plagiarist—of the late Georgette Heyer. Earlier in Rosemary's long career, she is said to have been (first by herself and, later, by others) a celebrated World War II correspondent and winner of the Wurlitzer Prize for Creative Journalism—an octopus in a plastic cube that adorns the mantelpiece of her study in New Orleans's fashionable Audubon Park. Thanks to Rosemary's canny way of mumbling Wurlitzer, the word has, over the years, turned to Pulitzer. As a result, Rosemary is famous. And means to stay that way. A legend, living.

During this conversation, Bellamy has stared raptly at the

stage as though listening to the music, which has not yet started. He keeps his back to the newcomers. He does not like the way that they look.

"You see my mother died in a snowdrift on Garfield Avenue . . ."

"With Edna Herridge! Yes, I know. I knew Edna slightly. She's in 'Duluth' now. Playing the judge's sister."

It is now the turn of Clive and Rosemary to be at sea. Too late, Chloris realizes that she has said not only too much but too little. Obviously, Edna does not want Beryl's son to know that she—Edna—is in a TV series that has not yet found its "legs," as they say in television circles. Chloris knows the feeling. When Wayne wrote the first "Chloris Craig" she had gone to Paris with an overnight bag filled with nothing but essential toiletries and Saks Fifth Avenue labels. When word came to her of the great success of *Nelson Eddy, a Fire in the Larynx*, she nearly wore her fingers out sewing in the Saks labels. In triumph, she returned to Duluth with a steamer trunk.

"Come and sit with us," says Chloris, realizing that with this one kindly gesture of hers, Rosemary and Clive will achieve, jointly, social position of the first rank in Duluth— the dream of Clive's mother, though Chloris could not know this but Clive could and does.

"I don't mind if I do," says Rosemary, seating herself regally beside Bellamy, who smiles at her. Chloris wishes, suddenly, that Rosemary's nose were smaller. She turns to Clive—his nose also cries out for surgery. What have I done? wonders Chloris, feeling faint, aware that the entire opera house is talking of nothing else but those extraordinary noses that Mrs. Bellamy Craig II has invited to her royal box.

Fortunately, the opera has now begun, causing the noses to lose their definition in the half-light from the proscenium arch. Bellamy shuts his eyes and sleeps the sleep of the just tired while Chloris racks her brains. What was it that Edna Herridge told her about Clive's mother, Beryl? Other than the fact that she is now in one of Rosemary's creations? But which one? She will have to ask Edna the next time she catches her in "Duluth." Unless Rosemary knows.

Chloris must feel her way very carefully with Rosemary. Chloris knows how inscrutable the creative process can be.

13

Captain Eddie is now at the spaceship. With him is his loyal sidekick Lieutenant "Chico" Jones and two scientists from Duluth University.

"Lucky for us no one ever comes near the spaceship," says Captain Eddie, surreptitiously. But there is no need for surreption because he is quite right. No one ever comes within a mile of the spaceship. By and large, people just don't like it. Certainly Captain Eddie doesn't like it. But he has a job to do.

"Chico" has placed a tall ladder against one side of the ship and he and the two scientists with their scanners follow Captain Eddie up the ladder to the top of the ship.

The view from the top is not at all breathtaking. The towers of Duluth are off to one side and the desert is off to the other side. Route 99 is more than a mile away, jammed with traffic, as always. In the distance, to the north, the Great Lakes resemble shallow finger bowls. To the south, the perpetual haze from the oil refineries and the rich gumbos hangs, as it always does, over New Orleans, the Crescent City.

"On a clear day," says Captain Eddie, trying to strike a

man-to-man note, "you can see the Pacific Ocean from up here."

"No, you can't," says one of the scientists, an uppity sort. He is walking carefully across the gummy top of the spaceship, holding a scanner in one hand. He stares at the instruments on the back of the scanner.

"What makes this thing so gummy?" asks Captain Eddie.

"Because it is made of an alien material," says the second scientist, a nice guy, all in all.

"*Illegal* alien?" "Chico" responds automatically, hopefully, in the sense that he hopes it is not all that illegal, as the prisons of Duluth are bursting with wet- as well as dry-backs. Lieutenant Darlene Ecks's strip-search expeditions are now yielding more aliens than anyone knows what to do with.

The scientist ignores "Chico."

Captain Eddie sighs. He has almost decided to run against Mayor Herridge for mayor. More than anything, Captain Eddie wants to ride around in the mayoral limo with the color TV and the wet bar in the back. He also wants power. So does his better half Mrs. Thurow. Captain Eddie thinks the world of that woman.

"Well," says the scientist with the scanner, "there's a lot going on inside of here."

"Like what?"

"Like . . . Well, it sounds like a party. Someone's playing an accordion, I *think*. I don't know what the tune is because I'm tone deaf. This is just off the top of my head because we scientists can't jump to conclusions but we can always hazard educated guesses."

"I see," says Captain Eddie, who doesn't see at all. What would people from outer space be doing in the Duluth desert just off ethnic Kennedy Avenue, he muses, giving a party? Why couldn't they do that on their home planet?

"What do they look like?" asks Captain Eddie.

"How the hell do I know what they look like?" This par-

ticular scientist is a bad-tempered man. But his companion,
Dr. Nice Guy, says, "The fact is, we can only get a *general*
shape with the scanner. And the pulse rates, of course, and
respiratory cycles. I would say," says Dr. Guy, thoughtfully, "that they probably look like centipedes."

"That's *not* an educated guess," says the bad-tempered
scientist. "And you know it."

"Well, *I* get a centipedal feedback on my scanner . . ."

"Dr. Guy, can we make communication with them?"
Captain Eddie is getting desperate. "Can't you ask them to
move on? After all, they are breaking every city ordinance
in the book. *And* they are making me look silly."

"Also, if the Chief here can get them to move," says
"Chico," "he's a shoo-in to beat Herridge for mayor."

"Well, now, I wouldn't say that . . ." Captain Eddie
is embarrassed. He doesn't want it generally known that
his hat might soon be in the ring. But the scientists do not
care one way or the other. They aren't even listening. Dr.
Nice Guy is now on his knees with a hammer. He raps
twice on the top of the spaceship, a hard thing to do because it is so gummy. "Knock, knock," says Dr. Guy.
"Who's there?"

From inside the spaceship there comes a hideous sound.
The four men freeze. They have never heard such a sound
before. Their faces are drained of all color. They dare not
move. *They cannot move.* The sound rises and falls. Then it
stops altogether.

"I don't think," says Dr. Guy, his voice trembling, "I'll
try that again."

"Better not," says Captain Eddie, really shaken. "This
is for the U.S. Air Force. This is out of my hands. I wash
my hands of it." But the red gumminess is sticking to all
their hands and clothes as they hurry down the ladder and all
four know that it will take each of them many hours to clean
themselves, with kerosene and turpentine, when they get
home.

"I'll bet it's Commies in there," says "Chico."

14

Chloris and Wayne are sitting in the Persian Paradise Houseboat, watching the ice skaters ice-skate on the frozen river. "Would you say, Wayne, that in *Mother Wore Tights*, Betty Grable's legs were too thin?"

"Depends on the way she was photographed. In *Coney Island*, the gams were gorgeous."

"But the left calf was too thin, I thought, in the Boardwalk scene."

"I think I now know who killed Betty." Wayne is something of a tease.

"Oh, Wayne!" Chloris has never felt closer to Wayne than she does now. "I knew you'd crack the case. Who did it?"

"First, it was, as you always suspected, a crime of passion."

"I love a crime of passion more than any other kind." Chloris does, too.

"Yes." Slowly, maddeningly, Wayne eats the last of the shish kebab on his plate while avoiding the flaming saber of some elaborate dessert, borne on high like Liberty's vibrator by an illegal alien as yet unviolated by Lieutenant Darlene Ecks.

"Wayne! I'm all ears."

Thoughtfully, Wayne sips his Cold Duck. Then: "Clyde Tolson." That's all he says. But his eyes are bright with triumph.

"Who the fuck," asks Chloris, "is Clyde Olsen?"

35

"Tolsón. With a 'T.' Remember the greatest love story never told?"

"If it *wasn't* ever told . . ." Chloris is getting cranky.

"But it *was* whispered. Whispered, baby. Clyde Tolson was the longtime live-in lover and flatfoot associate of J. Edgar Hoover, the director of the Federal Bureau of Investigation."

"Hoover?" Chloris frowns: that name keeps cropping up. Why?

"Now then, this is how I have reconstructed what happened. Oh, I'm missing a piece or two of the puzzle but the essentials are all there."

"Go on, Wayne. This is really hot stuff."

"Thank you. Now then, Betty meets Herbert."

"Herbert who?"

"Herbert Hoover."

"Oh, yes. How silly of me. I keep forgetting. The starched collar. Yes. Go on, Wayne. All these Hoovers!"

"They have an affair. A platonic affair. They really live it up. Vegas. Fairbanks. Waikiki. Anchorage. Palm Springs. Juneau. You name it. Wherever the lights are bright and the living's high, there was Betty and Herbert."

"God! What good times our ancestors had!"

"Yes. But there was one little detail that Betty was never able to master."

"How to have her left leg photographed so as it would not look too thin?"

"Well, that's *another* little detail. But the big detail, the one that cost her her life . . . Who is that waving at you?"

Chloris looks up. Rosemary Klein Kantor and Clive Hoover —that name again, thinks Chloris—are coming over to say hello. "Oh, fudge!" mutters Chloris. "Hi, Rosemary! Hi, Clive!" She greets them graciously. After all, she let them sit in her royal box at the opera. "This is Wayne Alexander. Now let's have one big flurry of introductions after which you two will split."

But this is not to be because the two newcomers think that

Chloris is simply full of fun. "I will have a brandy," says Rosemary, sitting down.

"I will have an after-dinner liqueur," says Clive to the waiter. He turns to Chloris. "Mother's will has been probated. I will inherit one hundred million dollars of oil money, which she was able to get from Dad after she took him to the cleaners, three years before his death."

"I like you, Clive," says Chloris, with all sincerity. "A whole lot. You are going to be quite an addition to Duluth society."

"I had hoped we could get him for the Crescent City, just across the causeway." Rosemary gives Chloris a somewhat challenging smile. This will be a fight to the death, thinks Chloris. But she will win. She always does.

"I have found Clive a mansion or home in Audubon Park," says Rosemary, in a steely voice, "our fashionable residential section . . ."

"Which has nothing like the view that our Garfield Heights has, the place where," Chloris plays her trump card right on Clive's nose, as it were, "your angel mother was planning to buy a home or mansion."

"That's absolutely right, Mrs. Craig." Clive stares at her—passionately.

"Chloris to you."

"Chloris . . ."

"Now, Chloris . . ." begins Rosemary.

"Mrs. Craig to you, Ms. Klein Kantor. Until we know each other well enough to be on a first-name basis."

"There is very little that I don't know about you, sweetie," says Rosemary, not one to take this sort of thing sitting down.

A cat fight, thinks Wayne.

Such style, thinks Clive, torn between the intellect of Rosemary and the social position and tits of Chloris.

Real sleaze, thinks Chloris, turning on the charm. "Clive will be happier here in Duluth, where we have tradition. Gracious living. Intellect." She indicates Wayne, who looks very brainy, as indeed he is. "And the seat of numerous government bureaus both state and federal."

"Including," says Rosemary, "U.S. Customs—if memory serves."

Chloris is stunned. How could this woman know about the labels? For once, no ready phrase springs to her lips. She is abandoned by her own *savoir dire*.

"I have always noted that you people in Duluth—the Grail, as it were, of my late mother, Beryl—have a distinction not to be found elsewhere and I must confess, in all honesty, that I am like my mother in every way save one."

"Really!" Rosemary blushes. Hard-hitting though she might be as befits the author of the Wurlitzer Prize-winning *Dateline Hiroshima*, she is still the authoress of Harlequin-style romances. Cock could no more make an appearance in one of her romances—other than as an unnamed and undefined part of the generalized male aura of one of her interchangeable dashing heroes—than it could ever come close to finding even temporary haven between her own thin lips.

Clive fixes Rosemary with a cold gaze. "I meant, Ms. Klein Kantor, my nose. Beryl's was changed. Mine was not. It was her dream that I change it *before* she established herself on Garfield Heights, socially."

Chloris is getting uneasy with all this talk of noses. She dabs the end of her own retroussé number with a bit of powder.

"When news came to me of Beryl's death in that snowdrift at the foot of Garfield Heights, I was—I confess this only to *this* table—checked into Dr. Jasper's Rhino Clinic at Long Beach, where I was ready to conform my—let us face it—flat potato nose with a *pomme soufflée* like Mother's. Alas. The morning I was to undergo the knife, word came that Beryl was as one with Nineveh and Tyre. I hurried home to Tulsa, where Beryl was to be interred. At the actual interment, imagine my surprise—and true excitement— to see Rosemary Klein Kantor, a stranger to me in person but one known to me, as to everyone, by repute. It was then . . ." Clive pauses. "You take it from there, darling." He turns to Rosemary.

"On the sad day of Beryl Hoover's death—" Rosemary says, taking it, as requested.

"That name!" whispers Chloris, to herself since the others seldom listen to anyone.

"—I was midway through Chapter Three of *Countess Mara*, which is set in the Swiss Alps at the clinic of a famed cosmetic surgeon, when Beryl suddenly entered the book, as a patient. Beryl made herself right at home. She claims to have been a friend of my heroine, Countess Mara, which I doubt—"

"Mother sometimes says—said—*says* that she knows titled people when she doesn't," confesses Clive.

"We shall know in Chapter Four," says Rosemary, a bit grimly. "But as I was fixing her to the page, as I do all my characters, with verve and magic, I—*sensed* the snowdrift. But as to her actual moment of death, she was not exactly forthcoming."

"Mother is—was—*is* a Christian Scientist. Death is not her bag."

"Anyway, she told me that due to a sort of fictional warp of the sort we plagiarists—I mean writers . . . What a funny slip!" Rosemary is getting rattled. "She still remembered, as I was writing her, her life here in *Duluth*. She wanted me to get an urgent message to her son Clive. What? I asked. But by then she was totally integrated in *Countess Mara*. Intrigued, I rang all the funeral homes in Tulsa and found the one where she was about to be potted for planting. And since New Orleans is a mere hop, skip and jump from Tulsa, I arrived just in time to join in the obsequies for my new character, very much alive, if I may say so, on the page, but . . ."

"Dead as a mackerel in . . ." says Wayne, wanting to contribute to this hen-fest.

". . . unreal life," Clive completes Wayne's sentence

incorrectly, a habit of his. "But I'm thrilled to hear that Mother is doing so well in *Countess Mara* . . ."

"But what was the urgent message?" asks Chloris, always practical.

Rosemary frowns. "I don't know. You see, Beryl is no longer autonomous. She is also out of *Duluth* forever."

"I don't think that is possible," says Wayne, who at least once a day reads aloud to himself the motto on top of the McKinley Tower. No one knows who put it there. No one knows exactly what it means. No one really cares except Wayne. He is positive that it is some sort of code, to be broken in time.

"Perhaps Beryl is just biding her time," says Chloris, hoping that the message from Beryl—if it is ever delivered—will reduce in no way Clive's one hundred million admittedly inflated U.S. dollars.

"Or," says Rosemary, "she may be about to make a second appearance in the serial I am writing for *Redbook*."

"Rogue Duke?" Chloris never forgets a title. She also remembers Edna telling her on television how Clive's mother is in *Rogue Duke*.

"Yes. My characters often do double—even triple duty. There is, actually, a character called Beryl—not Hoover—in *Rogue Duke* and if *she* is Clive's mother, there is still a chance that this urgent message . . ."

"Tell me," purrs Chloris, attention span snapping, "how you, with that—unusually—large—even—*enormous*—nose would know enough about plastic surgery in the higher social circles to be able to describe in *Countess Mara* the life and good times of a rhinoplasticeur? Do you work *entirely* from the imagination? Something that is not done here in *Duluth*."

Small as she is, Rosemary pulls herself up so that her chin no longer rests on the edge of the brandy snifter. "Mrs. Craig, I, too, have undergone rhinoplastic surgery."

"Surely you are putting we on!" Chloris is diverted.

"I was born of ancient rabbinical stock. Unfortunately, I

was also born with a tiny retroussé nose not unlike that sawed-off nose-blower you are wearing—''

''Ms. Klein Kantor!'' Chloris is now diverted to fury. ''This sawed-off nose-blower, as you call it—''

''—is a pop-model that went out in the late sixties. My own magnificently shaped and *flared* schnozzola took two years to build. The bone and sinews and cartilage of my left Achilles heel furnished the stuff of this magnificent nose. That is why I walk with a limp. But it was worthwhile, let me tell you! I am now a credit to my ancestors and I am not false, as so many others are here in *Duluth*.''

''But surely, Rosemary,'' says Clive, who now regards the authoress as a temporary stand-in mother surrogate, ''*your* nose is as false as all the others. I mean although it was built *up* rather than down, it is still not the nose that you were born with, is it?''

''No. But it is the one that I *should* have had. And that I now have . . .''

''A Platonic essence of a nose?'' asks Wayne.

Rosemary blushes. ''I am sexually pure, Mr. Alexander. All my relations are Platonic.''

''I think,'' says Chloris, rising, ''that we have exhausted the subject of noses. I am happy that Beryl Hoover—your mother, dear Clive—is in *your* book, Ms. Klein Kantor. Actually, I remember now that that was what Edna Herridge told me in 'Duluth.' So *bonne chance!* Now, Clive, I will take you to my bridge club . . .''

''Not The Eucalyptus!''

''Yes, Clive. The Eucalyptus, the ultimate refuge of the elite.'' Chloris sweeps Clive from the room. Clive is overjoyed. Socially, he has never dreamed of climbing so high. On the other hand, Rosemary looks grim at the thought of Duluth's latest new twosome while even the equable Wayne's nose is a bit out of joint.

Unknown to this ill-assorted quartet, every word that they have said has been recorded by the DPD. Later Darlene and ''Chico'' will listen to the tapes, hoping to catch a well-known drug-pusher who works out of that particular table aboard the Persian Paradise Houseboat.

Predictably, "Chico" is bored by all this high-society palaver but Darlene is thrilled to listen in on her favorite authoress and to find out that the woman in the snowdrift with Edna Herridge is now in *Rogue Duke*, which Darlene has just begun to read, as it appears in monthly installments in the brand-new old *Redbook*, a magazine for the romantic career woman.

15

Lieutenant Darlene Ecks, Homicide, is walking carefully along the high swinging walkway of Duluth's Regency Hyatt Hotel. Darlene has a fear of heights. Also, the recent collapse of a hotel walkway in nearby Atlanta, Georgia, during a Duke Ellington concert, is on her mind.

Darlene tries not to look down at the floor of the lobby far, far below but, of course, she can look at nothing else. She tries to think of her mission: Drugs are being dispensed in the Lunar Bar at the end of the walkway. Darlene—clad not in uniform but in a flashy B-girl outfit—is to make the connection with the bartender. Then the bust. This will be a feather in her cap if she pulls it off—and if she does not faint dead away with terror on the walkway.

Midway in her journey, Darlene does what she always does when she is fearful. She withdraws into romance. She conjures up the latest installment of *Rogue Duke*, set in Regency-Hyatt times, her favorite period.

Radiant in a tiara, Darlene enters the ballroom. Crystal

chandeliers are ablaze with light. All eyes are upon her. She wears a dress of ivory-white lace with a long train.

"Lady Darlene!" booms the major-domo.

Darlene—neck high yet arched like a swan's—moves through the room towards the fat Prince Regent-Hyatt. He holds up a monocle. She gives him a sweeping curtsy.

"Gad, Sir Hugh, she's a looker!"

"May I have this dance, Lady Darlene? I am the Earl of Grantford."

"Indeed you may, Earl, honey. I am Lady Darlene."

"I know."

"You know?"

"Yes."

"How?"

Rosemary Klein Kantor's dialogue goes on page after page like this and Darlene savors every word of it. As they sweep through a dance, Darlene is in utter heaven until she glimpses, as she swirls about, a familiar face—a face that ought not to be there but there it is in the crowd. A woman in black. Tall. Glowering. Obviously a Bad Person. But *who* is it? Darlene wonders, making a small moue, which the Earl notices.

"I see that you have espied her, Lady Darlene."

"Oh? Did my moue give me away?"

"Your face is like a crystal plate through which blazes the innocence of your soul."

"You are a doll, Earl. But who is that woman in black?"

"That is Beryl, Marchioness of Skye."

"Oh, Clive Hoover's mother. Or was until the accident. She looks—sinister." Darlene gives a tiny shiver.

"Lady Skye is a secret spy for Napoleon Bonaparte."

"For . . . ? Oh, yes. Him. Natch. I know the name," says Darlene, with a dazzling smile. But she is a bit disgruntled because she only expects to find people that she *doesn't* know when she drifts into a romance. After all, real life is bad enough.

Since Darlene is now at the Lunar Bar, she is able to step

out of *Rogue Duke*—and off the walkway—with a sense of relief. She definitely does not like Beryl.

Through the Lunar Bar's picture window—like a spaceship porthole—there is a spectacular view of the masses of pink cherry blossoms that line the ridge of low hills which mark the beginning of the Duluth Woods. It is now early March. Spring comes early in Duluth. On the other hand, summer comes late. It is thought that the spray from aerosol cans has altered the climate and Wayne Alexander has written a hard-hitting exposé on the subject that is now running in the *Blade*. On the other hand, KDLM-TV's *Six O'Clock News* has stayed away from the subject like the plague because aerosol lacquer hairspray is a big advertiser, although officially banned for some years. KDLM-TV always knows on which side its bread is buttered.

There are two bartenders. One is tall and black. The other is tall and white. They wear red jackets with pictures of the moon on them. A dozen chippies are seated at the bar or at the Formica-topped "moon" tables and quite a few men— many from out of town—are on the loose, picking up chippies. Darlene finds this sort of thing sordid. But then she knows that, sordid or not, there is nothing that she or anyone at the DPD can do to stop immorality in the Lunar Bar or anywhere else because everyone pays off Mayor Herridge, which disgusts Captain Eddie, who is powerless when it comes to challenging those of the Mayor's cronies who are vice lords.

As luck would have it, the *Six O'Clock News* is on as Darlene takes her seat at the bar and orders a Brandy Alexander from the tall black barman.

Mayor Herridge is being interviewed at City Hall by Leo Lookaloney, who has, recently, been doing fewer sports and more political interviews, to the disgust of his numerous fans.

Leo says, "The Air Force thinks that the spaceship may be a Russian secret weapon."

"I think not," says the Mayor, stubbing out the big black

cigar that he always smokes except when there is a camera around, as it is bad for the image of a corrupt politician to be seen smoking a long cigar like a corrupt politician. Mayor Herridge is a forceful man, with a mellifluous voice. "Two scientists from the University of Duluth examined the ship last February and one of them, a Dr. Guy, said it comes from another world."

"Which one?"

"He couldn't tell." Oh, the Mayor is smooth, thinks Darlene. "I mean there's no label on it that says what it is or even what's in it, which means that, wherever it's from, they have no Pure Food and Drug Act, which would point, I'd say, to an authoritarian or even maybe totalitarian type of government."

"Are you saying that the spaceship is edible?"

"Dr. Guy thought it might be. They're still examining this red goo it's made of."

"I see."

"Yes."

"It is rumored that Captain Eddie Thurow—"

"Yea, team," murmurs Darlene into her Brandy Alexander.

"—of the DPD is planning to run against you, sir, for mayor."

"If he does, I'll whip his bleep."

At this point, the tall black barman switches the station to a soothing filler about horses.

Darlene studies the barman carefully. He is the alleged drug-pusher. He is light mahogany in color with an Afro-style hairdo. He is quite handsome, with a snub nose. Basically, Darlene has nothing much against miscegenation. After all, she's been making it with "Chico" for years. But one cop getting into another cop—which is really all that Darlene is despite the romantic daydreams—isn't such a big deal. Besides, she knows too much about "Chico," his hopes, fears, wife, children, stamp collection, love of bondage and Heineken beer. They are like brother and sister by now. There is no mystery, no rapture.

"What can I do you for, miss?" The alleged drug-pusher has a twinkly, slightly fresh manner. He is quite the dude.

"I'm into winter sports." That is the code phrase.

"Yeah? But it's spring now. See them cherry blossoms?"

"Me, I like the snow."

The barman gives her a long look. Then he indicates with his head that she go into the pantry, which is next to the ladies' room. Darlene, heart pounding, goes, nonchalantly, into the pantry, which turns out to be a small windowless room with a sink and shelves full of glasses and cases of diet cola.

Darlene catches a glimpse of herself in a small mirror on the back of the door beside which hangs the steel comb that the barman uses to tease his Afro. Darlene decides that she has never looked lovelier. The pale blue eyes gleam with adventure. The cheeks are aglow with good health. At twenty-seven Darlene Ecks is very much a girl after her own heart.

The door opens. The barman slips in. Then he locks the door. Gives her a big wink.

"Hey, baby, how much you want?"

"One gram."

"That'll set you back one and a half Cs," he says, removing with a spoon one gram of cocaine from an open diet-cola can that she can see is filled to the brim with glittering white Peruvian Inca-proof cocaine.

"And that'll set *you* back five to ten in the slammer, with time off for good behavior after the twentieth month." Darlene has removed her trusty revolver from her handbag. Although the barman's jaw has dropped, he does not drop the precious cocaine. He stares at her, dumbly.

"I am Lieutenant Darlene Ecks, Homicide . . . And sometimes Narcotics Squad. Your buddy squealed—Big John." This is the barman's name to his confederates.

"That som' bitch," Big John mutters. Then he puts the ounce back into the diet-cola can.

"What else you got in here, Big John?"

"Nothin'."

"Nothin', ma'am." Darlene is a stickler for good manners.

"Ma'am." He gives her a look that is meant to kill.

"I don't believe you, Big John. So let's take a gander at all the open cans." As Big John presents each opened diet-cola can for her inspection, she plays, idly, with the handcuffs that, presently, she will snap onto his mahogany wrists—"Chico's" favorite foreplay. But, somehow, something—a little bird?—tells her that Big John isn't into bondage. At least not on the receiving end.

Once Darlene is satisfied that the various cans are indeed empty, she decides to indulge her sense of fun. She knows in her heart of hearts that she is exceeding the limits of her authority as laid down in black and white by the DPD but, in very special cases, a lieutenant does have the right to bend the odd rule, if it seems appropriate to do so.

Until now Darlene has never performed strip-search on any male other than a member of the okra and prunes set. As a result, truth to tell, she is getting a bit bored with the sameness of these capers since one alien's corn is very like another's. But Big John is tall and black—or glistening mahogany. He is also very definitely on the cute side. Yes, she thinks to herself, nothing gained, nothing ventured.

"All right, Big John, shuck down."

"What does that mean . . . ma'am?" He obviously has not grown up on a plantation, she thinks, or served any time in Kyle Onstott's *Mandingo*.

"It means you're going to get a total body search. I guess you know what that is because, according to your record, you've done time before."

" 'Cause I was framed by them white cats . . ."

"Well, this time you weren't framed, I caught you with the goods."

"That fuckin' stoolie . . ."

"So start stripping."

GORE VIDAL

"Start *what?*" Big John is not as fast on the uptake as she had thought on first meeting.

"Get out of those Goddamned clothes so I can see what dope you got stashed away on your person."

"I ain't got no shit on me. Honest Injun!" As he sweats, her silken panties moisten—she only wears the jockey shorts when she wears the Mainbocher uniform that is never out of style.

"We'll see. So let's start with that dumb jacket."

"Oh, shit." But he does as she tells him. Then, slowly, he takes off the clip-on bow tie and then, slowly, he starts to unbutton the white shirt. As Darlene gets her first glimpse of the smooth, shimmering, mahogany curves of his chest, she thinks to herself, To think! I almost took accounting in high school!

16

Beryl is somewhat taken aback by the coarse blond young woman—Lady Darlene—who stares at her at the Bessborough ball for the Prince Regent.

Although no longer in mourning for her late husband, Beryl, Marchioness of Skye, still dresses in black because black suits her natural white camellia skin. Black also suits her usual mood. Black is also easier for Rosemary Klein Kantor to handle, as she has, rather surprisingly for a best-selling authoress, no clothes sense.

Can this be the Prince Regent's new mistress? Beryl asks herself as Darlene passes her, whispering, "Beryl Hoover! What are you doing here?"

The Marchioness of Skye cuts dead the hussy. At the moment for the purpose of this true fiction—or false truth—our Beryl Hoover is still as dead as that proverbial mackerel. Later, of course, when she leaves *Countess Mara* for *Rogue Duke*, she will remember—in due course—who she was and the danger her son Clive is in.

On the other hand, Edna Herridge is a very different case. Currently, she is living at the Montecito Hotel in Hollywood, where all the best New York actors stay—she is from New York now, divorced, two children—and working in "Duluth," a series that is slowly beginning to make its mark. Edna likes the director. Edna needs the money. Edna hates the drive to Universal Studios at Burbank but she has no choice because that is where the series is being made. Since Edna has no depth perception, she fears a fatal accident.

Halfway through the fourth episode—one gives away no secrets because by the time this page is read "Duluth" will have been canceled—Edna is going to crash into a Santini moving van and die instantly. She will then be written out of "Duluth," the series.

Edna has had a bad run of luck with cars lately, as she would be the first to tell you, if she could remember. But when she collides with that moving van she will be absorbed once more into a continuum where the relative law of absolute uniqueness obtains and she will then be seen to good advantage in all sorts of texts, ranging from a compendious Michener yarn to a minatory tale of Gass.

At *this* moment, however, Edna remembers that she has had another life. Or a parallel life—she isn't quite sure which. She is astonished to see Chloris in bed with a vibrator. Somehow, Chloris is not the sort of woman that Edna—a bit of a prude in *Duluth* though a secret alcoholic and good-time matron in "Duluth"—would have thought capable of self-abuse. But Edna manages to keep her cool as she looks through the TV set at Chloris, who looks back at her, too surprised to shut off the vibrator.

After their chat, Edna tries to ring Mayor Herridge in *Duluth*, only to find that the city of Duluth in her new true fiction is not her old Duluth—and *our* only Duluth, never to be left or lost. Edna is relieved, in a way. Yet she is also haunted every moment that she is on the set of "Duluth" by the thought that someone from her old or parallel life might suddenly pop up out of the camera's lens. Should she go back into analysis? To tell the truth, Edna Herridge is now fearful for her sanity.

On the other hand, the Marchioness of Skye—to whom the name Hoover still means nothing—is enjoying very much the plot of *Rogue Duke*. But then there is hardly a character alive or dead who does not enjoy being—for the first few pages anyway—in a Klein Kantor book.

"Like a breath of purest ozone," Captain Eddie will say when he makes *his* appearance as Napoleon Bonaparte in *Rogue Duke*. But that's some pages in the future.

17

Meanwhile, Captain Eddie Thurow has thrown his hat into the ring. "That's right, boys, my hat is in the ring!"

This is said to the gathered media in the banquet room of the Ramada Inn. There is a smattering of applause, as well there should be, for Captain Eddie is the first police chief in twenty years not to be indicted at least once for acts of corruption. In Duluth that's something of a record.

The Occidental newsperson—a man as it happens—from KDLM-TV holds the microphone close to Captain Eddie's mouth.

"Captain Eddie, do you foresee a tight race between you and the Mayor in the coming primary?"

"Well, I always run scared." Captain Eddie grins. At the back of the room "Chico" gives him the thumbs-up gesture.

"Actually," says Wayne Alexander, butting in, "you've never run at all before."

"I've never denied that." Captain Eddie keeps his cool.

"Will you reopen the libraries and massage parlors if you are elected?" asks the Occidental newsperson.

"Those that should be opened will be opened. I'll be acting entirely on a case-by-case basis."

"Will you hire more police in order to fight the crime wave caused by the illegal aliens in the ethnic Kennedy Avenue section?"

"That is my firm intention. We need law and order. We need more police. More prisons. And," Captain Eddie pauses dramatically, "more public executions of the kind which our forefathers here in Duluth were famous all over Minnesota—and even nearby Louisiana—for!" By now there is bedlam in the banquet hall. This is a winning speech. Only Wayne Alexander, a professional liberal and spoilsport, sneers. But no one notices the sneer.

"What," shouts Wayne, "are you going to do about that spaceship?"

"I will, if elected mayor, see that it is moved across the border into Mexico . . ." The cheering begins again. ". . . where it will be such a tourist attraction that our little neighbors down ole Mexico way will say *gracias* to their Uncle Sam as they pay off the interest on the money they went and borrowed from the First Duluth National Bank!" Captain Eddie's hat is in the ring all right.

A bullet's flight away from the Ramada Inn, a dozen little neighbors from ole Mexico are seated in the back room of a hovel in a barrio where, in the front room, their stoic women are endlessly folding enchiladas, ironing tortillas, stitching tortillas.

When Darlene Ecks pressed Pablo's *membrum virile* inside him, the iron, as they say in Puerto Vallarta, entered his soul.

"I wish to kill," says Pablo to the newly formed Aztec Terrorists Society. As a single Terrorist, the others nod, and their expressionless Aztec faces twist with a shared hatred of Darlene Ecks.

As a part of each Terrorist's initiation into the Society, a large picture of Darlene in her always stylish Mainbocher uniform is placed upon a used serape. Then, one by one, the humiliated youths spit on the photograph while Pablo actually relieves himself upon the hated image.

Once the original of the photograph is captured, the Aztec Terrorists plan to gang-rape, mutilate and kill her. As they discuss all the awful things that they are going to do to Darlene, their okras become heated, their prunes taut.

Mucho macho is now at stake. To each Aztec Terrorist, his okra is a plumed serpent, ever ready to serve and be serviced by the dark gods of the blood. But then it is no secret that from Yucatán to Tijuana the prophet of the macho man is no other than D. Herbert Lawrence, author of *Kangaroo*, the bible of every illegal alien everywhere.

18

The Eucalyptus Bridge and Backgammon Club is in an old mansion on Garfield Heights, overlooking the Duluth Woods. The mood at The Eucalyptus is very different from that of the hovel in the barrio.

Chloris and Clive are getting along famously. They play

backgammon in the tastefully appointed library of the club—formerly the home of an old Duluth Creole family now defunct. But the *crème de la crème* of the still funct Duluthian socialites often spend many a happy afternoon and evening at the bridge and backgammon and chemin-de-fer tables as well as in front of the row of one-armed bandits that Mayor Herridge gave the club—illegally—after a raid on an illicit gambling den. The only *legal* gambling in Duluth is at The Dude Ranch, near Lincoln Groves. The Ranch is the largest casino in the world as well as the most mysterious, since no one knows who The Dude is. He—or his answering service—telephones in his orders to the maître d'hôtel, who has never laid eyes on him. It was Beryl Hoover's misfortune to stumble upon his identity.

At The Eucalyptus, black servitors in livery, from nearby New Orleans, stagger about, carrying trays of mint juleps and Dr Pepper, the two favorite tipples of the club members. The perpetual drunkenness of the black servitors is a byword in Garfield Heights.

Chloris has just won eight thousand dollars from Clive at backgammon and she is in a very good mood indeed. "I do wish I'd known Beryl, your mother."

"You would've been real pals," says Clive, lying.

"Anyway, Beryl's gone now. Forever. But the place that she dreamed of for herself here in Duluth . . . yes, right up here on Garfield Heights! That place can be yours."

"Oh, Chloris!" Impulsively, Clive takes her huge hand in his tiny one. Aware that one of the drunken servitors in livery is watching this potentially compromising gesture—in Chloris's social position she must be above suspicion, like Caesar's Palace—Chloris withdraws her mitt and says to the servitor, in French, the language of New Orleans's vieux carré as well as of all the old-guard Duluth families—not for nothing was Chloris born a Duluth des Bois—"*Portez-moi un Docteur Peppé.*" With alacrity, the liveried servitor obeys.

"What it must be like to have total *savoir faire* as well as *savoir dire!*'' exclaims Clive. Is he in love, he wonders? Is she?

Am I? asks Chloris of herself, already starting to think a tiny bit in French. Lately, Wayne Alexander has been more of a typewriter-cum-vibrator to her than true lover. After all, Chloris is now thirty or forty years old, depending on which dentist will fink on her, while Clive is only twenty-five, small but perfectly formed, a pocket-sized John McEnroe. Chloris is a tennis buff and loves the bad-tempered current champion, except for the nose—Clive's, not McEnroe's, though she doesn't like the tip to John's all that much— which will have to go. She will deal with it, she decides, tactfully. ''About your nose,'' she begins tactfully.

''My *what?*''

Chloris remembers, suddenly, the one hundred million dollars. ''About your clothes,'' says Chloris smoothly. She will get to the nitty-gritty in due course. ''Bellamy's tailor is crackerjack.''

''Mother always bought my duds at the boys' department of Bon Marché on Canal Street.''

A cold hand clutches at Chloris's heart. ''Clive,'' she says. He puts down the backgammon cup when he hears the familiar name.

''Yes?''

''Was your mother clinging, possessive, overpowering in her love for you?''

Clive nods. ''That would just about describe Beryl.''

''Was your father weak, passive, absent from home a lot?''

''You mean before he died?''

''Yes. Naturally, he'd be away from home a lot *after* he died.''

''Well, yes. That just about describes Dad not only before he died but also three years ago when Mommie took him to the cleaners during the divorce and got the hundred mill.''

''I see.'' Chloris slowly sips her Dr Pepper. The taste-fully appointed library with the crackling fire, velvet drapes, rare antiques and distinguished socialites has suddenly lost all its warmth and security for her. A shadow perceptible even to the intuitive Clive now crosses her face where only an instant before all was brightness. Chloris begins to see Wayne in a new light. Although he's something of a bore nowadays, they do have the Betty Grable book to finish—and the odd good time in bed and . . .

"Chloris." Clive's voice is urgent.

"Hmmmh?" Chloris has drifted off.

"I know what you're thinking. You're thinking that I'm some sort of sissy boy. A mother's boy. Immature. Unable to respond to warm mature *hetero*sexual love. Confess, now. Isn't that what you are thinking?"

Chloris nods, slowly. "You took the words out of my mouth."

"Well, I just want you to know that I'm into pussy all the way."

"*All* the way, Clive?" Chloris's eyes are now aglitter.

"Absolutely and totally the whole way, no holds banned or barred."

"Why did I doubt you?"

"Beryl, I suppose. The clothes from the boys' department. But you should've known right off that with a nose like mine, I'm all man!"

"Clive, you darling!" Chloris is in love—for the first time. An absolute first, she thinks. But then who is counting? "Promise me one thing, Clive."

"I'll promise you the moon, Beryl . . . I mean Chloris."

"*Never have your nose fixed.*"

"Sooner lose my weenie, Chloris."

"So young and yet so wise." She raises her voice. "*Encore, serviteur noir en liverie, un Docteur Peppé.*" Chloris is happy. So is Clive. The black servitor is stoned out of his head.

19

Beryl, Marchioness of Skye, still has no memory of *Duluth*, her son Clive, the terminal snowdrift. She is now totally involved in the Chapter Four house party of *Rogue Duke*. All fashionable London is there including the immensely gross but most engaging Prince Regent, known to his intimates as Reggie.

It is teatime. Handsome men in ruffs with glittering orders about their necks, drink tea and laugh with—but never at—Reggie. Glorious women, wearing tiaras, sit about the huge room enjoying the crackling fire and one another's witty discourse. They eat a lot of chocolate fudge cake and biscuits.

Beryl pretends to take part in the teatime happy-hour at Blenheim Palace but, actually, she is keeping an eye on Lady Darlene, a hussy if Beryl has ever seen one. Also, and this is Beryl's secret fear, Lady Darlene could well be a counterspy.

Worse, that morning, while hunting carrion in the park, Lady Darlene had made an unmistakable pass at Reggie. Too shame-making, thinks Beryl, who has always had a soft spot in her heart for the Heir to the Throne. Since her widowhood, he has taken to confiding in her his hopes and dreams. He wants to reconquer France. "After all, it's really ours, don't you know?" he said to her at breakfast in the very first installment, which set the plot moving at such a cracking pace.

"You *must*, sire!" she had said. Little does he suspect

that she is an agent of Napoleon Bonaparte, soon to be played by Captain Eddie Thurow.

"I mean what's a regent for, what? Conquering stuff. Like to have Paris, eh, what?"

"Oh, yes, sire!" she had said. As characters go, Beryl, Marchioness of Skye, is not one of Rosemary Klein Kantor's all-time page-turners, but Beryl has her uses and her use at this particular moment is to get the goods on Lady Darlene and drive her not only out of Blenheim Palace but out of Regency Hyatt society altogether.

The previous evening, at bedtime, Beryl had noticed that the link-boy who had lighted Darlene's way up the grand staircase had been a tall, handsome mahogany-colored Negro youth—of a sort seldom found in this sort of novel, as it is set in Regency Hyatt England. But then ever since the collapse of the Equal Rights Amendment, Rosemary has been integrating her books like mad, upgrading every ethnic and/or woman that she can.

Is it my imagination, Beryl now ponders, that Darlene and the dusky youth chatted for a moment longer than was entirely necessary as she stood in the flickering light of his enormous link just outside the massive oaken door to Darlene's bedroom at the end of the long upstairs hall at Blenheim Palace?

Suddenly, from her place beside the open-hearth fire, Darlene rises; looks about furtively; then darts from the room.

A rendezvous! Beryl smiles tightly. Now is her moment to catch the baggage in the act. Since all eyes are on the Prince Regent, who has never been wittier, Beryl is able to slip rather than dart unnoticed from the room.

Just as Beryl enters the long corridor, Darlene shuts the door to her bedroom. On tiptoe, Beryl hurries to the massive oaken door on which hangs a curious sign which says "Pantry." What is a pantry doing up here, a puzzled Beryl asks herself, amongst the tastefully appointed guest bedrooms of the nobility? But then Beryl hears footsteps. She is just able to secrete herself behind the nearest arras an instant before the dusky link-boy appears on the scene, mischievous eyes atwinkle, moist lips parted with lust.

Powerful link in one hand, he opens the door marked "Pantry" with the other.

20

Lieutenant Darlene Ecks, Homicide, is having a good deal of trouble keeping her cool in the pantry of the Lunar Bar at the Duluth Hyatt. Big John is having his problem too—fear being predominant, with lust, as always, a close second.

Big John is now bare as a board. Darlene has never seen anything like him—the beautifully defined but slender muscles, the pelvic line of Mars, the long, rather storklike Watusi legs, the musky sweat pouring down his sides from armpits modestly decorated with what look to be black wires—his hands are locked behind his neck so that she can get the full frontal view in all its African splendor.

Darlene affects—without her customary thespian skill—a lack of interest that is supposed to be based on disinterest in the powerful organs of generation that hang halfway down the sinewy thighs. But she cannot help but notice that the slightest nervous shifting of weight from size twelve to size twelve causes them to swing, pendulumlike, from right to left in a half arc, the result of the superior size and weight of the left prune . . . Prune! she exclaims to herself, wondering how—and why?—she has wasted so much of her time in the land of olé and okra.

Baseball is more like it. No, tennis ball, she decides, as

she allows the huge scrotum to rest gently on the palm of her left hand while in her right hand she still clutches the trusty pistol that she always packs.

"One false move, jungle bunny, and you lose these!" says Darlene, lifting the heavy mass in her search for drugs, as she rationalizes her—for absolutely the first time, ever—totally awakened lust, so different from the mere titillation achieved by the breaking down of the macho pride of your average third-world Latin prune-carrier—a pleasant enough way to while away the odd idle hour but no big deal.

Darlene holds high Big John's tennis balls—except tennis balls are not oblong. No, she decides, they are more like . . . She racks her brain. *Alligator pears!* That's it! She has struck upon the exact simile. Darlene has always preferred similies to metaphors, the result of her first and only year at Duluth U., where she almost took accounting.

Two avocados, one larger than the other, in a warm damp capacious black chamois bag—she is now getting a verbal purchase on the reality that overflows her hand. She also notes, in passing—not that she plans to go anywhere for the moment—that the bag is far too large for its contents. Could this be due to the heat of the pantry? Prunes always shrink and tighten up in her masterful hand. Perhaps Big John is on drugs. But then terror tends to minimize turgid powers. And he is terrified—if sweat is still the bottom-line index.

Darlene presses the heavy burden up against Big John's flat belly to a point that proves to be a mere whisker to the south of the protuberant navel, revealing the glossy perineum, dotted with black wiry hairs—so many cactuses in desert country, she similes to herself, noting, more in anger than in sorrow, that packets of hard drugs have not been hidden in that overprotected area.

"Why . . . ?" Big John's voice is now lacking in sufficient breath to complete a sentence. What, she wonders, is he really afraid of? What is he trying to tell her?

"Yes?" Darlene gives him a winning smile and, simultaneously, rolls the larger avocado against the smaller one. Boys, she has discovered, really hate this.

Big John gasps. "Ow!"

Darlene decides that they even *feel* like alligator pears, a soft texture over a hard stonelike interior. How often Darlene has thought what fun it would be to open up one of these sacs and remove the contents for a good look! But permissive as the DPD is about killing blacks and third-worlders on sight, opening up a scrotum just for fun is a departmental no-no. Forbidden fruit. Not for the first time does Darlene realize just how sexist the DPD is. It is a man's world, after all, though it must be said that at this particular moment it is *not* Big John's world. The oyster, as it were, is in the other court now. She squeezes hard. He gasps.

"Yes?" Then Darlene drops the heavy sac. Back and forth it swings between the lean legs while the *membrum virile*—on police duty Darlene is always careful to call a spade by its technical name—moves from side to side like a pendulum. Without blood, the *membrum* must weigh a pound. She notes that it is black like the scrotum—in marked contrast with the rest of Big John's pale mahogany body.

Then, slowly, Big John's manhood asserts itself. Darlene gasps at what she sees rising toward the pantry ceiling. She is, after all, all woman. He is, after all, more than all man. In fact, Big John, erect, is something altogether else. Can this be—Darlene is now thinking faster than she has ever thought before—*love?* The love that she has never known. "Chico" is large, certainly, in the love department but Big John is beyond anything that she has ever seen before even in the highly detailed centerfolds of those family magazines whose pages she often idly riffles, always on the lookout for electrical appliances with which to furnish her nest just back of McKinley Center.

They confront one another. Man. Woman. Darlene knows in her heart of hearts that the shortest distance be-

tween two points is still a straight line—an incredibly long
thick straight line.

Beryl, Marchioness of Skye, tries the handle to the massive
oaken door to the "Pantry." She smiles, maliciously. The
dusky link-boy has forgotten to secure the door with the key.
She opens the door. In the half-light that is teatime light at
Blenheim Palace, Beryl sees a sight that no one has ever
seen before in a Klein Kantor novel. Although the authoress
is always deep into Romance, nothing is ever really shown
in any detail because Rosemary's kind of reader's imagination, as Rosemary well knows, is so much less than her own
due to all the television that the average Romance reader has
absorbed since birth.

Beryl gasps. But the couple on the bed are oblivious to all
but their own illicit passion—not to mention miscegenation,
punishable by death by impalement for both parties in Regency Hyatt England.

Lady Darlene's white shapely legs are wrapped in a full
nelson about the tawny lithe back of the link-boy—alias Big
John in *Duluth*—who pounds in and out of her with the
speed of a giant hummingbird who has just made it with a
white magnolia.

For a single instant outside time, Beryl is transfixed. She
has never seen such turgid powers—blurred as they are due
to the speed with which the link-boy deploys them. Napoleon Bonaparte hasn't a patch on this stud. Although Beryl
has been the "Little Corporal's" passionate mistress for
over a year (as well as his number-one spy who will assist
him in the coming invasion of England—it is the fateful year
1914), she is forced to admit in her heart of hearts that even
in her limited experience of noblemen and royalty—some
five hundred erotic encounters by her own, admittedly
vague, count—Napoleon is the chipmunk of the lot, while
the other four hundred ninety-nine, including the late March
of Skye, though somewhat better than the "Little Corpo-

ral,'' do not begin to compare to what that slut Darlene has managed to get a full nelson on.

I shall tell Emma, Lady Hamilton, Beryl says to herself, as she slips, albeit reluctantly, from the room. Emma, who is my personal friend, she thinks, will know what to do. England must be cleansed of this menace! Preferably by impalement.

The lovers on the pantry sink take no more heed of Beryl's departure than they did of her arrival. But then the simultaneity effect in this fictive instance was blocked by a sudden change in Rosemary's mood as she hunts and pecks her way toward the ultimate goal of every creator, the Kozinski Communal Effect, perfected in the early years of the Central Intelligence Agency at Langley in Virginia.

21

Edna Herridge—Beryl's death partner of some pages ago—is having lunch in the Bistro Garden of Beverly Hills with Rosemary Klein Kantor. Although in character *this* Rosemary is identical in almost every way to *our* Rosemary, she lives not in New Orleans, the Crescent City, but in Beverly Hills, where, instead of composing romantic tales like *Rogue Duke* and *Countess Mara*, she is the creator of numerous television miniseries. Currently, she is the producer-writer of "Duluth."

This Rosemary and this Edna have known each other for years. They worked together in the Golden Age of Television some thirty years earlier, which means that each girl is, as the French would say, of a certain age. But neither looks to be more than thirty years old, thanks to the wizardry of a certain surgeon in São Paulo, Brazil.

Edna's character in ''Duluth'' is called Hilda Ransome, the judge's widowed sister. When not in ''Duluth'' Edna is the well-known character actress Joanna Witt. In order to avoid confusion, we shall continue to think of her, as she herself does from time to time (hence, the migraine headaches), as Edna Herridge.

The Bistro Garden is crowded with Beverly Hills's beautiful and not-so-beautiful people. ''Good taste abounds,'' as Rosemary observes, ordering a light breakfast wine. Then she turns to Edna. ''You are really making an impression on the viewers, Joanna.''

''Oh, Rosemary! You know and I know it's your words, your heavenly magical words, that make primetime America drop whatever it's doing to look and to *listen* to us 'Duluthians.' '' Edna turns to the waiter. ''The chef's salad, please, without the ham, the cheese or the lettuce.'' The waiter knows Edna's eating habits. He smiles, knowingly.

Rosemary orders the *confit d'oie*. As usual, she is on a diet.

E. G. Marshall, the well-known actor, passes their table. He and the two ladies exchange greetings. At different times the three have worked together. ''What are you up to?'' asks Rosemary. ''Aside from making those lucrative commercials—in the high six figures?''

''I'm doing a one-man show,'' says Mr. Marshall, ''on Ezra Pound.''

''Oh, that's a fab notion!'' says Rosemary. She has heard the name Pound before, somewhere.

''I hope there's a part in it for me!'' says our Edna—their Joanna and ''Duluth's'' Hilda—giving Mr. Marshall a winning smile. He moves off to his table.

''I miss live television,'' says Rosemary thoughtfully. ''Remember Florence Britton?''

''One of the all-time great story editors.''

"Yes."

"Rosémary."

"Yes."

"You've been in analysis?"

"For thirty-one years now. Ever since I wrote my first *Danger* script for CBS."

"It's done you a world of good."

"Yes."

"You're still going to the same analyst?"

"Heavens, no! He died before *Playhouse Ninety*. I'm on my fifth analyst now—with a bit of est, but not too much, on the side." Rosemary looks at Edna—it should be noted that *this* Rosemary has retained the delicious upturned nose that mother nature in one of her extremely rare benign moods has contrived for her. "You have a problem. I've noticed it in the rushes. There are times when you don't seem to be in the script."

"Oh, God! I hope it's not hurting the series!" Edna is agitated, truly.

"No, darling. We just edit those little moments out. But there are these lapses."

"I need help."

"The sky's the limit at Universal."

"They'll pay for an analyst?"

"Santa Claus is our leader Lou Wasserman's middle name."

"I know. I was a fool to ask. Rosemary, I keep thinking that I'm someone else. Selling real estate, in *Duluth* . . ."

"Who is Mayor Herridge?"

Edna is aghast. "You know? How?"

"In that last seg we taped, you went off into this rap about how he mustn't do what he's planning to do to Captain . . . uh . . ."

"Eddie Thurow!" The dam breaks. Edna has someone to reveal all to. "It happens only when I'm on camera. Suddenly, I see through the lens and I can see them back in *Du-*

luth watching me in 'Duluth' and then I can talk to them and they can talk to me.''

"That's a new one, I must say," says Rosemary, all ears.

22

Mayor Herridge is nothing if not the ideal family man. He has a wife who is devoted to him and three children in high school. He has a perfect home life. Like all the great figures in life and literature, he is very domestic—Gargantua, John F. Kennedy, Beowulf, you name him or her and he or she will be a good family man, or as Julius Caesar, the rhetor, once asked, "If you fail at being a husband and parent, what on earth have you got, life-wise?"

But when it comes to politics—good family man or not—Mayor Herridge plays hardball. He is seated now in his study, feet up on his desk, puffing his cigar, watching the TV—and plotting—when, lo and behold! there is his sister Edna smaller than life but very much more alive on the TV.

The Mayor sits bolt upright. "Sis!"

"Oh, my God, it's you!" gasps Edna.

"Of course it's me," says the young man who plays her son, adlibbing.

"I'm up for reelection."

"How does it look?" Edna is relieved that—good family man or not—her brother shows no particular interest in how she has been able to get from the family vault in Lincoln Groves to prime time. She is tired of explaining that to which she has no answer.

While Edna's son in "Duluth" jabbers away about a girl

he has knocked up, Edna looks past him at the lens of the camera where, clear as a bell, she sees her brother through the usual haze of cigar smoke. Since Mayor Herridge likes to do all the talking, Edna can listen to him while waiting for her next cue.

"Captain Eddie's hat is now in the ring. Well, if he thinks he's going to beat me in Duluth, he has another think coming. Edna, you won't believe what I've got on him!"

Edna looks inquisitively at Mayor Herridge. He gets the point. Although a good family man, he is no fool. "You can't talk because the other actor will notice?"

Edna smiles and nods, which disconcerts her son in the miniseries who has just said he is going to kill himself. On the other hand, later, when Rosemary sees the rushes, she will exclaim, "God, she's great! Look at the way she smiles instead of cries! I haven't seen anything like that since Kim Stanley in the Golden Age of Television."

"Whatever happened to Kim Stanley?" asks her co-producer.

"I think she's teaching," says Rosemary.

"I liked her in *Planet of the Apes*."

"That's Kim *Hunter*," says Rosemary disgustedly. These young people have no sense of history, she thinks.

Mayor Herridge is really wound up now. "Police brutality. That's how I'm going to get him. Calculated, *depraved* brutality. Worse than Houston. Captain Eddie's got this sadist on the force. Lieutenant Darlene Ecks, Homicide. She's into S and M with these wetbacks she catches. Roughs them up. Gives them a hard time. The barrios are ready to explode. Well, I'm going to see to it that they do explode. I got Bill Toomey of the Central Intelligence Agency on the job. When the barrios go up in flames, I'll call out the National Guard—at the eleventh hour. Then a couple of neutron bombs and that's the end of the Sixth Ward, where they don't vote for me anyway. That's also the end of Captain Eddie."

"But is all this really Captain Eddie's fault?"

When Rosemary hears this line in the screening room, she

says, "There she goes again! She's into some other script." She turns to the director. "Edit that out." But of course, the line will still be on screen when Mayor Herridge watches "Duluth." Although millions of other viewers will hear the line, none will notice it, because although television is often heard it is never listened to.

"Of course it's his fault! He's supposed to run a tight ship. Anyways, thanks to Lieutenant Darlene Ecks, the barrios are now so much tinder ready to be set ablaze by a single match. When Bill Toomey strikes that match, Captain Eddie—if he survives their senseless rage—will retire to Boca Raton, Florida. And I will be reelected."

Edna's scene is over. She vanishes from the tube. Idly, Mayor Herridge wonders just what Edna is doing in "Duluth" when she should be in the family vault at Lincoln Groves. Most men when they see a dead sister alive in a brand-new miniseries would think that they were going crazy, but not Mayor Herridge. He thinks that Universal TV is crazy for hiring the late Edna Herridge.

Chuckling softly, the Mayor studies the latest reports from his undercover agents in the barrios where Darlene has wrought such havoc. He knows that Pablo has just been elected the chief of the Aztec Terrorists Society.

" 'There'll be,' " he hums, " 'a hot time in the old town tonight.' "

23

Darlene herself is now in a state of havoc unlike any that she has ever before wrought—or had to endure, for that matter.

In the course of two hours—it seems like two seconds—Big John has mounted her five times and each time delivered the goods. Darlene's pink delta feels a bit raw, while her right hand is paralyzed from holding the trusty revolver to Big John's head for two straight hours of absolute ecstasy. Darlene is never *not* the professional policeperson. Yet now she is something else. Something altogether new. Something . . .

As they lie side by side on the pantry sink—not the most comfortable of love nests but still sufficiently large enough for them to essay a number of variations on that missionary position which is the essentially conservative Darlene's usual choice—Darlene realizes, gazing into the eye of her first spade lover ("Chico" never really counted because of the handcuffs and bondage scenes), that she is, at last, a woman. Warm and mature. Loving and giving. And taking. She can take quite a lot, apparently. In fact, she can take a lot more of Big John, she decides, just as soon as she goes to the bathroom.

Darlene desperately needs to tinkle. As she puts the revolver to Big John's temple, she is, suddenly, tender. "Get off me, you black bastard," she whispers.

He obeys with alacrity. She notes that the avocados are still full. Ready to go again. She tries to recall the policeperson's oath. But her head is now all fuzzy. This is what it means to be a real woman, she thinks.

As Darlene squats over the sink, relieving herself, trusty revolver aimed at the source of the ultimate ecstasy, she is thinking hard. Big John in the slammer for twenty years? No way. Scratch. But she *is* a policeperson. She believes in law and order. Yet the thought of those turgid powers enjoying no release for twenty vital years save the odd sock has her up in arms.

"What we gonna do now, fox?" Big John's macho is making a comeback. For an instant, Darlene debates whether or not to pull the trigger. She *has* been raped, after all. And she has every right to blow away the source of her humiliation for which she would be sure to receive the Civic Achievement Medal while Big John, if he survived the loss of his turgid powers, would then not mind the slammer all that much, while his socks would arrive once a week at the prison laundry unsullied.

But even as Darlene Ecks is thinking of the ultimate solution, she knows that she cannot detach from the rest of Big John that which she has come to love. More important, she thinks, as she climbs down off the sink, he has not only managed to slake a lifetime's lust while, simultaneously, awakening it, he has made her the woman she has always dreamed that she might one day be, absolutely after her own heart.

"Put your duds on, dude," she says, watching with sorrow the quick covering-up of all that had been, for two hours, hers.

Darlene puts down her trusty revolver. "Take those handcuffs," she snaps. "Snap them on me."

He does not need to be told anything twice. In an instant, Darlene—mistress of bondage—is handcuffed. She is surprised how much she likes it.

"O.K., Big John, this is the cover story. I caught you dealing. You wrested my trusty revolver away from me. You tore my clothes off. You raped me. Then you split."

Big John looks down on her. He is again masterful in his red jacket with the Lunar Bar logo on the back. He has even got his clip-on bow tie on right.

"Yeah," he says. The mischievous eyes twinkle.

She waits. For what . . . ?

"You sure nobody came in while I was pleasurin' you?" he asks.

Darlene does not quite like the way he takes it for granted that her fluffy delta is getting more pleasure than it gives, but then he is a black dude. "Not to worry," says Darlene, as crisply as a woman who is handcuffed can be crisp.

"But I swear while I was pumpin' away this woman came in the door . . ."

"The door's locked. What you saw was like you were on acid . . ."

"Oh, yeah." He knows what she means. " 'Cept I don't take no acid."

"But you deal. It rubs off. Anyway it was only that bitch Beryl, Marchioness of Skye, who is a spy for Napoleon." Although Darlene is only halfway through Rosemary's *Redbook* serial, she has worked that one out.

"Huh?"

"Split, Big John." Darlene tries to sound hardboiled. But her voice quavers. Then when he kisses her tenderly on the lips, she dissolves into tears. Passively, she allows his masterful hands to gag her with her own exciting panties. She shuts her eyes for a moment. When she opens them, he is gone. Forever? She cannot bear the thought. She is racked with sobs. Silent sobs, due to the gag.

Suddenly, Darlene's eyes become very dry. And round. And glazed. She has just remembered something. She is suddenly panicky. She *must* get to her accessories. Fast. But she cannot move. Cannot call out for help. And who knows when the other barman will enter the pantry in search of cocaine or diet cola?

Darlene is in a state of utter terror because, that morning, Darlene, who won't take the pill, forgot to pop in her diaphragm.

Only foam can save me now, she thinks, desperately. But it must be soon because she is positive that she can actually feel what must be a full gallon of Big John's private proof racing through the dark to that pair of golden eggs which have never before been, but once, by man's essence, brought to *complete* life with, as it were, a kiss.

24

Captain Eddie has decided to handle the whole thing with dignity. Also, he wants to make his peace with Wayne Alexander and the *Duluth Blade*, whose editorial support he is now seeking. Since Mayor Herridge has KDLM-TV all sewed up, Captain Eddie has invited only the print media to his office, where he is about to bestow on Lieutenant Darlene Ecks the department's medal of Civic Achievement.

Lieutenant "Chico" Jones is the only other officer in the room. Captain Eddie likes to play his cards close to his vest. The rest of the Duluth Police Department will learn from the press and the radio that Darlene has been honored. Then full departmental congratulations will be in order. Captain Eddie likes to make everything as complicated as possible. That is his way.

Darlene takes her place in front of the desk where Captain Eddie stands, medal in hand. She is very much aware that she has never looked better. "Rape agrees with you," said one of her fellow policepersons—a woman—earlier that day, a bit snidely, Darlene thought at the time.

Needless to say, Darlene is looking forward to the onset of her next period with more than usual interest. If Big John did not achieve a bull's-eye, she will eat her always fashionable Mainbocher uniform. She will also kill herself, as she is a Roman Catholic and cannot have an abortion, ever— abortion being worse than contraception or suicide in the words of his Eminence Bishop O'Malley of Duluth, who should know. On the other hand, if she has the child—with no father—who will change the diapers and act as a role model? Darlene is a disturbed if awakened woman under the cool exterior that she presents to the clicking cameras of the print media.

Captain Eddie makes a little speech. Darlene says, "I just did my duty. That's all. Win some. Lose some. That's what we're all here for in this department."

Captain Eddie pins on the medal. Then Wayne Alexander comes forward. "Lieutenant Ecks, what you did was very brave. And you've got a lot of spunk, carrying on like this, as if nothing happened."

"So what do *you* think happened?" Darlene is cross; and suspicious.

"Officially, you were violated by a black man—"

"He was more a light mahogany. And I resent what you said about being violated."

"Well, that's what the hospital report said. You were raped."

You could hear a pin drop in the chief of police's office. Until now, euphemism has always been the name of the game at the DPD.

Darlene blushes. "I don't know what you mean," she stammers. "I was just going through S.O.P."

"What's that?" Wayne is a relentless news hound.

"S.O.P. means Standard Order of Procedure," snaps Darlene.

"I know," snaps Wayne, "but just what is the procedure when you have caught a drug dealer or illegal alien dealing in drugs or, maybe, just being alien and illegal?"

Darlene looks at Captain Eddie. But cat has got the Chief's tongue. Since he, too, has seen some of the same reports that Mayor Herridge has been accumulating, he knows that if he lets on that he is aware of what she's been up to, he will be culpable, too. Yet Captain Eddie has always been behind Darlene one hundred percent because, like everyone else, he knows that the only way you can get an illegal alien

72

to cross the Rio Grande and go back home is to hassle him. And Darlene is tops at that.

On the other hand, Captain Eddie has not yet seen the Secret FBI—ears-only—Report which describes the bloodbath of all the gringos that is now being organized by one Pablo Gonzales, whose youthful *membrum virile* Darlene once pressed inside of him, where it remained, of its own accord, for some seconds, making him, for all intents and purposes, during those seconds, a woman. Pablo will not forgive or forget this total insult to his plumed serpent, not to mention the dark gods of the blood. Pablo, according to the FBI, has gone underground in the barrios. The Aztec Terrorists Society is now collecting dynamite and razors. They are also importing barrels of Mexico City tapwater which they intend to introduce into the Duluth reservoir. Beyond that, the FBI knows nothing. Pablo himself has vanished, and the date of the attack on the gringos is unknown.

The FBI has suggested, unofficially, to Mayor Herridge that Darlene be withdrawn from the service for a while—put on sick leave, say, as she is not only truly sick but she is also the match that will ignite the dry tinder that is the hatred in the barrios. But Mayor Herridge has said no, because, of course, he wants a bloodbath. He wants to be reelected over—if necessary—the dead bodies of the entire DPD. Good family man that he is, Mayor Herridge has a dark side to him. But all of this is unknown to the unsuspecting Captain Eddie and Darlene at the medal-giving ceremony.

After Captain Eddie's summing-up policeperson's role model speech, Wayne says, "What's with the spaceship?"

"Nothing new. It's still there. In the desert."

Absently, Captain Eddie removes the red thumbtack. Thoughtfully, he holds it in his hand.

"No news?" Wayne is sharp.

"No news." Captain Eddie is serene.

"Thank *you*, Mr. Chief of Police!" says Wayne, using the age-old phrase that ends every press conference with the chief of police of Duluth. Then Wayne goes.

"Smart bastard," says Darlene.

"Maybe you should go easy on the illegal aliens," says Captain Eddie, putting the red thumbtack not where the spaceship actually is in the desert on the map but in the Duluth Woods. Captain Eddie is no stickler for detail, never has been.

"I will, Chief. I promise." Darlene means it, too. Once a girl has dined, as it were, on a sparerib with yams, the very sight of okra and prunes is nauseous. "Any news of Big John, my rapist?"

"He was seen," says "Chico," "in the barrios last night."

"What's a black man doing there?" Darlene is surprised—and a little perturbed. Hostility between black and brown is a constant in Duluth—and will remain so if Mayor Herridge has his way. After all, should the two groups vote together in one election, they would out-vote and out-elect The Man—as white folks are known to black folks. But this is not about to happen, because Herridge is planning to start a race war—a small manageable race war.

"Yes, it is funny," says "Chico." "I got ahold of his record."

"How old is he?" asks Darlene. At twenty-seven she does not want to be older than the man she loves.

"He's twenty-seven," says "Chico" from a memory that is photographic.

"Married?"

"Never. But he's got three steady girl friends."

"White?"

"Black."

"Oh." Darlene hides her delight. It is well known that black dudes delight in blond goddesses.

"He's also got . . ." "Chico" pauses, awkwardly.

"Clap?" Darlene's subconscious has now broken through and the thought that she has been able to suppress since—and even during—those two hours of ecstasy in the pantry of the Lunar Bar surfaces, dragging in its tow not only syphilis but the dreaded herpes, the lifelong torment of half the DPD's gals.

"Well, maybe. It doesn't say in the report." Captain Eddie has now gone to look out the window, not wanting to pry into the private lives of his subordinates, one of whom now sports the newly bestowed medal of Civic Achievement.

"I gave a smear at the hospital. But sometimes it doesn't always show . . . I mean, Wassermann-wise, all's well, but a lot of the blood's still out and . . ."

"Darlene, you're babbling," says "Chico." "All I was going to say is that Big John, as he is called in the drug world, is the acknowledged father of twenty children for whom he pays the three mothers a generous allowance for clothing, housing, food, schooling. He's some mother, that Big John!"

"Some father," Darlene whispers—and she can feel one of the golden eggs inside begin to glow with a new— unwelcome? —life. Darlene sits in the chair where Captain Eddie grills suspects. Dried blood over the years has given the walnut-veneer surface a rich aubergine sheen.

"He also owns a string of dry-cleaning establishments."

"Acme Cleaners?"

"The same."

"There's one near me. They always do my Mainbocher uniforms for me. They are careful of the fibers—always." A question—egglike—begins to swell in Darlene's brain. "If Big John owns Acme . . . ?"

"He's rich, all right, your rapist." "Chico" is plainly— *obscurely* plainly, that is—jealous.

"So why is he—was he—a barman at the Lunar Bar?"

"That's the biggest drug dispensary in town. And Big John's got a big family to look after."

"And Acme . . . ?"

"There's no better place this side of a Vegas casino or a Hollywood movie studio for laundering hot money than a cleaning service."

"I see," says Darlene. She is now in over her head. She is a changed woman. She will never strip-search again. She has found her man. But she must share him—if he stays out of the slammer—with three black women and twenty children. This is a lot more than Lieutenant Darlene Ecks ever bargained for when first she held, so idly, so frivolously, so contemptuously, those alligator pears in her tiny girlish hand.

Darlene weeps and neither "Chico" nor Captain Eddie knows why—or knows how to comfort her.

25

It is a warm day in June and Chloris and Clive are riding together in the Duluth Woods, as always at this season of the year loud with birdsong and the cries of muggers and their victims. Naturally, Chloris and Clive are armed to the teeth in their expensive (Huntsman Ltd. of London) riding togs. They have just been to see the foundation being laid for the palatial home that Clive has engaged the world-famous architect Philip Jackson to build for him high on Garfield Heights. It is to cost twenty million dollars. Made of a wide assortment of costly marbles, semiprecious stones and Byzantine mosaics, the house, when finished, will contain one bedroom, a drawing room with wet bar and a loggia from the Minoan period (1500 B.C.) newly found at Thera in the Aegean Sea and smuggled to Duluth, as most beautiful rare things are nowadays.

"I don't want a dining room or a kitchen," says Clive, "as I like to eat out."

"Oh, you are so wise, darling," says Chloris, who is deeply in love despite what *might* be a difference in age of a quarter century if anyone is counting—and no one would dare, outside Duluth's high society.

"I mean if I want a snack, I can always send out to Jack-in-the-Box and then eat it in my loggia—or painted stoa, which is the right name, I believe."

"I think I love a stoa more, even, than a loggia."

"Chloris!"

"Clive!"

In love, they ride through the noisy greeny woods.

"I don't want a guest bedroom either," says Clive, returning to the subject of the new house.

"Because you don't want an overnight guest?" laughs Chloris, fishing like mad.

"You're fishing like mad, you minx! No, I want you all to myself. In *my* room. *My* bed. *Mine!* Divorce Bellamy. Marry me."

"Oh, child!" Chloris frowns. Clive has been going on about this ever since their love affair began that afternoon at The Eucalyptus Club. "We have an open marriage, after all," she explains, yet again.

"Well, I want you to shut it. With you and me inside."

The boy's ardor stirs her. She wonders how she could ever have disliked his huge flat nose. Nevertheless, Mrs. Bellamy Craig II is an institution not only in Duluth but as far afield as Georgetown and Sausalito. Could Mrs. Clive Hoover—the name makes her think, guiltily, of Wayne Alexander and the perhaps forever-interrupted Betty Grable bio—take the place of Mrs. B.C. II? Would it sound right? Would it *be* right? Bellamy himself would not care. But if he took another wife she would then be . . . Warm though the greeny June day is, Chloris shivers. It is as if someone had started to do the hully-gully on her grave.

"Look!" says Clive.

Chloris looks and there, up ahead, in a clearing where once had been a Japanese teahouse, is something huge and red and round. Something absolutely out of place. But familiar. Chloris racks her brains. As she is racking them, Clive says, "It's another of those spaceships! It's an invasion!"

But then "Chico" Jones comes into view. He has been making a circuit of the ship, a walkie-talkie in his hand through which he talks to Captain Eddie back at headquarters. "No," he says, in answer to Clive's cry. "It's not another spaceship. It's the same one."

Chloris and Clive tether their horses. Then, adjusting their togs, they join "Chico" at the spaceship, which is just as gummy and disagreeable-looking as ever.

"When did it move here?" asks Chloris.

"Not long ago," says "Chico," vaguely. But he's beginning to suspect just when it moved. In a minute, of course, Captain Eddie will know for sure and he will tell "Chico."

Captain Eddie's voice comes crackling out of the walkie-talkie. "Does your present position conform to position previously suggested by this headquarters?"

"Yes, Chief. To the last parameter," says "Chico."

"Stand by," says Captain Eddie. As the three stand by, the spaceship rises slowly in the air. Then it disappears. There is no sound of a motor or engine or anything. The thing just goes away.

"Curious to know on what principle it runs," remarks Clive, who has always had a yen for engineering, discouraged by his mother, Beryl, in her restless search for higher and higher social position.

26

The Prince Regent takes Beryl, Marchioness of Skye, and leads her toward the gazebo in the rose garden at Windsor. It is the sort of lowering day that Mondrian might have painted.

"Beryl, you're my kind of gel, you know?"

"Oh, sire!" Beryl's ready wit has already made for herself a place *sans pareil* at the Regency Hyatt court.

The Prince Regent laughs uproariously at this sally. "You make me laugh. You make me cry. I don't know what I would do were you ever to leave me."

"Sire, I can go no higher," says Beryl, lying.

The Prince Regent, sides heaving with mirth, sits down on a bench beneath a marble statue of Queen Victoria. He pulls Beryl down beside him. "I think I should tell you, I am going to invade France *before* Napoleon Bonaparte invades England."

"No!"

"Yes!"

Beryl's eyes narrow. This is pretty heavy stuff, spy-wise. "Have you . . . made a plan?"

"It's all here." The Prince Regent removes a sheet of paper from his pocket.

"In writing?"

"Yes, you delicious slyboots!"

Beryl knows now that she must, out of love for Napoleon and France, gain possession of that sheet of paper.

27

Meanwhile, back in Duluth, Captain Eddie now understands the principle which caused the spaceship to move from the desert to the Duluth Woods. But to be absolutely sure, he has looked it up in his old high school physics textbook, where he finds that, according to Pynchon's lesser corollary to the law of gravity, whenever a spaceship (macro) is represented by an object (micro) on an *exact* chart of where gravity insists it rest when not under propulsion, then *macro* will move on its plane exactly as *micro* moves on its representational plane. But due to the law of fictive coincidence, the converse does not hold: Though *macro* moves, *micro* cannot, held down, as it is, by the gravity that *macro* is freed of under propulsion. Naturally, Captain Eddie had learned all this back in P.S. 49 but he thinks it a good idea to crack the old books again, just to confirm his "gut instinct."

After ascertaining by walkie-talkie from "Chico" that the spaceship is indeed in the Duluth Woods where, not thinking, he had stuck the red thumbtack, Captain Eddie picks up the red thumbtack and holds it for a moment in the air. Where shall he place it now? If the map showed anything but the Greater Duluth area he would stick it in the middle of the Pacific Ocean twenty miles to the north. But he is limited to Greater Duluth. The desert off ethnic Kennedy Avenue seems the logical place to put it. After all, that's where the monster centipedes—which is how Captain Eddie pictures the crew of the ship as a result of Dr. Guy's report—put it in the first place.

But then, suddenly inspired, Captain Eddie plunges the red thumbtack into that corner of Lake Erie which joins with the Colorado River at the edge of the Fifth Ward where the black folks live.

"There!" says Captain Eddie. "Now maybe those centipedes will drown."

28

It has been a long lunch at the Bistro Garden. Twice Edna has sent back the chef's salad. The first time to remove the shreds of cheese. The second time to remove the lettuce.

"You always were a picky eater," says Rosemary, admiringly. She likes temperament in an actress.

E. G. Marshall has finished his lunch and as he passes their table, he says, "So long."

"I'll be auditioning for your one-man show," says Edna, a twinkle in her eye.

After Mr. Marshall has gone, Edna levels with Rosemary. "I'm not getting enough lines in my scenes with the judge."

Rosemary sighs. She has heard all this before. She gives her standard answer: "For my stars, I write, as you know, a ratio of two to one per page of dialogue. First page: judge has two lines to your one. Second page: you have two lines to his one."

Edna has heard all *this* before. "Yes, angel. But there's such a thing as *word count*. My lines are always broken. I have twice as many three dotses as he has. He'll give a long speech. Then I'll say, 'you mean dot dot.' "

"But that's not just two dots, that's actually two dots plus a real biggie, a *question mark*, which gives you a lot more to play as an actress."

"Don't con me, Rosemary." Edna now mounts her high Emmy-winning horse. "I've got, technically, one line, yes. But it's only two lousy words plus two lousy dots, and as for being able to play one of your sleazy question marks—" Edna breaks off. "My God! It's happening again."

Edna stares at a couple who are being shown to a better table than theirs by Kurt, the creator of the Bistro Garden as well as of its flagship up the road, the Bistro.

"What's happening?" Rosemary sees only an elegant young man, dressed by Armani, with a wide flat nose, and a chic older woman dressed by Valentino.

"It's Mrs. Bellamy Craig II, the social pinnacle of *Duluth*. The real Duluth, that is. Where I used to be. She's one of the ones I see in the lens of the camera. But now—there's no lens! She's here. This means that I can go back to selling real estate in *Duluth!*"

"And give up your career?" Rosemary is aghast. She is also tough as nails. "You've got a contract with Universal, sweetie. You're committed to thirteen episodes of 'Duluth' . . ."

"Shove it," says Edna, hurrying toward Chloris and Clive at their better table.

Rosemary is alarmed. It will be a lot of work writing Joanna Witt, Emmy Award-winning actress, out of "Duluth" at this point in the series. But, she decides, grimly, if she has to, she will. Not for nothing is Rosemary Klein Kantor queen of daytime television. She is ruthless when it comes to her art.

Clive and Chloris have just jetted in on the private jet Clive has bought as a tax shelter: not only do you get an enormous amount of depreciation and write-off on a jet as well as being able to deduct the salaries of the crew which they then kick back to you a part of but you can also pick up some extra change by renting out your jet to people with money to burn.

Chloris has had, for days, a hankering for the chef's salad at the Bistro Garden. Since Clive is in love, the sky's the limit as far as Chloris goes. The day before they went riding in the Duluth Woods they lunched at the Bistro Garden. Then, after attending the spring sales at Ted Lapidus's elegant shop, they jetted back to *Duluth*, making good use of the very same anomalous fictional warp that is driving poor Edna out of her gourd.

Edna is now beginning to see double, as she is now—true to the warp—in two narratives at once. But she is nothing if not game. "Chloris, darling! It's me."

"What's that?" asks Clive, aware of Chloris's discomfiture.

"She is the TV star Joanna Witt, out here," explains Chloris to Clive, "but when she's in 'Duluth,' the TV series, she is, sometimes, I don't know why, the late Edna Herridge, realtor, or so she says. Hello, Edna, or should I call you Miss Witt?"

But the now total double-exposure is too much for Edna, who slips to the floor in a faint. Rosemary Klein Kantor and two waiters hurry over. "I'm so sorry," says Rosemary. "But Miss Witt is not herself today."

"Quaaludes," whispers Clive to Chloris. In his day he has hung out more than he'd like Chloris to know in the West Hollywood Hills. Neither, fortunately, recognizes *this* Rosemary Klein Kantor nor does she recognize them, as the classic fictive law holds absolutely firm in this case, due, in large part, to her small nose.

29

Mayor Herridge enters the kitchen of his modest but comfortable home. The two sons and a daughter who are having their lunch—they are home for the start of the summer holidays—spring to their feet with cries, "Kiss me, Daddy!" and he kisses all three little shavers warmly while Mrs. Herridge stands at the stove, stirring her lovingly prepared Campbell's home-style minestrone. There is a tear of joy in her eye as she watches this warm tableau. She married a winner, and she knows it. But, best of all, together she and the winner have produced three grand little shavers. While every other shaver in Duluth has been sent away either to summer camp or reform school, the Herridge shavers will be staying home to be with their loving Mom and Daddy. "I sure lucked in," she thinks to herself, as she stirs the soup. "And I'm the first lady of Duluth to boot."

But their happy family life is abruptly suspended by the arrival of Bill Toomey, the Mayor's right hand. Even though it is a Sunday morning—time for church—the business of the city never lets up.

"Your Honor, can I speak to you privately? Mornin', Mrs. Herridge. Mornin', three shavers."

"Mornin', Bill Toomey!" the happy family sings out, always glad to see Daddy's right hand, even if it does mean that Daddy won't be going to church with them, where he joins in the hymns, lustily. They are Lutherans.

Mayor Herridge—whose not very Christian name used to be Mayor until he dropped it by deed-poll after his election

as mayor on the sensible ground of redundancy—and Bill
Toomey go into the Mayor's study.

"What is it, Bill?" The Mayor lights up his long black
stogy.

"The spaceship."

"That fucking thing! What now?"

"It's moved again."

"From the Duluth Woods?"

"Yeah. It's in Lake Erie now, a few yards from the
waterfront."

"*Under* water?" For a moment Mayor Herridge is hope-
ful. In a way, he and his archrival Captain Eddie are quite a
bit alike.

"No. It's floating on the water. The fishermen are belly-
aching like mad."

"I never get their vote anyway. What's the Chief
doing?"

"He looks like he's just swallowed a canary. It seems he
predicted—this A.M.—that the spaceship would end up in
Lake Erie."

"That can mean only one thing. He's in cahoots with
those Communists inside the spaceship. Bill, this is our
breakthrough!" Mayor Herridge is genuinely excited. Like
all politicians he thinks only of elections. He has long since
decided that, for his purposes, the spaceship is filled with
Russian Communists and he has been extremely gratified
that at least one of the many presidents of the United States
has agreed in public that this is probably the case.

"Call up KDLM-TV. I'll go on the *Six O'Clock News* tomorrow night. As this is a major emergency, tell them I will
want the full ninety-second crisis slot between the standard
downtown fire and the child-in-jeopardy spots."

"You got it, boss."

"But I don't want Leo Lookaloney for the interview."

"Consider him dead. Now then, your Honor, you got a
second?"

"Well, I *should* be joining the wife and the little shavers at church . . . ." Mayor Herridge's eyes fill with tears as they always do when he thinks of his family and his closeness to them. "A second for what, Bill?"

"Operation Chile-con-Carne." This is the secret code name for the plan to inflame the barrios, and destroy Captain Eddie.

"Yeah. I got a second," says Mayor Herridge, stubbing out his cigar in the bronze ashtray given him by the Teamsters Union the previous summer. "Shoot, Bill."

30

Darlene has taken to hanging out at the Acme Cleaning establishments. But none of the employees—all black—will give her so much as the time of day.

"Big John? Who he, honey?" was the longest and least pungent response that she has been able to elicit from any Acme employee in the McKinley area.

Disconsolately, Darlene crosses busy McKinley Avenue with its numerous elegant shops and movie theaters. It is a brilliant summer day. Supposedly, she is investigating a murder in the McKinley Plaza Hotel but her heart is not in that particular murder. Truth to tell, Darlene's heart is now only in one place. She is in love. Head over heels in love. She has not conducted a single strip-search since she found perfect love in the pantry of the Lunar Bar.

Although Darlene has lost all interest in illegal aliens, they have not lost all interest in her. By night, Pablo moves throughout the barrios, inflaming the already overheated wetbacks. Posters of Darlene can be found in the back rooms of every hovel, covered with spittle—and worse! The illegal alien women are all getting a bit uptight. Who is this blond beautiful gringa who is bringing out the macho beast in their men? they whisper to one another as they iron their tacos. What can it all mean? they ask, as they stitch their tortillas. What is her strange power over their men? they ponder, folding their tortillas with practiced fingers. Every last one of them would give an eyetooth to be able to get such a rise out of her man, for is not hate, as they say in the barrios and nowhere else, akin to love?

Unaware of the dangers that lie in store for her once she crosses McKinley Avenue and enters the barrios, Darlene walks, as in a dream, which she is—of love—into what Duluthians call Little Yucatán.

Obsidian black inscrutable eyes in age-old Mayan or Aztec faces immediately recognize Lieutenant Darlene Ecks, Homicide, whose recipiency of the Civic Achievement Medal has not gone unremarked in the local Spanish press. As Darlene, a dazed smile on her moist lips, pauses at a colorful outdoor market where chiles and peppers and black beans are bought and sold by women in the colorful black dresses of their original homeland, Pablo and two accomplices materialize just back of the chickpea stall.

Pablo whispers, in Spanish, which they all speak to one another when they are alone together, as they are all illegal aliens, "There she is! Ours," he adds, "to do with as we will!" A little smile crosses his face and yet, for reasons he cannot fathom—is not the shoe definitely on the other foot now?—he can feel a certain shrinkage of his okra and a definite tightening of the prunelike *cojones*. He realizes, with shame, that he is still afraid of her and he knows that there is but one way to exorcise that fear. Slowly, from beneath his serape, he draws a long knife. "This is it, muchachos," he mutters to his two accomplices. The plumed serpent that Darlene once pushed inside of him will now be avenged, with blood.

As Darlene—still in her stupor of love—enters an alley

which is, unknown to her, a dead end, the three young Mexicans follow her.

Halfway down the deserted alleyway, Darlene realizes that it is a dead end. As she turns to go back to the market, she sees three figures, blocking her way. Illegal aliens, she notes in a flash. Although she has given up strip-search, she cannot control what is for want of a better adjective or cliché a Pavlovian response. After all, has she not been a crackerjack policewoman for six years? She still has a duty to perform. She starts toward them.

But when she sees three drawn knives, three menacing leers, she stops in her tracks.

Darlene calls for help but there is no help for Darlene in the barrios—only hate, and death.

31

Bill Toomey leads Mayor Herridge into the high school gymnasium. Although it is shut for the summer, the smell of dirty socks and marijuana is stifling.

Mayor Herridge holds a handkerchief over his nose as he enters the basketball court. Then, in his own tracks, he stops —unable to believe his eyes. Bill Toomey has done it again.

Twelve uniformed policemen and twelve uniformed policewomen are lined up in front of him. Each of the twelve women is a dead ringer for Darlene Ecks. Each of the twelve men looks as if he could be Darlene's twin brother. All of them are blond—some peroxided, of course, but the effect is the same—and all of them are blue-eyed. Each of the twenty-four is in the absolute pink of condition.

"Jesus!" Mayor Herridge is reverent through his hand-kerchief. "Where did you get them, Bill?"

"FBI, CIA, DIA, DEA, Treasury agents, Bureau of Nar-cotics agents—every single federal spy agency was able to contribute its Darlene look-alike."

"How are we going to keep Captain Eddie from finding out?"

"Simple. If caught, the cover story is that they are federal agents investigating the Communists inside the spaceship. But they won't be caught because we're counting on sur-prise. The second you give the word, Operation Chile-con-Carne will be operational. The men will strip-search the women. The women the men. By nightfall, Duluth will be in flames. Then we send in the national guard. Nuke the bar-rios. And you will win the election as the Law-and-Order candidate."

"Bill, they don't don't make them like you anymore."

"No. They don't," says Bill, who knows his value. "Meanwhile, these folks here are undergoing intensive training in the Duluth desert."

Bill turns and addresses the intensively trained twenty-four Darlene look-alikes in a loud voice, "Men and women of the special brigade, it is my honor and pleasure to intro-duce, at this time, his Honor the mayor of Duluth, Mayor Herridge."

Mayor Herridge is not certain whether or not Bill—in his sly way—has managed to use his original forbidden-to-all-employees-of-the-city first name. But if Bill has, the Mayor will forgive him this minor transgression because Bill Toomey has really come through with the goods.

"My friends!" Mayor Herridge's orator's voice is like honey, pouring from a glittering Steuben glass "Bernard X. Wolff original design" pitcher.

There is a lot more in this vein, of course.

32

Chloris is alone with Wayne in her expensive but chic drawing room overlooking the city. A buffet is being set up by Mexican servants in the dining room, which is next to the drawing room. Chloris is giving a small *intime* party for Rosemary Klein Kantor, who is coming in from the Crescent City for the weekend. Rumor has it that Rosemary is contemplating moving to Duluth. The Eucalyptus Club is divided over this. But Chloris, all in all, welcomes the idea of another famous author in her city.

"I'll have someone to talk shop to," says Chloris to Wayne. Chloris is somewhat uneasy with Wayne, as well she should be. After all, she has, more or less, dumped Wayne, who does not like being dumped.

"You'll have to learn to read first," snaps Wayne, whose snap is a lot worse than most people's snap.

Chloris winces. "You know how to hurt me, don't you?"

"Yes."

"Actually," says Chloris, defensively, "I can read a great many *short* words. After all, I was taught the look-say method in school. But since I have had so much to think about since I was in school I now don't remember anything that I looked at or said except, for some reason, the three-letter words. Not only can I recognize *every* single three-letter word, I can say it, too. So that's not doing so bad, is it?"

Maliciously, Wayne writes on his reporter's pad in big

90

block letters C-A-T. ''What's that?'' he asks, holding up the pad.

''I refuse to be tested in my own residence.'' Chloris is very huffy indeed. She is also not entirely sure just what the word is. She has seen it before, of course, many times. She also knows that she has always liked the way the first letter curves. It is one of her favorite letters. She has never liked the middle letter, which often trips her up. The last letter she can take or leave alone, she has no feeling about it one way or the other.

''*What is this word?*'' Wayne stares at her intensely.

''Don't use that tone with me, Wayne.''

''I'll use any tone I damn well please, you two-timing bitch.''

''Then I shall call for the butler.''

''Just try.''

''The word,'' says Chloris, upper lip as close to a snarl as her plastic surgeon would allow her, ''is 'cat.' ''

''No,'' lies Wayne, triumphantly, ''it's 'cow,' which is what you are!''

''I can't believe we're quarreling like this!'' Chloris bursts into tears. She is also nearly one hundred percent positive that the word on the pad is 'cat.' This means that if Wayne is lying to her about 'cat,' he is capable of lying to her about almost anything. Strange, she muses, now no one ever really knows anyone in Duluth. She blows her nose, carefully.

Wayne is now pacing the floor. ''What if I were to expose to the world that not only does 'Chloris Craig' not write the 'Chloris Craig' books but she can't even read them or anything else?''

''You know, Wayne, that that is blackmail.'' Chloris is now very cool.

''So?''

''You can end up in the clink.''

''Have I asked for money?''

''Not yet.''

"Then you have no case."

"But I can *say* that you asked for money. And who will believe Wayne Alexander over Mrs. Bellamy Craig II?"

Wayne stops his pacing. "What do you see in that pansy?"

"*Which* pansy?" Chloris is now total mistress of herself. She has nerves of steel.

"Clive Hoover."

"Oh, Clive? He's sweet. He amuses me. That's all. We're simply friends. We play backgammon at The Eucalyptus Club, where no journalist has ever set foot."

"Do you deny that you're having an affair with him?"

"Well, he *is* a pansy. Or so *you* say, and you should know, working on a *newspaper* . . ."

Clive Hoover, the subject of the conversation, enters the room. He is wearing a violet silk caftan and six strands of pearls. A tiny frown crosses, briefly, Chloris's face. Maybe there *is* something in what Wayne says. But, no! How could there be? Those hours of passion they have known together could not be simulated. Yet, even so, why did Clive steal her vibrator? She is positive that it was Clive who took it their first night together. At first, she was thrilled by the symbolism of the gesture. But now . . . Wayne Alexander has succeeded in his mission. He has sown the seed of suspicion in fertile soil.

"Darling!" Clive kisses Chloris's cheek. As he does, he whispers in her ear, "What's that creep doing here?"

Like most one-eared men, Wayne has uncommon hearing. "I'm here to discuss Chloris's new book on the murder of Betty Grable."

"Oh." Clive is taken aback. He had not wanted Wayne to overhear him because it has been his policy to stay on the right side of this particular creep, who is, after all, a journalist who can make or break a social figure and, truth to tell, Clive is, at heart, the same social climber that his late mother was—as well as something much more, which she was, too.

"Yes, Wayne is my invaluable researcher," says Chloris.

"Who is this Betty Grable?" Clive is too young to remember Betty. Impatiently, he fingers his pearls, as he is told about the dead star at great length. "So," he says, when they finally shut up, "who killed her?"

"*I* know," says Wayne, smugly. "In fact, I am the only one now alive who knows."

"Well, who did it? After all, I'm paying you as a researcher," snaps Chloris, no mean snapper herself.

But at that moment Rosemary Klein Kantor, in a Pucci afternoon teagown, limps into the room, a bright smile on her lips. They greet her effusively. Clive is midway through the latest installment of *Rogue Duke* in *Redbook* and he has recognized his mother, thickly disguised as Beryl, Marchioness of Skye. He says as much to the creatrix.

"Oh, is *that* your mother?" Rosemary looks thoughtful. "Yes, it's possible. As you know, I thought that she had got into *Countess Mara* but, lately, as I've been assembling that gorgeous tale on my word-processor, I've been having this sense that she never really did join that book, in spite of there being the reservation in her name. And, of course, you're right. She did become the Marchioness of Skye in the middle of installment two. I was aware of that at the time. Has she sent you a message from Regency England?"

"Not so far. But I think that she now knows that I'm reading her, which is something."

"Well, I won't spoil your fun by telling you how the story ends." Actually, Rosemary never knows in advance how—or even if—her stories will end. As a result, some of them never do end, to the consternation of those of her characters who are left to mill about in limbo, unable to move on to new assignments. In the memory bank of Rosemary's elaborate word-processor, ten thousand historical novels are on deposit, and once Rosemary is at the controls, dexterously stealing plots, characters, sentences, words, no one—least of all she—can tell what will happen next.

Chloris notices Wayne's reporter's pad on the sofa. She picks it up and shows Rosemary the word that he wrote. "Darling, I left my glasses upstairs. What is this word?"

" 'Cat,' " says Rosemary, whose reading skills are well above the average in Duluth.

"Swine!" Chloris rounds on Wayne—who cringes.

"No, cat," says Rosemary. "As among the pigeons. What a lovely caftan," she says to Clive. Rosemary likes very rich people even more than she likes just plain rich people.

"Thanks, Rosemary. I have always had a feeling for rare stuffs. Exquisite fabrics. Costly jewels."

Chloris tries to avoid Wayne's eyes but cannot. Clive is now flying about the room. "Rare *objets d'art*. Bibelots. Masterpieces of the cabinet-maker's art. These are the very essence of my being. Why else would I be in Duluth?"

"Politically," says Rosemary, sitting down in a stiff chair and arranging her lame leg on top of an exquisite Chippendale milkstool, to the horror of Clive, who stops flitting, and of Chloris, who is too polite to say anything but does look a dagger or two at Rosemary, who is now dominating, as she always does, the social occasion, "I have always refused to give up my principles."

"Which are what?" asks Wayne Alexander, retrieving his journalist's pad from the sofa.

"Well known to most of my readers, I should think." Although Rosemary likes nothing better than to repeat herself, she usually prefers to do so on her own terms. Nevertheless, she is polite to Wayne because she, too, likes to stay in good with the press. There is not a book reviewer in the Crescent City who has not been at least a dozen times to Rosemary's home to eat one of her homemade gumbos while listening to her tall stories of the great days when she alone in the United States stood up to Hitler. "It was lonely, yes," she says, rocking the bad leg back and forth, causing the Chippendale to creak ominously. "But I'm used to battling alone. I don't run from a fight. I knew Hitler was bad news as early as

'29—I mean '39. Not," she says quickly, "that I was much more than knee-high to an azalea at the time, on my mother's plantation near Baton Rouge . . . Oh, the smell of those azaleas! You know, even now, their heady fragrance recalls to me those happy days . . ."

"Azaleas have no scent," says Clive, who is growing bored. He is also worried about the Chippendale stool.

"That's what I said." Rosemary, like all great writers and highly paid processors of words, is a quick and ingenious liar. "It is the scent of peonies that always recalls to me our plantation in the spring . . ."

"Peonies don't grow in Louisiana," says Clive, getting very snippy indeed. He has now decided that Rosemary is tacky. He also remembers that his mother, Beryl, would not allow a Klein Kantor novel in their Tulsa home. Now poor Beryl is stuck in *Rogue Duke*. Clive feels compassion for his late mother. After all, she left him an empire.

"Those *particular* peonies were grown at great expense in our extensive greenhouses!" snarls Rosemary, causing the stool to crash beneath the weight of her lame leg.

In the Crescent City Rosemary Klein Kantor is known to one and all as "Our Lady of the Flies."

33

"Chico" Jones and his policeman buddy are driving their police car down ethnic Kennedy Avenue. As they pass the stretch of desert where the spaceship first landed, "Chico" says, "I wonder what's inside that thing."

"The spaceship?"

"Yeah. I don't think it's centipedes."

"No," says the buddy, who has a subscription to *Popular Mechanics*. "I mean how could a centipede drive something like that?"

"It doesn't look really Russian either," broods "Chico."

"Well, it *is* red—and gummy."

"That's true. The Chief has got to go and get it out of Lake Erie, somehow."

"Yeah. The fishermen say it's scared away all the salmon."

At that moment a stolen car pulls out in front of their police car and races towards Route 99, which crosses the desert at this juncture on its way to Pittsburgh.

"Follow that car!" commands "Chico." On skidding, smoking tires they take the hairpin curve that connects Kennedy Avenue with Route 99. In no time at all the driver of the stolen car loses them.

"All right," says "Chico" glumly, "let's go back to the city."

Little does "Chico" suspect that Darlene is in an abandoned warehouse at the edge of the barrios.

Darlene is scared, really scared. This can't be happening, she thinks. This is all a dream. But it is not a dream.

Darlene's own handcuffs handcuff her hands—so different from the last time when they were *lovingly* handcuffed by Big John. It's like it was another world, the Lunar Bar, she muses, as Pablo and his two accomplices use their long knives to cut to shreds the always-in-fashion Mainbocher uniform.

"Scream all you like, gringa, no one can hear you!" shouts Pablo. "This abandoned warehouse is a million miles from nowhere." Pablo's English is much improved since he has taken over the leadership of the Aztec Terrorists Society.

Darlene is now down to her jockey shorts and bra. The illegal aliens laugh when they see the jockey shorts. "Some kind of a degenerate,'' says one accomplice in Spanish to the other.

"This could well explain her highly perverse psychology which has resulted in those plainly psychotic—there is no other word—assaults on our Latin manhood.''

"Soon to be avenged—and terminated,'' says the other accomplice. They speak excellent Spanish, thinks Darlene, who can order a meal or arrest a killer in Spanish but has as hard a time speaking fluent Spanish as they have speaking English.

At the time that Pablo Gonzales was strip-searched the only English word that he really had a grip on was "what.'' He has now learned a lot more words, which he proceeds to use on Darlene.

"O.K., gringa. Let's see them titties!'' He tears away her bra. She gasps. He gasps. "Mother of God!'' he exclaims raptly. "So big!''

"They are indeed perfection itself,'' says the first accomplice, whose name is Calderón Gonzales, a muscular youth. "Roseate nipples,'' continues Calderón raptly, "of a sort we never get to see except in the 'girlie' magazines which the Cardinal Primate of all Mexico has forbidden to us.''

"Do you actually obey him?'' asks the second accomplice, Jesús Gonzales—each is named Gonzales but they are not related to one another; even so, they are like brothers. Jesús fondles one of Darlene's jugs while Pablo feasts with hungry mouth on the other, like an unweaned piglet home to the sty.

"Oh, indeed I do,'' says Calderón, pulling down the jockey shorts.

All three stare, rapturously, at the delta's golden fur—dry as Death Valley at the moment. This is definitely *not* Darlene's sort of scene. Although she is able to follow in a general way the idle drift of their conversation, she does not really know the language well enough to make any particular contribution to what, basically, is now a theological discussion.

"Yet I feel," says Calderón, stretching wide Darlene's delta so that the dainty clit is fully exposed, "that the Cardinal Primate's intent was to deny us not the pictures in *Playboy* so much—"

"I like *Hustler!*" says Jesús.

"Now that *is* vulgar. No, his Eminence, I think, when he issued his bull, was more concerned with the secular humanist values expressed by Señor Hefner in the *text* of *Playboy* rather than in those basically anodyne shots of blond beaver."

"Speaking of blond beaver," says Pablo, lapsing into his native tongue, "we've got us a winner. Spread them legs, Calderón."

Calderón—a crypto-admirer of the *Playboy* philosophy, which is so markedly unlike that of Aquinas—shoves Darlene's legs apart. Darlene is now too terrified to scream. She is also a tad, as they say at police headquarters, curious. She has never seen an erect okra. Will there be a surprise in store for her? She watches, with alert eyes, as three sets of trousers and drawers drop to six pointy shoes, which are never removed, voluntarily, by illegal aliens during a rape or even a housecall due to the embarrassing ubiquitousness of corns.

Pablo's *membrum virile*, fully erect, measures three inches. The other two okras are somewhat larger. Darlene notes that Calderón's foreskin does not retract in either the turgid or tumescent state while the Cardinal's exegesist's *membrum* bends slightly to the left. Well, one thing, thinks Darlene philosophically, I'm not going to *feel* much of anything.

Pablo, leering, okra in hand, now poises himself at the rim of Darlene's capacious honeypot.

34

Chloris's reception for Rosemary Klein Kantor is not getting off the ground. For one thing, the guest of honor has not stopped talking since the Chippendale stool broke.

But Clive, thank God, thinks Chloris, has stopped flitting and is now staring bleakly at the view of Lake Erie where the spaceship is plainly visible. Clive cannot make up his mind which red is in the worst taste—the spaceship's or mother nature's lurid sunset.

Five alien maids—led by dark-eyed Carmencita, the La Pasionara of the barrios—cater to every gustatory whim of two dozen of the best couples in Duluth society who have fallen upon the buffet like biblical locusts. Even Bellamy has forsaken his Jean Harris Diet for the elk's heart and onion pâté that is the sine qua non of Chloris's kitchen.

Chloris notices, grimly, that hardly anyone stops very long near Rosemary's chair. Only Wayne has not left her side. He scents a story, somewhere, somehow.

Chloris wonders what on earth has got into Rosemary. Ordinarily, she is good if boring company. But at this socially important function in her honor she has suddenly shown her true colors. Not only is she a living legend, she is a fabulist. Chloris would not have believed this metamorphosis if she had not witnessed it.

"I was in Hiroshima when the first atomic bomb fell. You probably remember the story I filed the day after. *Dateline Hiroshima by Rosemary Klein Kantor*. I was with Hearst in those days. Boy, was Ernie Pyle pissed off that I had scooped him.''

''But wasn't Ernie Pyle already dead by then?'' asks Wayne, who had done rather well in the history of American journalism course at Rutgers, admittedly a short course.

''That's what I said,'' says Rosemary, irritably. ''If he wasn't dead, how could I have scooped him? It was Quentin Reynolds who was livid . . .''

''But, surely, Mr. Reynolds was in London, wasn't he?''

''Quentin Reynolds was—and is—where I say he is—or was. I could drink him under the table in those days. Where was I? Hiroshima. Yes. I had been parachuted into Japan by General Doolittle some months before. In disguise, of course. My Japanese was fluent in those days—and my features were out of *Madame Butterfly*. If I say so myself, I was exquisite in my blue and green pagoda, with the joss sticks stuck in my thick glossy hair.''

35

''Chico'' Jones and his policeman buddy are driving aimlessly along the edge of the barrios, stopping a few crimes, starting a few others. You never know what you set in motion when you take an action of any kind, as ''Chico'' often says, when he is in a reflective mood.

''Say, whatever happened to that spade who raped Darlene?'' asks his buddy.

''Darned if I know,'' says ''Chico.'' ''He's hiding out, I guess. The narcs are after him.''

''They say he's about the richest man in the colored community." "Chico's" buddy is white and very sensitive to "Chico's" sensitivity about the word "black," which "Chico" hates, preferring "colored" as more descriptive.

"Oh, he's rich all right. But he's greedy. For money. Women. Power."

"That's me you're describing," says the buddy, with a chuckle.

Just then—at the very edge of the barrios—"Chico" hears a familiar scream. "My God," he exclaims, "that is Darlene's scream. They've got her!"

"Where?"

They turn on their police car searchlight. Up ahead, they are able to make out an abandoned warehouse.

"That abandoned warehouse," says "Chico," grimly. "She's in there, I'll bet." There is a second terrified scream. But this one is exactly like a police siren. The sort of scream that can split the eardrums of any normal person. It is Darlene's special inimitable scream.

"Chico" drives the car with a crash into the wall of the abandoned warehouse. Slightly dazed from the impact, the two policepersons leap out of their totaled police car and, guns drawn, go looking for some way of getting inside the abandoned warehouse.

36

Inside, things have been going from bad to worse for Darlene. The rape part was annoying but not all that bad. For a minute or two, she felt as if she was being jabbed to death with pencil stubs. As a result, her nerves are now all on edge with frustration as well as terror. It took Pablo eighteen seconds to achieve orgasm, while his two accomplices did not last much longer in the saddle.

But then, greedy things, she thought, they insisted on seconds. And this time Darlene was forced to commit oral sodomy on all three, which took them, marginally, a few seconds longer than vaginal rape took them. They may be tiny but they are virile, Darlene thinks. Even so, she is getting testy. But not until the third rapist—Jesús—slips out of her mouth due to the bend in the okra and her lovely blond hair suddenly gets the full benefit of his manhood—and she has just had her hair done that very A.M. like the Princess of Wales!—does she think to herself, *this is too much!*

Darlene is also starting to feel really icky. Enough is enough, she decides. They have had their way with her. Pablo has had his revenge for the way she pushed his okra inside him. Time to call it quits, she decides. Shake hands. Be good sports. Let bygones be bygones. But they have no way of knowing that Darlene—their nemesis—is a changed woman and no longer a nemesis but a pussycat.

The three youths pull up their shorts and trousers and buckle their colorful silver buckles.

"Now," says Pablo, "for the fun."

"No, no!" says Darlene, doing her best to be a good sport. She understands Pablo's Spanish quite well. Calderón's is too flowery for her. "You've had your fun, muchachos," she says. "You have raped a beautiful blond gringa, the dream of every lusty youth from south of the border so . . . Olé!" she exclaims, to show that she bears them no ill will. On the other hand, she does not like the look of that knife in Pablo's hand.

Pablo squats down beside her. He lifts her beautiful left titty. Delicately, he pricks the nipple with the tip of the knife. There is a tiny drop of blood. There is also a great scream from Darlene. "You pervert!" she yells. "And I thought you were three straight-shooters. Three regular-guy rapists. Now . . . this!"

Calderón, whom she has, somehow, trusted—because of his spiritual and religious bent?—has spread wide her legs and stares, goggle-eyed, at the admittedly untidy interior. She wishes he wouldn't stare like that. But then when he aims his knife directly at the clit, Darlene lets go with her police-siren scream.

"No one can hear you, gringa pig!" Pablo giggles like the degenerate he is. "This is an *abandoned* warehouse."

But Darlene's voice has been heard. It is a loud voice at all times. But faced with dismemberment of her beautiful body, the voice is now louder than the regulation DPD siren.

In retrospect, the three Aztec Terrorists will agree that their error *número uno* was not to have gagged her. But that was Pablo's fateful decision. As a pervert and male sexist swine, he wants to revel in her screams and pleas for mercy as he goes about dismembering her. Instead, *he* is obliged to listen to a police siren coming out of her throat. At first, he just giggles. But then when Pablo thinks that his eardrums may burst, he lets drop Darlene's left titty as if it is a hot tamale. Even the cool Calderón is forced to stop his ears with his hands. The sound is truly deafening—frightening, too.

Just in the nick of time for Darlene—who is running out of breath—"Chico" and his buddy burst into the abandoned warehouse. "All right!" shouts "Chico." He fires at Pablo—fires to kill, which is S.O.P. for the DPD when dealing with illegal aliens and other dark-hued types. But "Chico" misses by a good twelve feet. He could never hit a barn door, he likes to joke. But it is true, He can't.

Darlene screams again, knowing what force her scream has when she means to demoralize.

The three muchachos drop their knives and make flying leaps out of the nearest window with "Chico" and his buddy in fast pursuit. As the two policepersons leap out the window, "Chico," who is accident-prone, wrenches his ankle. "After them, buddy!" he shouts. And the buddy obeys, leaving "Chico" on what turns out to be a pile of rubber tires in the dark. It takes him a long, painful time to get down off those tires.

Inside the abandoned warehouse Darlene is in a real snit. Here I am, she thinks, a blond goddess, raped by Mexicans and this dumb "Chico" comes in and starts firing away, without even asking, 'Are you all right?' or taking these handcuffs off. Darlene grinds her teeth. So far, this has not been her day.

Suddenly, Darlene sees a rat. It is watching her with bright clever eyes. Darlene is not into rats. In fact, the whole rodent family, including the much-loved-by-some chipmunk, leaves her cold. Quick as a flash, Darlene crosses her long beautiful legs. After all that's been going on between those legs in the last hour, she would not put it past this particular rat to try for a piece, too.

Slowly the rat approaches her, eyes glowing like burning coals. Darlene feels an inadvertent scream welling up inside her. But will this rat get the message? Darlene's police-siren scream can empty a room of illegal aliens in a second, but would a rat detect the very real menace underlying the scream? Would the rat *know* the difference between the DPD-siren scream and a just ordinary siren scream? Things are beginning to look hairy again, thinks Darlene, filling her lungs.

But before she lets loose, "Chico" hobbles back into the abandoned warehouse. And the rat walks away, mad as a wet hen, she can tell, about something.

"Darlene!"

" 'Chico.' "

"Chico" takes off the handcuffs. "My poor baby!" He holds her tenderly. But she does not want to be held tenderly by anyone except Big John and not even by him in her present condition.

" 'Chico.' I was raped. By all three. Twice. Twice each, that is."

"What's that in your hair?" "Chico" sniffs at the golden tresses he so much admires.

"Guess."

"Ugh!" "Chico" makes a face; then he scowls. "Just let me get my hands on whoever it was and I'll break his—"

"The third rapist. He did that to my hair. By mistake. The leader is called Pablo. They thought I didn't know any Spanish." Darlene has pulled on her jockey shorts. She now does the best that she can to reassemble her torn-to-bits but still fashionable Mainbocher uniform. "I must look a sight," she says.

"You look good enough to eat," says "Chico." He's still carrying a torch for Darlene.

"How did you find me?"

"Just luck. I mean I *heard* you, God knows. But it was just luck my buddy and I were over in this part of town."

"Let's get out of here," says Darlene. "I need a nice hot bath and maybe a tetanus booster shot. They were going to cut off my boobs."

"They wouldn't dare!" "Chico" is horrified.

"Yes, they would've dared. I sensed," says Darlene, slowly, thoughtfully, "a good deal of hostility. Particularly in the ring-leader, Pablo. I have a vague memory of strip-searching him. But, my God, there have been so many. You know, in the line of duty."

"Was it a plot, do you think?" "Chico" is holding the handcuffs. There is a gleam in his eye that Darlene recognizes and does not like.

"Yes. I think that they had been waiting for some time to get me alone and, of course, it's really all my fault for skipping out on that homicide case that Captain Eddie assigned me to. But I wasn't in the mood. So . . . Well, come on, let's split, 'Chico.' " Darlene is restive. Although her delta is not particularly sore, it is certainly not a showpiece at the moment.

"We can't go until my buddy comes back."

"He'll never find them in the barrios. So why don't we take the car? I mean, he'll figure out that we've gone and

. . . I mean, for God's sake, ''Chico,' I'm in shock. I've been raped. Mutilated—almost.''

''We wrecked the car.''

''How?'' Darlene's eyes become very narrow slits indeed. This is no time for ''Chico's'' accident-proneness to raise its ugly head. Unfortunately, that ugly head is raised a lot higher than usual. The car is a wreck and the buddy has vanished in hot pursuit of the rapists and Darlene, after all that she has gone through, must sit on a crate in an abandoned warehouse filled with rats, uniform in shreds, while ''Chico'' begs, ''Please, put them on.'' He holds out his wrists.

''No!'' Darlene snarls.

''Chico'' begs, piteously. Finally, Darlene, grimly, wearily, fast approaching tether's end, snaps the handcuffs on him.

''Revile me,'' he whispers.

Darlene, with, for once, some real feeling, tells ''Chico'' just what she thinks of him for wrecking the car, spraining his ankle, forcing her to remain at the scene of her near-death.

''Chico'' writhes about in ecstasy during this verbal abuse. But the arrival of the buddy puts a stop to these shenanigans. The buddy is sweating, and breathing hard.

''They got away,'' he says.

''Of course!'' yells Darlene. ''What is the DPD coming to?''

''We better go,'' says ''Chico,'' scrambling to his feet.

''What are you doing with handcuffs on?'' asks the buddy, who knows nothing about bondage.

''I was just trying to see if I could . . .'' As there is no real explanation, ''Chico'' turns to Darlene. ''Honey, will you unlock me?''

''I don't have the key.''

''Chico'' stares at her, mouth ajar. ''But I *gave* you the key after I took the cuffs off you.''

"No. You did not give me the key." Darlene is precise in her fury. *"You kept the key."*

"I'll look in your pockets," says the buddy. But the key has vanished and two members of Duluth's finest are obliged to help their limping handcuffed colleague out of the abandoned warehouse and walk him to the nearest bus stop on ethnic Kennedy Avenue.

While waiting for the bus, Darlene gives a little cry.

"What is it, sweetness?" asks "Chico."

"I wasn't wearing my diaphragm."

"Aren't you on the pill?" asks the buddy.

"I hate the pill. Oh, Jesus!" Darlene is distraught. First Big John. Now three illegal aliens. If she has a baby, whose will it be? Softly, Darlene begins to cry and there is nothing that "Chico," handcuffed as he is, can do or say to console her.

37

Back at the Bistro Garden, lunch is now turning into dinner. Edna has been too unwell to leave the table and go back to the Montecito. Fortunately, the owner, Kurt, out of the kindness of his heart, has allowed the two ladies to occupy the same table while the help cleans up after the lunch crowd and prepares for the evening crowd.

"You do feel better?" Rosemary is more than a little concerned. After the wedding in the fourth segment, she can write Edna out. But to lose Edna any time before the wedding would seriously alter the tone of the series—which *Variety* has already called "classy."

Edna smiles bravely. "Yes. I'm all right now. I was, suddenly, two places at once, two people at once . . ."

"I know the feeling," says Rosemary, lying as always. Every single Klein Kantor identity—and they are, literally and simultaneously legion—is totally separate from every other Klein Kantor identity. Yet they have certain character traits in common. For one thing, a few months earlier, Hollywood's Rosemary almost optioned *Rogue Duke* for a series to be made in England with Lew Grade. But at the last minute the deal fell through and so she was never obliged, thanks to the fictive law of uniqueness, to confront *Duluth*'s Klein Kantor. Only poor Edna has fallen totally afoul of the fictive law and it will be a great relief for her—and everyone else—when she collides with that Santini moving van just off Barham Boulevard and leaves "Duluth" as well as *Duluth* for good. "I'll have the onion soup now," says Edna to the waiter.

When the onion soup arrives, Edna takes her spoon and carefully breaks the crust of yummy toasted French bread, liberally sprinkled with a piquant cheese, and then she begins to stir with her spoon the steaming soup, slowly, first from right to left and then from left to right. She does this until the soup is ice-cold; then she stops and puts down the spoon. She has done what she likes to do best with a rich onion soup. Then the waiter takes away the soup that Edna has not tasted. Rosemary wonders, absently, if Edna is anorexic, too. Rosemary understands talent; admires it, too.

38

Pablo and his two accomplices have vanished into the barrios. On every side they are protected by one million illegal aliens with their age-old Aztec eyes and unbreakable code of *omertà*.

Pablo is like a god in the barrios, his every wish fulfilled by black-eyed señoritas. Whenever he appears for a *cerveza* in a *cantina*, young and old surround him, giving him *abrazos*. He has made his headquarters at the Daridere Italo-American social club, once the hangout of Duluth's Italian demolition experts—now all moved to the suburbs, so that the illegal aliens can fill up with Little Yucatán what was once Little Italy.

But Pablo is frustrated. As he and Calderón sit and watch joyous young couples dance the colorful tarantella, he broods over his *cerveza*.

"What is wrong, my leader? You seem down in the dumps after your successful rape of our nemesis."

"I *am* down, Calderón."

"You wanted more?"

"Much, much more."

"You wished, in your heart of hearts, to dismember her with your knife?"

"Si." Actually, Pablo uses the English word for the Spanish 'yes.'

"As they say in the Antilles, 'There will always be another time.' "

"She'll be guarded, closely."

"So we wait. Bide our time. Disrupt the gringos. I have poured three gallons of Mexico City tapwater into the Greater Duluth Reservoir."

"You are a man, Calderón." Pablo gives his friend the supreme accolade.

"So are you, Pablo."

"Si." Pablo lapses into English. Then lapses back. "We must begin a reign of terror. But there are so few of our people who are willing to lose all hope of getting nonforged green cards and the welfare." Pablo looks with a cold eye on his own people, dancing to a mariachi band beneath colored lanterns. "All they think of is to live for today. They don't have this fire in the belly that I have."

"I have it, too, Pablo," says Calderón. "When I think of the nightmare culture that these gringo Protestants—no, they are not even Protestants. They are . . . they are . . ."

"Secular humanists," says Pablo, who, unlike Calderón, is still a bit hung up on Aquinas.

"Yes, secular humanists, sometimes known as—atheists!" Calderón spits with disgust on the sawdust floor. "When I look about Duluth and see what they have created. Massage parlors, adult book stores, a symphony orchestra—I am revolted, Pablo, *revolted* by a culture that has no strong basis in faith. Oh, not just religious faith . . ." Calderón knows that if he gets Pablo onto religion, Pablo will start on Augustine and not stop until he gets the stigmata on his left hand, the first sign, in his childhood, that he was destined to be something pretty special, as illegal aliens go in Duluth.

"You are really more of a Thomist in your thinking than you suspect," says Pablo, absently. As he thinks of what a joy it would be to dismember Darlene, the plumed serpent twitches in his trousers.

"No, not really. I think of myself more as an early Christian. In that blessed time when moral values were really absolute. When there was a natural spontaneous moral consensus. There is no such thing here . . ." Calderón spits

110

into the sawdust again, to show his contempt for Duluth, "and to tell the truth, we are not much better south of the border, down Mexico way."

"What we need," says Pablo, finally beginning *not* to think about Darlene in small pieces suitable for mailing parcel-post to her colleagues in the DPD, "is a program. Idle terrorism is not the answer."

"We've done precious little of that, my leader," says Calderón. "Idle or not. After all, one desultory gang-rape does not a destabilization make."

"You've done your work at the reservoir. Don't forget that. But what we need now is real organization—and strategy."

"To do what?"

"To seize the city hall and police headquarters. To occupy the palatial homes on Garfield Heights."

"Then what?"

"We will make the rich and powerful gringos our hostages."

"Then what, my leader?"

"Then what—what?" Pablo is irritable. He sees nothing wrong with his master plan. But Calderón tends to be picky.

"What do we ask *for?*"

"Oh." Pablo frowns. Action, not theory, has always been his long suit. "Equality?"

"What form will it take?"

"Equal wages."

"That means we become U.S. citizens."

"Yes."

"But you hate this country and all that it stands for. So why get citizenship? Why get a Social Security number when it is an open secret that by the time you and I are eligible—at sixty-two—"

"Sixty-five," Pablo corrects him, "if we want the full benefits."

"Sixty-two of one, sixty-five of the other, my leader, this government will not pay anyone anything when you and I are old, and our lifetime contributions to Social Security will long since have been eroded by inflation and bureaucratic waste.''

''At Washington, they speak with forked tongue,'' nods Pablo, aware that his loyal sidekick is not idly beating his gums.

''I would suggest,'' says Calderón, carefully, ''that we strike a—and I know this goes against the basic spirituality of your nature—a materialistic note. That we seize and hold for ransom Mayor Herridge, Captain Eddie Thurow, the socially prominent Bellamy Craig IIs, the Oklahoma oil-rich newcomer to Duluth, Clive Hoover . . .''

''A fagola.'' There is nothing that is not known in the barrios. If so much as a hairpin falls on Garfield Heights, it is known in that alien and stark yet joyous and life-enhancing quarter between McKinley and ethnic Kennedy Avenues.

''Actually, he's not. The silk caftan was a mistake. My Carmencita, who was serving the canapés, heard him say to his inamorata Chloris Craig that he had only wanted to make a statement.''

''How much do we ask for them?''

''A million a head.'' Calderón thinks big. He also thinks a lot.

''How many heads?''

''As many as we can round up. That is where your strategy is all-important, my leader.''

''It must be soon.'' Pablo is thoughtful. ''The barrios is a tinder box. One match and . . . Pffft!''

''So before the match is lit, we strike.''

''Then we get the money. Then . . . What?'' Pablo is really *very* short on theory. He is all action.

''We go back to Mexico. I'd like to open a string of massage parlors. Nice ones like they have here . . .''

''I thought you were early Christian . . .''

''In the absence of an agreed-upon moral consensus, the

categoric imperative is self-interest.'' Not for nothing is Calderón's father back in Guadalajara a Jesuit priest.

"We must," says Pablo, "make a plan."

39

Beryl, Marchioness of Skye, pushes back the purple velvet curtain, lined with ermine. On top of a malachite table is the casket of inlaid ivory in which the Prince Regent keeps his most important papers as well as the Great Seal of England.

Beryl looks about the sumptuous room. She is, suddenly, afraid. Why? The Prince Regent is unconscious. She has drugged the decanter of brandy which he has just finished drinking. Reggie, as she and his other intimates call him, is now collapsed in an armchair beside the fireplace. Fat chins overflow his stock; he snores heavily.

Overcoming her sudden irrational fear, Beryl takes the tiny key that she has lifted from Reggie's pocket and, quiet as a mouse, she turns it in the tiny lock. Then she opens the casket. Inside she finds millions of pound notes, some jewels, love letters, mostly from her to him though there seem to be some from him to her but never posted. She wishes that she had the time to read them. But *la France* before *le plaisir*. Stuffing a million or so pounds in her décolletage with one hand, she rummages about the casket with the other until she finds—under the Great Seal—the single sheet of paper with the straightforward inscription ''Secret Plan for the Invasion of France.'' Quickly she stuffs the priceless document in her décolletage, which is now becoming a bit crowded.

Like a pistol's retort, a log snaps in the fireplace. She gasps. With trembling hands, she shuts and locks the casket and returns the tiny key to Reggie's pocket and slips out of the room and then walks out of Windsor Castle to where a carriage is waiting to drive her to Dover and the boat which will transport her to France and to her eternal love Napoleon Bonaparte. Everything goes without a hitch except for one thing. She is observed leaving the Prince Regent's chambers with an unnatural-looking poitrine. Since Beryl has enemies, word spreads.

Beryl, Marchioness of Skye, is arrested at customs in Dover.

"My lady," says the commander of the port, "we have reason to believe that you are a spy for France."

Beryl talks her way out of that one but it is touch-and-go for quite a time. Fortunately, her charms as a seductress stand her in good stead and even during her most intimate moments with the commander of the port, she is able to keep her poitrine to herself, the trick of the week, admittedly, but Beryl is *sans pareil*.

Rosemary's word-processor is on the blink and she is not getting the sort of scenes that *Rogue Duke* needs. But *Redbook* is pressing her. So Rosemary tries to dredge up some Georgette Heyer channel-packet stuff. Instead Rosemary gets a Bulwer-Lytton trireme, by mistake.

"Too enraging!" she cries, with vexation. But *Redbook* waits for no authoress so poor Beryl is shoved onto that trireme. Luckily, the rows of asterisks are working perfectly. "That will get her to France," says Rosemary, banging out three rows of asterisks. The trials of authorship, she thinks.

40

Clive and Chloris have taken to meeting secretly at The Eucalyptus Club. That is, everyone knows that they see each other there but everyone thinks that they are really there for the annual backgammon tournament, which they do take part in.

It is a hot day in July. Clive wears a light beige linen suit with pleated lapels from Carlo Paluzzi while Chloris wears a golden bit of summer frou-frou, run up for her by the Princess Galitzine.

"How is the house coming along?" asks Chloris, as if she hasn't been with Clive a dozen times to the site.

"Mr. Jackson is in Africa. He's trying to find me some Nubian porphyry, which is nicer than the Sudanese, they say."

"I like porphyry." Chloris is always direct. A black servitor brings her a Dr Pepper.

The lovers sit side by side in one of the comfortable leather sofas that face the big windows through which can be seen the palm trees that line the busy waterfront. The spaceship is still there in the lake, doing nothing.

"Have you heard from Rosemary?" asks Clive.

"Not since the reception." Chloris frowns. "I don't know what got into her."

"She sent me a copy of the latest *Redbook* with *Rogue Duke* in it."

"Is your mother Beryl in it?"

"Yes."

"How is she?"

"All right." Clive has got Beryl as far as Dover and he is ready to shut the book on her right then and there because if she does have a message for him she is certainly taking her time in transmitting it.

"Rosemary finally left your party with Wayne Alexander," says Clive. "My Mexican maid is a friend of your maid Carmencita and she told me."

"Yes." Chloris almost says "Good riddance!" She is sick of Wayne. But she is still hung up on Betty Grable. So she will have to make her peace with him. Only the night before she and Clive had watched a cassette of *Mother Wore Tights* and Clive now sees what she sees in Betty and he is just as curious as she is to find out who killed that wonderful girl.

"Rumor hath it," says Clive, "that Wayne is doing a big story for the *Blade* on Rosemary's early career as a war correspondent."

"I wouldn't put it past him."

"I wish he'd do a story on me." Clive is wistful.

"But, darling, you'll have to do something first."

"I know. I know. Don't rub it in. I think that's why I was so . . . on edge at the reception. Partly, it was the caftan . . ."

"A mistake."

"Yes. It created a false impression."

"Not to mention the pearls."

"Oh, but they're real!"

"My God. I thought they were Teclas!" Chloris is hugely impressed.

"No, angel, those pearls are the real McCoy from Grandma Hoover."

That name, thinks Chloris. "Well," she says, with a smile, "if you got 'em, show 'em!"

"But mostly I wanted to make a statement. To say—what next? I've accomplished everything I set out to do. The money. The house—when it's finished. The twin Lear jets. The social position . . ."

"You are at the very top here in Duluth," says Chloris, who put him there. "I feel like Joan of Arc with the Dolphin."

"But is this enough?" Clive is filled with an ongoing identity crisis. Or so he wants her to believe. Actually, Clive is busy as a bee, enlarging the empire that his mother left him. Social-climbing is simply the front that he maintains for the world. Although Chloris wants to help Clive, she is, after all, only a woman. As he tells her about his latest tax shelter, she yawns, mouth shut but nostrils wide.

Absently, Chloris stares out the window. Idly, she studies the spaceship beyond the palm trees. Suddenly, a round door opens in the side of the ship just level with the water.

"Clive . . ."

"I wanted a life of splendor. Rare fabrics. Exciting people. Devastating denouements. So what do I get?" The question is rhetorical but Chloris is quick with an answer.

"Well, for starters, you've got a ringside seat to the spaceship whose door just opened."

"When?" Clive stares at the spaceship. The open door looks like a round black hole in the side of the ship.

"About the time you were laying it on me about that tax shelter that went sour."

"Actually, I think that that shelter's going to be all right."

"Michigan oil leases?" Chloris snorts. "Everything good up there's been bought twice over. Those were dry holes you went and bought."

Clive is growing irritated. "One hole has already come in. The others, if you prorate them over the next two tax years . . ."

41

Captain Eddie and "Chico" Jones are down at the waterfront where the local blacks are sitting under the palm trees that line Lake Erie, staring at the spaceship and waiting for something to come out of it. So far nothing has. Meanwhile, every black youth is playing his transistor radio and disco music makes the palm fronds shudder.

Captain Eddie holds up his binoculars and trains them on the round black hole.

"What do you see, Chief?" asks "Chico."

"Nothing. Just a—a black hole. That's all."

"Was there any warning?" It is Wayne Alexander, now Captain Eddie's ally in the struggle with Mayor Herridge for the hearts and minds of Duluth next November.

"None that the DPD can reveal," says Captain Eddie, cautiously. He must be cautious because it would be just like the FBI to know what was going on and then not tell him in order to make him look silly.

There is a great noise of sirens as Mayor Herridge and the news team—live—of KDLM-TV arrive at the waterfront.

The blacks chuckle among themselves at all this activity on the part of The Man. They themselves are content to sit on the beach, fishing in the late afternoon sun. They don't really care one way or the other what's inside the spaceship on the sensible ground that whatever it is it's going to be white, which will just mean more trouble for the brothers. When word spread that there were centipedes inside the spaceship, Big John is said to have said to certain members

118

of the colored community, "You can bet your black ass that they is *white* centipedes!" This was much appreciated at the time.

While the camera crew sets up—it is now five o'clock, almost prime time—Mayor Herridge strides over to Captain Eddie. "Well, Chief, what have you done now?"

"I've done nothing so far. What have you done, your Honor?"

"Notified the Pentagon. The FBI. The CIA. And one of the presidents."

"Which one?"

"The fat one. You know . . . What's his name?"

"So?"

"Air Force should be here any minute. They will want to make contact first, they said."

"I'm afraid, as chief of police, that's my job. Get me a boat, 'Chico.' A motorboat. That . . . uh, Chris-Craft over there will do just fine."

"Yes, Chief." "Chico" hurries off to get the boat for Captain Eddie. The Mayor is fit to be tied. He shouts to one of his aides that he wants a boat, too.

Then, at just about the same time, the Mayor and the police chief get into their separate boats—and race each other to the spaceship.

Captain Eddie's boat is the first to arrive at the spaceship. After the boat's engine is cut, the boat bobs up and down beside the round door whose sill is about a foot above the surface of the lake.

"Hi!" says Captain Eddie, a bit nervous, even though he knows that "Chico" is standing behind him with a machine gun at the ready in case these really illegal aliens turn ugly. "Anybody home?"

But there is not even an echo from inside the ship.

Captain Eddie peers into the darkness.

"Can you see anything, Chief?" asks "Chico."

"Nothing. Did you bring a flashlight, 'Chico'?"

"No. I thought they'd have their own lights. You know, inside."

"Maybe their generator's on the blink." Captain Eddie is getting nervous. Just what *is* inside there? And is it—or *are* it, or they—dangerous?

The Mayor's boat is now next to Captain Eddie's. "Well, what've you done *now*, Chief?" The Mayor is always on the offensive with Captain Eddie, blaming him for everything that goes wrong in the city from petty larceny to arson and loitering.

"I am trying to make contact," says the Chief. "Only nobody's answering."

"Idiot!" Mayor Herridge puts one foot gingerly on the rounded door sill, careful not to let the red gumminess mess up his shoe too much. "Welcome!" he shouts, "to Duluth! The Venice of Minnesota!"

There is silence from inside.

"What're you going to do now?" asks Captain Eddie, enjoying his rival's discomfiture.

"I'll think of something. Don't you worry, Chief."

The Mayor takes his foot off the door sill.

Back on the beach, Darlene and another policewoman are reporting for duty. They are slightly late because Darlene has missed her period. Having missed her period, she is filled with foreboding. En route to the waterfront, Darlene stopped off at a clinic where her worst fears were promptly confirmed. She is pregnant.

KDLM-TV anchorperson Leo Lookaloney is delighted to see Darlene, who is a perennial favorite with the local news media.

"Here comes Lieutenant Darlene Ecks, Homicide. Long time no see, Darlene!"

"Hi, Leo. Hi, everybody out there." Darlene musters a weak smile for the TV audience.

"What do you think is in the spaceship?"

"What do I think is in what?" Darlene is thinking about one thing and one thing only and that is the baby that is now assembling itself inside her, and just what color it is going to be, brown or black?

"The spaceship," says Wayne Alexander, stepping into the shot, much to Leo's anger, as the TV media does its best to ignore the print media and vice versa. But Wayne is ambitious, despite the missing right ear.

"Oh, that," says Darlene, recognizing Wayne. "Hi, Mr. Alexander!"

"The Chief and the Mayor are out there now in those two boats," says Wayne, whose lead sentences are read in classrooms all across the country in journalism schools.

"Well, I guess if anyone knows *they'll* know pretty soon." Darlene wishes she could get interested in the spaceship but it has always been a blank spot with her. And today—of all days—it is a total nothing.

Leo is getting annoyed—and a little desperate. Usually these two make good television, able as they are to talk off the tops of their heads for seconds on end. But now—today of all days—he has a pair of dummies on his mechanical hands. "What," he asks, "is the editorial position of the *Duluth Blade* on—"

But Leo has been had. "In the coming election, the *Blade* supports for mayor, one hundred percent, police chief Captain Eddie Thurow." Wayne is triumphant.

Leo looks as if he has been poleaxed.

"Yea, team!" says Darlene, starting to cry. Although a devout Roman Catholic, she has already had one abortion. She can't face letting down God a second time.

"I should also say," says Wayne, inexorably, right into the camera, "that my three-part exposé of the famous Crescent City writer Rosemary Klein Kantor will start appearing in the *Blade* this Sunday . . ."

"Did she write *Rogue Duke*?" asks Darlene, through her tears. Unable to remember any writer's name, she is equally unable to forget any title.

"Yes, and two hundred other tales of high costume romance as well as a lot of hard-hitting Wurlitzer Prize-winning creative journalism.''

Leo is beside himself. ''Here you two are, going on about someone from the hot-print media when the most exciting event in the coldest media there is is taking place right here on Lake Erie!''

''But nothing's happening at the moment, Leo,'' says Wayne, enjoying total TV exposure. ''So I think it might be interesting for your viewers to know that Rosemary Klein Kantor was never a war correspondent in Japan, which is where she made her original reputation the day after the bomb fell on Hiroshima. She was actually at the Mark Hopkins Hotel in San Francisco, where she faked an eyewitness account of the bombing of Hiroshima and then got it onto the wire service through . . .'' At this point Wayne breaks off, with a little laugh. ''Well, I don't want to give away too much of my own story but it's hot as a cracker.''

Not as hot as you're going to be, says Rosemary to herself. She is seated in her luxurious word-processor room with its view of Audubon Park in the Crescent City. She picks up the telephone from her Regency desk and dials the home number of Louis Nizer, the ace lawyer.

''I'm going to own the *Duluth Blade* before I'm through!'' Rosemary shouts at the TV screen, which is now showing a commercial. ''Just you wait and see.''

By now, the director of the special news program, high atop the McKinley Communications Center Tower, has already told Leo to get those two creeps off the air and switch back to the spaceship, where Captain Eddie and Mayor Herridge are having a quarrel.

''You're the mayor. You're the one who's come out here to welcome these—things to Duluth. So you go on in there.''

''But you're in charge of security and . . . Hell! Who knows what kind of dope these types are trying to smuggle into Duluth? So you go on in there and bust a few heads, O.K.?''

The two boats are bobbing up and down so much that Mayor Herridge, never a good sailor at the best of times, is feeling sick to his stomach. He turns to his aide. "Get me Bill Toomey. Tell him to get his ass out here. And tell him to bring the key to the city, which I forgot."

The aide tries, vainly, to contact Bill Boomey by walkie-talkie. "He's not in his office, your Honor."

"But he is. He has to be. He . . ." Suddenly, like an icy hand about his already queasy stomach, Mayor Herridge remembers something. "What . . . what day is this?" he asks, knowing already the answer.

"Monday," says the aide, helpfully.

"No. No. The day and the month."

"It's July the Fourth, your Honor. Remember? You were supposed to be at the baseball stadium right now, saluting Old Glory. But then we got the word about this door here opening up and . . ."

Mayor Herridge sits down on the walkie-talkie, breaking it. He mops his brow. He is feeling very ill. Today of all days, he has unleashed Bill Toomey.

By nightfall the barrios will be aflame. What kind of impression is that going to make on world television? Not to mention on the aliens from outer space? Although in the long run, Captain Eddie and his department will get the blame, this is now the shortest of short runs.

Mayor Herridge has got to do something. Quick. Since it is too late to stop Operation Chile-con-Carne, he must now create a diversion—anything. He looks at the round dark hole in the side of the spaceship. He shudders because he is, very simply, a coward. But now—*this is it*. Over the top!

Mayor Herridge gets, shakily, to his feet. For a moment, he thinks he will throw up. But then he remembers that, no matter what, the spaceship won't be bobbing up and down the way this Chris-Craft is . . . He clutches now at straws.

"Gentlemen." The honeylike tones of Mayor Herridge's official voice can be guaranteed to send a tingle down any spine connected to a pair of ears that happens to be within listening range. Even Captain Eddie's spine feels a reluctant tingle. "The mayor of Duluth is going in there to welcome these aliens to the Venice of Minnesota."

With that, Mayor Herridge hops up onto the sill of the ship. Then he takes a long stride into the dark interior. "Anybody home?" he asks in a cheery voice.

There is silence. Then the dark round hole vanishes. The door to the spaceship shuts so swiftly that it is not possible for anyone's naked eye to see on what principle it works. Where an instant before there was a round opening, there is now only a red gummy curved surface.

"Well," says "Chico," in a whisper to the Chief, "if he don't come out you got the election in the bag."

"True." But Captain Eddie is a lot more subtle and farsighted than his loyal aide. "On the other hand, if he *does* come out, having pulled off some kind of deal with these aliens, then I'm a dead duck come November."

"I hadn't thought of that," says "Chico."

Captain Eddie turns to the driver of the boat. "Back to shore."

On the waterfront, the black faces are delighted at what has happened. If their votes were not regularly burned at each municipal election, Mayor Herridge would never have been elected in the first place. Now, perhaps, those lost votes will be, in a metaphysical if not electoral sense, added up.

Leo is excited. It is six o'clock. Time for the local news. All sets in Duluth are now switched on. "Our popular mayor of Duluth has just entered the spaceship," he says to the camera, "for a pow-wow with the aliens. As he entered the spaceship, the door shut behind him so fast that no one's naked eye could follow it. So here's a replay of the shutting door *in slow motion*." Not for nothing has Leo been doing sports for the last five years.

At The Eucalyptus Club, Chloris and Clive are watching the *Six O'Clock News*. The other members are playing back-gammon and bridge. They are not interested in the spaceship. But Chloris and Clive both have intellectual curiosity to spare, which sets them apart from their fellow socialites.

"It looks better on TV than through the window," says Chloris.

"Yes."

They watch the slow-motion replay. There is no door in any earthly sense. What happened was the red gummy material of the spaceship just comes together in the twinkling of an eye and shuts the hole but not before—in slow motion, of course—Chloris and Clive and everyone else watching the replay could see a short thick-set man, shaking hands with Mayor Herridge just inside the ship.

"Well, at least these aliens are human beings like us," says Clive.

"*And* white," adds Chloris significantly, in a low voice, so as not to be heard by the black servitors.

"He looks sort of familiar, the man who was greeting the Mayor."

"Yes," says Leo, almost as if he has heard Clive. "He does look familiar and you can bet your bottom dollar that the highly trained analysts here at KDLM-TV will be analyzing that one shot in depth until we know for certain who—and most important, *what*—the thing is that greeted our gutsy Mayor."

On the waterfront, life is returning to normal. It is now accepted as a fact of life that either the Mayor will come out of the spaceship or he won't.

Captain Eddie strides vigorously to his car. He catches sight of Darlene. "Honey, you've been crying," he says. "I didn't know you liked our late Mayor all that much." Captain Eddie has decided to act, in public, as if the Mayor is a goner.

Darlene throws her arms about the Chief. She sobs into his neck. "I'm pregnant!"

"Gosh! I'm sorry."

"And I don't know which one it is."

"There were the three Mexicans . . ."

"And . . . Big John."

"That makes . . ." The Chief counts slowly on the fingers of the hand that holds Darlene to his fatherly breast. "Four. So get an abortion. Yes, I know Duluth is Catholic. But you can always get an abortion in the case of rape and/or miscegenation. You're in business, honey."

"But I want the baby," Darlene wails, "if it's . . . it's . . ."

"Big John's?"

Darlene nods. Then she pulls away from Captain Eddie. She knows that he is sickened by what he has heard.

Captain Eddie *is* sickened. But he doesn't blame Darlene. It is the shock that she's been through, he decides. "You'll snap out of it, honey," he says. He turns to "Chico." "Go to Federal Judge Hawkins. Tell him I want a search warrant for that spaceship. And while he's about it, he might just give us a *habeas corpus* for the Mayor."

"Yes, Chief."

"Busy times," says Captain Eddie, as he gets into the car, with a brisk "no comment" to Leo, who has managed with his artificial arm to insert the hand mike inside Captain Eddie's mouth, spoiling somewhat the briskness of his "no comment."

Captain Eddie does not know just how busy the times are. If he did, he would be out of his skull with anxiety because Mayor Herridge—even *in absentia*—has totally outmaneuvered him.

Unaware of his peril, Captain Eddie returns to police headquarters to await instruction from whichever president happens to be on duty at the time. It is possible, of course, as this is the Fourth of July, the day of our national independence and a holiday, that there are no presidents at all in the White House, which would suit Captain Eddie just fine, as he is in no hurry to save Mayor Herridge.

42

Bill Toomey's command post is in the Little Yucatán district, where he has taken over the Daridere Dance Hall. Here he presides over the radio communication center that connects each of the twenty-four agents with Bill's command post. As Bill barks out his orders, a Darlene male look-alike, in DPD uniform, has half a dozen dark-eyed señoritas lined up, stark naked, against the dance hall wall. The Darlene male look-alike is plainly having a ball as he pinches and probes with stubby, insensitive fingers. "We're looking for drugs, señoritas!" he says in Berlitz Spanish. "And," he adds, smiling, "*I'm* looking for a virgin to take to the Policeman's Ball."

That boy should have studied gynecology, thinks Bill Toomey, admiringly, as the señoritas scream with horror while the false cop continues his quest for drugs and intact hymens.

This is the way to make enemies for the DPD—not to mention Captain Eddie, thinks Bill Toomey, contentedly. He is now confident that Mayor Herridge will be a shoo-in come November. But Bill Toomey does not know that Mayor Herridge has disappeared. Perhaps for good. Bill Toomey worships the ground that Mayor Herridge walks on.

Meanwhile, Pablo and Calderón are being bagged at their command post in the dimly lit cellar of an Indian moccasin shop. As the Darlene look-alike girl flings open the door to their hide-away, she trains a gun on the astonished youths.

127

Needless to say, she does not know that she has captured the leadership of the Aztec Terrorists Society. But then she is new to town, a student nurse from nearby Fond du Lac.

In his desire to create *total* rage in the barrios, Bill Toomey has spent a number of weeks conducting a series of in-depth discussions with a team of FBI psychologists whose work in the prisons of America and elsewhere is the envy of their colleagues in the KGB. Since Darlene's rather haphazard and impromptu strip-searches have been the life-giving spark, as it were, to Operation Chile-con-Carne, the team has taken it from there.

After numerous tests and studies, the team was able to un-earth twelve male Darlene look-alikes whose passion for dark female flesh knows no bounds. But even more impor-tant than this sexual imprint which mother nature has wound like poison ivy around their double helices, each is a male chauvinist who takes absolute pride in never allowing his fe-male partner to achieve orgasm.

To weed out the liars and the just plain pushy—and there are always a few—lie-detector tests were given and the bad apples were soon separated from the good. Bill Toomey is now well satisfied with his twelve blond—some dyed, of course—storm troopers. If they cannot outrage, terminally, the innate modesty of the dark-eyed señoritas no one can.

By nightfall, Bill Toomey—a one-time classical scholar from Fairleigh Dickinson University—expects the streets of the barrios to be filled with screaming Bacchae—dark-hued women intent on the mutilation and murder of every white man in Duluth, particularly those wearing the DPD uni-form.

The twelve women chosen presented more of a problem. Out-and-out Sapphics were rejected. Fortunately, the wom-en's movement knew nothing of this, as the operation was hush-hush, and so there was no picketing or bad-mouthing. In strictest secrecy, Bill Toomey impressed on all twenty-four Darlene look-alikes that they are fighting terrorism and in the battle against terrorism *anything goes*. Twenty-four tongues eagerly licked forty-eight lips when this good news was imparted to them.

The twelve women are not enthusiasts for the masculine principle. Many are tomboys—highly competitive and resentful of the fact that even when they were wee lasses the wee lads could run faster and yell louder than they. Resentment rather than lust rules their psyches.

Midge— the name of the Darlene look-alike who captures Pablo and Calderón—is a student nurse who is known in the male ward at Fond du Lac General Hospital as "a mean mother." There is nothing she won't do to undermine the male spirit.

Midge is delighted with her present assignment. For one thing, it is a welcome break from hospital routine. For another, she has never had a good look at the so-called Latin Lover—her own love life is well provided for by a Swedish-American widower of substance whom she refuses to marry because she likes her independence. But they spend every Saturday night at his house, watching television, and all day Sunday, resting and eating waffles.

Midge confronts her first two Latin Lovers. She is delighted—if slightly surprised by their obvious terror. What has happened to Latin macho?

Little does Midge know that *Pablo and Calderón think that she really is Darlene,* come back for revenge. Although Midge in her blond Princess of Wales wig resembles Darlene only slightly, to the two illegal aliens it is the real Darlene. But then blond gringas all tend to look alike to your average inscrutable Aztec rapist.

"O.K., rapists! Up against the wall!"

The word "rapists" nearly brings on heart failure in Pablo. This is death, he thinks, as he leans against the wall for support, knees turned to water. He does not know that all Darlene look-alikes have been instructed to denounce the illegal aliens as rapists in order to put them on the defensive. Pablo and Calderón are convinced that their last few minutes on earth are now at hand.

Since Midge has not been trained in police work, she is ignorant of many of the telltale signs of terrorists at work. She pays no attention—to Pablo's surprise—to the bombs that they have been assembling or to the veritable arsenal of rifles and canisters of Mace. Perhaps she is waiting till we are dead, thinks Pablo. Then she will say that she killed us at the very heart of our terrorist ring.

Midge rather likes Pablo's looks. The whites of his narrow eyes are luminous with fear. Calderón, she notes, is more muscular but his features are less handsome.

Midge approaches, revolver aimed at Pablo's heart. Then—she has been well briefed by Bill Toomey—she stamps hard with her heel on the pointy shoes just where she knows the corns are. Pablo squeals. Midge turns to Calderón—another cry as his corns are mashed beneath her sturdy heel. The boys double up with pain until a mild pistol-whipping soon straightens them to attention again.

Midge removes a stack of rifles from a chair—she does not even begin to wonder what those rifles are doing there—that is not her assignment. Then she pulls up the chair in front of the two muchachos and goes into her act.

"Start peeling, rapists!"

"It was an accident," says Pablo, trembling fingers unbuttoning his khaki Fidel Castro revolutionary shirt. "I mean we didn't know it was you. I swear. In the abandoned warehouse . . ."

"We thought it was this girl friend of ours," says Calderón, helpfully. "Pretending she was police."

Midge doesn't know what they are talking about—and doesn't care. "Hurry up," she shrills. "I've got a lot more house calls today."

43

Edna is sitting in a car on the set of "Duluth." It is the fourth episode. She is about to play a scene where the car she is driving goes off a bridge because she is drunk but she will be saved at the last minute because Rosemary wants her at the wedding in the next episode.

There is a technical hitch. The back-projection that gives the impression that the car she is sitting in is actually moving down a country lane and then across a bridge is on the blink so Edna has nothing to do for the moment but sit in the car and wait for her cue to start pretending that she is, drunkenly, driving the car. There is no dialogue. Just a lot of screaming. A close shot. And that's it for the day.

Rosemary has been unusually kind since the hallucination in the Bistro Garden. Edna's lines are now much longer than "you mean dot dot question mark." Rosemary has made a lot of interesting variations like "For Heaven's sake, Silas, you can't *mean* that dot dot question mark." Like all actresses of the first rank Edna wants to be able to use the name of the character that she is acting a scene with as often as possible because this gives immediacy as well as keeping the other actor on his toes.

Edna enjoys the busy-ness of a TV set at Universal. Cost is no object. She has at least one costume change in every one-hour segment. Edna sits back in the car seat. Through the windshield, she sees the camera, waiting to photograph her first scream. To her surprise, the red light is on. This means that the camera is live even though the taping has not begun.

Automatically, Edna turns her left three-quarter attractive side to the lens. As she does, a familiar figure appears, inside the lens.

"Chief Thurow!" Edna exclaims. Try as she might—and her attempts have been successful ever since the Bistro Garden—to exorcise her previous life in *Duluth*, it keeps cropping up the way that lines from an earlier play by Sumner Locke Elliott, say, will suddenly quite obliterate a section of the Tad Mosel script that she is working on, putting her in two dramas at once, to the chagrin of the director and her fellow mummers. Hazards of show business.

44

Captain Eddie is napping in his office with the television set on. He has had a full and, all in all, happy day. Because it is the Fourth of July, no one in the military or the government has started to hassle him yet. Mayor Herridge is locked up safe as houses in the spaceship and all is right with the world. Captain Eddie is sound asleep when "Duluth" comes on the air.

Although the fictive law of simultaneity requires that the time it takes for one character on another plane to speak to a character in the immediate field of force always be the same, a pause in the making of that segment of "Duluth" where Edna runs her car off the bridge can be used to timely advantage *if* each character is in precise conjunction with the other. As Captain Eddie, suddenly, opens his eyes, he becomes visible to Edna, who becomes visible to him.

"Edna Herridge! What are you doing on TV?"

"I'm in this series, 'Duluth.' "

"Well, congratulations! Better than real estate here in Duluth, I guess."

"Well, it's different." Edna looks about nervously to see if it's time for her cue. Fortunately, the back-projection is still broken. She has a moment to talk to Captain Eddie—and she is glad. She has always liked him. They grew up together. Went to the same schools, dances; smoked their first pot together back in the good old Eisenhower days. "Listen, Eddie."

"Yes, Edna?" Captain Eddie is still a bit dopey from his nap and all the activities of the day. He knows *something* is not quite right. After all, people on the TV can't see and talk to you even though you can see and talk *at* if not to them. "I must be dreaming," Captain Eddie says, comfortably. He has completely forgotten that he attended Edna's funeral last winter.

"I don't have much time. This scene is going to start any minute . . ."

"What happens in it?"

"I'm drunk and I drive a car over a bridge . . ." Edna is getting a bit irritable at all this palaver.

"Car?" Captain Eddie frowns, beginning to remember something about a snowdrift.

"You know that Mayor and I never did get on."

Captain Eddie nods. "That's common knowledge here in *Duluth*."

"Partly is was that bitch he married. Partly those insufferable little shavers . . ."

"One of them's on methadone right now."

"Let's hope it ODs." Edna never liked children in *Duluth*. On the other hand, in "Duluth" she dotes on her son while, as Joanna Witt, she has a good one-on-one relationship with each of her two actual children back East in New York City.

"Now I saw Mayor a little while back. He's out to get you."

"You can say that again. But I've got a trick or two—"

"Shut up, Eddie. My cue is coming up. He's hired a bunch of thugs. Police look-alikes. They're supposed to go through the barrios . . ." Edna's voice changes suddenly: she coos to the floor manager. "I'm ready, darling. Whenever you are." Edna looks back into the lens. "They're going to hassle the Mexicans. They're going to create a bloodbath. And blame it all on you and the Duluth Police Department."

Edna is now back in "Duluth." Captain Eddie stares, dumbly, at the screen as Edna's car seems to be going faster and faster. There is a close shot of her face. She is leering; she is plainly drunk.

"Oh, Edna!" Captain Eddie feels something awful is about to happen.

Edna's eyes widen, like new-poached eggs. She screams. Captain Eddie shouts, "Watch out!"

But Edna's car has gone through the railings of a bridge. There is then a process shot of the car slowly sinking, followed by a commercial, which Captain Eddie switches off. For a long moment, he broods. Then the telephone on his desk rings. He picks up the receiver. A voice says, "Wayne Alexander here."

"Where is here, Wayne?"

"All hell's breaking loose in the barrios. Your men and women are strip-searching every illegal *and* legal alien in sight."

"They are *not* my men—"

"Chief, I've seen them with my own eyes in Little Yucatán. They're in uniform, for Christ's sake!"

Captain Eddie hangs up. Edna's warning is true. But it has come too late. Captain Eddie looks at his wristwatch.

Midnight. He picks up his private line. "Get me 'Chico' Jones. Quick."

Then Captain Eddie goes over to the map of Greater Duluth. He stares at the red thumbtack just off the waterfront. "You son of a bitch!" he shouts at the Mayor, who, dead or alive, is inside that thumbtack of a spaceship.

Suddenly, a light goes on inside Captain Eddie's head. Why get mad when you can get even? he thinks.

Captain Eddie pries loose the thumbtack. For a second he holds it poised over the deserted swamp at the far edge of the Duluth Woods. No one ever comes within a mile of that swamp and by the time he has put it off limits due to . . . radioactivity from the Duluth Nuclear Plant? no one will ever see or hear of the spaceship and Mayor Herridge again. Viciously, he jams the thumbtack as deep into the swamp as he can. He hopes that he has managed to give the aliens and Mayor Herridge a real shaking-up.

"Chico" Jones reports for duty. "What's up, Chief?"

"Get my car. We're going into the barrios."

"At midnight, Chief? Unarmed?"

"Four squad cars. Tear gas. Mace. Nerve gas . . ."

"Well, that's better," says "Chico," brightening.

45

Midge is very grim as she examines the naked Pablo. She now sees what Darlene saw—or didn't see. As for Calderón, although his distinguishing marks of gender are visible to the naked eye, they are in a state of total retraction.

Both Pablo and Calderón are now beyond mere embarrassment. Handcuffed and helpless, they know that Darlene is about to revenge herself for the gang-rape. They understand her feelings. An eye for an eye. A cock for a cunt. It is the code that they have lived by. Now it is the code that they are about to die by.

"I hope," says Pablo, "that our suffering will be brief." His attempt at a few well-chosen last words, full of dignity, is marred by the convulsive twitching of his legs, which turns into St. Vitus' dance when Midge, taking a sharp knife from her reticule, approaches the center of Pablo's macho being—or where she thinks the center must be lurking.

Midge plunges her left hand into the wiry bush and finds the objects of her search. She grasps the tiny genitals in one hand—they barely fill the heel of her palm. With the other hand, she poises the knife over the unprotected pubis. Pablo's inadvertent scream would have been music to Darlene's ears though she would have pointed out, with some pride, that her own sirenlike scream when faced with dismemberment at Pablo's hands had at least succeeded in summoning the police, while Pablo's scream is merely thrilling to Midge, who, with a practiced deft touch, cuts away, in three strokes, all of Pablo's pubic hair, revealing what Midge refers to, scornfully, as "Smaller than your average unborn male at the start of the second trimester."

Pablo is now babbling in Spanish, praying for mercy. But Midge has moved on to Calderón. As she clears his pubic area with her knife, she decides that Latin Lover-wise, Calderón is almost interesting. She grabs the tip of the okra pod.

"What's this? Can it be what is known to those of us in the medical profession as psilanthropism?" Calderón gasps an affirmative, eyes bulging under narrow Mayan brow. All that he worships she now holds in her hand—the plumed serpent, the dark gods of the blood.

"I have just the cure." With a wrench, Midge pulls back the recalcitrant hood, which splits like a cracked lip in winter. There is a splash of blood. Calderón crumples to the floor in a dead faint.

Midge is delighted. But she is not yet finished. Although she has more than once got away with, literally, murder in the male ward at Fond de Lac General, there are still certain perimeters and parameters that she is obliged to observe. But here, on this special assignment, everything goes.

Midge opens her reticule and, as Pablo watches, knowing that Darlene means to kill him slowly, with ten thousand cuts, she removes her favorite bit of equipment.

"No!" Pablo screams. "I am ready to die like a man. But not—not that!" Pablo's screams and pleas fall on deaf ears as Midge prepares.

46

Shortly after midnight, the barrios are in actual flames. The section along ethnic Kennedy Avenue has gone up like dry tinder when a match has been applied to it, which is exactly how it did catch fire. One of the Darlene male look-alikes, under orders from Bill Toomey at the Daridere, has set the blaze. "But be sure it's on the desert side," Bill barks into the radio. "We don't want it spreading over to McKinley Avenue."

Needless to say, Leo and the KDLM-TV crew are on the spot. They are ecstatic. Although almost any fire will win a prize on television, a conflagration is certain to win new advertisers. Should the conflagration burn for more than a week it becomes a bona fide holocaust—and a whole new ball game, numbers-wise.

"This," shouts Leo into his hand mike, "is a conflagration!"

Meanwhile, Captain Eddie and his men are spread out through the barrios. So far they have caught only one of Bill Toomey's men and he is cucumber cool. Toomey has trained his troops well. "FBI," says the captive, flashing an FBI badge and identity card.

"Hold him," says Captain Eddie. "That ID could be a forgery. Like the uniform," he adds. Captain Eddie, like every police chief in the nation, hates and fears the FBI even more than he hates and fears Communists.

The sky over ethnic Kennedy Avenue is bright with flames. "Well, they did it," says Captain Eddie, half to himself, half to "Chico."

"Did what, Chief?" asks "Chico."

"I've still got a card or two left to play." Captain Eddie is grim. He tells the men in his fleet of police cars to arrest every false policeman and -woman that they can find in the barrios.

As Captain Eddie is addressing his troops a stone's throw from the Daridere, not a stone but a Molotov cocktail is hurled at him. Luckily for Captain Eddie, the cocktail falls just short of him. In the bright sheet of flame from the cocktail, which singes Captain Eddie's eyelashes, two slender Mexican youths can be seen, hurrying into the winding streets of the barrios where no gringo dares to go unarmed.

"And keep an eye out for the illegal aliens. They have been deliberately inflamed against the DPD by these false policemen who have been hassling them."

"Why?" asks "Chico," naturally.

"No time to explain," says Captain Eddie, leaping into his command car, giving orders right and left.

As the fleet of police cars carooms off, the two Mexican youths who threw the Molotov cocktail stand in the shadows, watching intently. One is Pablo. The other is Calderón. To their astonishment the gorgeous blonde whom they had taken to be Darlene did not dismember and kill them in the cellar of the moccasin shop.

"No more than what we actually deserved," says Pablo.

The light from a burning warehouse in the next street flickers across his now impassive face. Pablo is always fair in these matters.

"Perhaps the gringa lives by a different code," muses Calderón. With one hand inside his pocket, he clutches his tortured *membrum virile*, still damp with blood. The plumed serpent is now forever plumeless.

"Or maybe she will come back a *second* time to kill us," says Pablo, always one to examine all the angles. "But I will die first rather than go through what I went through."

"What *did* you go through, muchacho?" Calderón is genuinely curious. When he himself regained consciousness after a thirty-minute faint, he found Pablo on the floor, curled up in the fetal position, sobbing uncontrollably, and babbling meaningless words.

"You will never know. No one on earth will ever know what she did. But," says Pablo and he swears a mighty oath, "I will die or be avenged!"

Little does Midge—still making her rounds and having a ball—realize what she has done to the leader of one million illegal aliens. She does notice that there seem to be quite a lot of fires in this particular section of town but no worse, she thinks, than downtown Fond du Lac on your average Saturday night.

47

High atop the McKinley Communications Center, the president of KDLM-TV and a dozen of the city's most powerful figures are meeting in the boardroom. Paneled walls of laminated plywood frame picture windows through which, beneath a gibbous moon, the barrios can be seen in flames.

Thoughtfully, the rulers of Duluth look down at their city and each asks himself (in his own way): what does it all mean?

Bellamy Craig II, after ordering a bullshot from Rastus, the loyal black servitor, takes his place at the head of the table. The dozen other very important people sit to his left and right, each with a pad of paper and a Dr Pepper, unopened, in front of him. Only Bellamy gets the bullshot. But then he is the owner, through a series of complex trusts, of KDLM-TV as well as of the *Duluth Blade*. Until tonight not even Chloris—who is present—has realized the extent of his holdings. Bellamy exerts total control over all the media in Greater Duluth.

Chloris is impressed. Chloris is wearing her Givenchy Mao suit suitable, the *vendeuse* told her at the time that Chloris bought it, for the more casual sort of cultural revolution or longish march. Next to her on the sofa behind Bellamy's thronelike chair, Clive is in riding tops, complete with spurs. As devoted as Chloris is to Clive, this is Bellamy's night. She has never before seen her husband exude so much crude naked power. Until now she has never really been sure just what Bellamy does do other than lead Duluth society—which he actually leaves to her to lead—and play polo. Now she knows. And she in inordinately proud to be his humble helpmeet.

As the bullshot is set on the table in front of Bellamy, he says, "We've got to keep up our strength. This is going to be a long night. You may go, Rastus." The black servitor cringes from the room.

Bellamy presses a button on the console in front of him. A curved television screen descends from the ceiling, causing ahs and ohs from all of the very impressed very important people.

Bellamy takes a sip of his bullshot. Then he says, indicating the screen, "We shall be able to keep track of events throughout Duluth in the course of the night. My KDLM-TV crews are stationed at strategic points around the city. As I press these different buttons on my console here, we will be able to see any given sector of the city. What shall we look at first?''

"Garfield Heights," says Chloris. "To make sure that no looters have penetrated our wealthy enclave."

There is a murmur of satisfaction from the others. Bellamy, always amiable in regard to Chloris despite—or even because of—their open marriage, says, "Very well." He presses a button.

The screen fills with a long shot of Garfield Heights, serene in the moonlight. Then, due to the magic of KDLM-TV, not to mention a very expensive private monitoring service, there are a number of shots of the different streets and mansions as well as of the homes in this highly desirable neighborhood. All is peaceful. As per usual, two tanks from the national guard are stationed at the entrance to the Heights, cannons at the ready. Only one thing is odd. Rather too many Mexican maids seem to be busy running errands. They hurry from house to house. Before Chloris can ask *why* their maids are prowling about, Bellamy says, "Don't worry. They only *look* like Mexican maids. Actually, they are plainclothes persons from Captain Eddie's special squad whose sole task is to guard the Heights."

There is a patter of applause at this. "Bellamy thinks of everything," says Chloris in a low voice to Clive, who glowers. She is treating me like a lounge lizard, a fancy boy. If she only knew, he thinks. But she doesn't. She can't. Clive is morose.

"Now," says Bellamy, "I think it's time to check in at the scene of the conflagration."

The screen is suddenly ablaze with yellow and red and orange flames as well as wonderful smoke effects. For sheer beauty there is nothing like a burning barrio. There is rapt applause from the rulers of Duluth in that boardroom. Although, to a man, they own every single building—hovels to one side—in that part of the city they are, to a man, as land-lords, insured to their eyeballs. In fact, one of them lets just a whisker of pussy out of the bag when he says, "I wouldn't like to be Lloyd's of London tonight." This witty sally is greeted with giggles and sniggers.

Captain Eddie, who has been in the background, directing the fire, to the annoyance of the fire chief, a traditional rival, comes toward the camera, where he is given a headset and hand mike so that he can both hear and talk to Bellamy high atop McKinley Tower.

"Good evening, Chief." Bellamy always speaks to servants as if they were servants. This means that he is very polite in the way that he talks to them but impolite in that he never listens to a word that they say, as he knows that they will lie about all the things that they have broken and all the food that they have toted. "How is the conflagration?"

"Pretty bad, Mr. Craig. But we're getting it under control."

"I see." Bellamy is not listening. "Who started the fire?"

"Provocateurs. From the Federal Bureau of Investigation. Posing as DPD officers. They came to create havoc *and* a conflagration in order to reelect Mayor Herridge, who put them up to it."

"I see," says Bellamy, nodding; he has heard none of this. "Keep up the good work, Chief. And remember. Anything you want, you'll get. The sky's the limit."

"Thank you, sir." Captain Eddie trembles respectfully, as Bellamy switches to another channel.

"I'd like a bullshot," says Chloris to Rastus, the black servitor, who has reappeared, only to disappear.

"What about me?" asks Clive, who is thirsty.

"This is very serious," says Chloris, warningly.

On the screen now is the palm-lined waterfront, all lit up with the special lights that Captain Eddie had ordered installed to make sure that the black population does not follow the Chicanos into open rebellion against their white masters. But the blacks never do anything that the Chicanos do. If one group riots, the other looks to its own knitting.

From under the palm trees at the edge of the lake, "Chico" Jones speaks into the camera lens. "Lieutenant Jones, Homicide."

"How are things with the nig-nogs at the waterfront?" asks Bellamy, coming straight to the point.

"Everything's quiet here in the *colored* section." "Chico" uses the word "colored" as often as possible even though he knows that it annoys the brothers who are—now that welfare is being cut back—more than ever into blackness. One of these days the black inner city will blow sky-high. Everyone knows that. But everyone also knows that it will never happen on the same day that the barrios are aflame. No way, as they say under the palms. This particular night when the blacks should have made common cause with their brown brothers against the common white enemy, they are all crowded into the Martin King Holy Grace Mortuary Auditorium, listening to a lecture on Total Love by yellow Yoko Ono, who is in town, signing Frisbees and offering her message of Total Love to all people on earth and in Duluth.

"That's good to hear, Lieutenant . . . *Uh?*"

"Jones, Mr. Craig."

"Well, keep up the good work and now—"

"One minute, sir," says "Chico," interrupting the most powerful man in Duluth.

"How about thirty seconds?" jokes Bellamy. "Time is money."

"I'll be quick about it. I think you should know, sir, that the spaceship is gone."

There is consternation in the boardroom. "Gone?" says Bellamy, listening for a change. "What do you mean by gone?"

The crew at KDLM-TV has now cut to a long shot of Lake Erie and it is true that where the spaceship has been there is now only algae and garbage as before.

"But when? Where?" Bellamy is on edge.

"About eleven o'clock, it just disappeared. We don't know where. Maybe back to outer space or somewhere."

"With Mayor Herridge inside?"

"Yes, sir, as far as we know, sir, his Honor was still inside."

Bellamy snaps off the picture, which is now of "Chico" Jones, in a very tight shot, beaming happily at the neat elimination of his boss's rival. "Chico" does not yet know that the spaceship is only a mile away in the middle of the Duluth Woods swamp.

48

In the burning barrios, Pablo and Calderón—like swift shadows—make their way from illegal headquarters to illegal headquarters. The muchachos are all at their posts, waiting for the word from Pablo to occupy Garfield Heights. But the word does not come. The sudden strike by the Darlene look-alikes has wrecked Pablo's master plan to seize the Heights. On top of that, the barrios do not need to be inflamed any more since they are already on fire for real.

Pablo collects thirty men. The hard core of his Aztec Terrorists Society. They are selfless. They are armed. They have *cojones* to spare. Pablo leads them to the abandoned warehouse where the flames—and the police—have not yet arrived.

"We must turn what could be potential disaster into victory!" Pablo is standing on a crate just a yard from where he raped Darlene on the floor. For an instant, he is excited as he thinks of that ecstatic moment. Then he frowns. Dismemberment rather than rape is on his mind now. But this time it will not be for pleasure, or even kicks. This time it will be for Mexico and for all that Mexico has suffered at the hands of the gringos from the war of 1847 to the present day of green cards withheld.

Palbo inflames the muchachos with a long speech, dwelling upon their past sufferings which, according to the muchachos themselves, do not begin to compare with the suffering that they have undergone this very night when seventeen of the thirty were stripped and humiliated by the Darlene look-alikes, often in the presence of their women, who were, in turn, humiliated by the thick red probing fingers of the male Darlenes.

Pablo deftly enrages the already inflamed men.

"The only thing that we need now," says Calderón, *membrum virile* hot and throbbing—probably infected, too, he thinks glumly—"is a plan."

At that moment Carmencita, Calderón's woman—how he is to explain to her the loss of both pubic hair and plumed serpent's plume is a bridge that he refuses to cross until it has come to him—enters the room, mantilla aflame.

Deftly, Calderón enfolds Carmencita in a sack and rolls her about the floor until the flames are out. "Are you hurt, my *paloma?*" he asks, as she gets to her feet.

"No, my *toro*," she answers, "only disheveled. I must warn you that the fire is approaching this abandoned warehouse by leaps and bounds. But before we flee, I have news." They are all speaking Spanish, of course, a language more formal than English.

"What it that?" asks Pablo, assuming again his role of leadership

"The entire power establishment of Duluth—led by that obscenity of an obscenity my employer Bellamy Craig II . . ." Carmencita spits on the floor to show her disgust. The others spit, too. "They have fled from the Heights in terror—"

"Of the fire?" asks Calderón shrewdly.

"No, of us!" Carmencita throws back her head proudly and gives the Aztec war cry. The others shudder and know in their hearts that Mexican Woman Aroused is as ten men or even one Darlene.

"Where have they fled to?" asks Pablo.

"The boardroom of KDLM-TV high atop the McKinley Communications Center Building. My leader," she says to Pablo significantly, "they are, for once, all together."

Palbo smiles, tightly. "Our time has come. The hour has struck. The enemy is ours. Operation Montezuma is now operational."

49

Unaware of the approaching danger, the very important people in the boardroom are munching canapés and discussing what next to do.

Bellamy is trying unsuccessfully to make contact with Captain Eddie, who is on the move, firing at looters and loiterers alike, making no distinction between the two as dead men tell no tales to the American Civil Liberties Union or even to the *Duluth Blade*.

"Strange, Yoko Ono never let me know that she was in town," says Chloris to Clive, miffed.

"But you don't know her," says Clive cattily.

"Even so . . ." Chloris does not need to say that she *is* Social Duluth. "Imagine lecturing at the waterfront, to darkies."

Bellamy, bullshot in hand, joins his wife and her lover.

He smiles in a kindly way at both of them. "Having a good time?" he asks.

"It's very exciting, isn't it?" says Chloris. "You're so masterful, Bellamy. Really. I mean it."

Clive wants to throw up. Instead he hurries to the bathroom, where he spoons some Pakistani coke into his huge nostrils. He feels better immediately. But then "a cold nose is a happy nose" is not just a proverb restricted to the denizens of the canine world.

In the boardroom, there is a newcomer—Wayne Alexander. He goes up to Bellamy, who smiles, always nice-tempered, and Chloris, who frowns, not always nice-tempered by any means. She will never forgive him for C-A-T. But she will have to dissemble, she remembers, if she is ever to find out who killed Betty Grable. Chloris puts on a smile.

Wayne is nervous. "I didn't learn till just now, sir, that you are the owner of the *Blade*."

"Hope you don't go printing that, Wayne!" laughs Bellamy, who knows that nothing can get in the paper without his O.K.

"Oh, I wouldn't dream of it, sir . . ."

"SEC and the FCC and all the other Communists in Washington would say that I had a monopoly of the Duluth media *if* they knew I owned both the paper and the TV so we've got to pretend I don't." Bellamy laughs his good-fellow laugh. "Say," he says, "we haven't been seeing you at our home so much lately. Why is that, Wayne?"

"Well, there's been a lot of work at the paper and . . ."

"Now, now, boy." Bellamy is understanding. After all, he himself had almost kissed Wayne once, mistaking him from the back for Evelyn Stellaborger. "Chloris has her moods. But they pass like summer clouds, don't they, Chloris?"

"Indeed they do, Bellamy." Chloris is trying to think when it was that she last made it with Bellamy. Certainly not since their marriage was declared open and that was at least ten years ago. She wonders, idly, if he has improved. She is impressed by his power tonight—and masterfulness. He is on top of the situation.

"I have something to report, sir," says Wayne, humbly, to Bellamy. But he is not able to report this something because the TV screen has lit up suddenly. There is a large round picture of what looks to be a jittery chicken looking over its shoulder. There is writing all around the picture which no one can read. Then a voice off-camera announces, "Ladies and gentlemen of Duluth, the president of the United States."

Then there is a pregnant pause, which soon gives birth in the boardroom to murmurs of "Which one?"

They soon find out—although, as usual, no one can remember his name. Of the many presidents, this is the very old one that they use on the television to read cue cards through shiny contact lenses.

"Hello there, Duluth!" The old television president flashes his capped teeth.

"You'd think that our importance as an industrial center and lake port would let us rate the fat one, what's his name?" says Bellamy, irritated.

"But, sir, Duluth voted against this particular batch of presidents." Wayne keeps track of this sort of minutiae.

"You think this could be their revenge?"

"Yes, sir."

". . . remember a story when I was reporting this basketball game—that was for radio. Remember radio? The funny box that didn't have any picture on it? So I was there in the stadium and it was half-time . . ."

Bellamy switches off the old TV president who never stops reminiscing. He turns to one of his aides. "Call the White House. Say we want the fat one. *Or nothing. This is Duluth!*"

"Yes, sir, Mr. Craig, sir."

How masterful, thinks Chloris, yet again.

"You were saying, Wayne," says Bellamy smoothly, "before Mr. Show-biz interrupted us . . ."

"There's been a breakthrough on the spaceship story."

"They find it, Wayne?"

"No, sir. But they think they've identified the man who was seen greeting Mayor Herridge."

"What man?" Bellamy gestures for Rastus to bring him another bullshot—his fourth. Chloris is counting—proudly, truth to tell.

"You remember that quick glimpse we got during the slow-motion playback?"

"Oh, yes. That."

Wayne presses a button. The huge curved screen shows the lab at one end of the cavernous studio—which is located in another part of the McKinley Tower. A technician, aware that he is on the air with the owner of the station, bows very low to the camera. "Mr. Craig, sir. I'm the head of the technical lab, sir."

"Nice to see you," says Bellamy. "I'm told you now know just who the man is who was greeting Mayor Herridge inside the spaceship."

"Well, sir. Yes and no. As you'll see, sir." The head technician presses a button and on the screen behind him— clearly visible on the screen in the boardroom—is the shot, in very slow motion, of Mayor Herridge entering the shadowy interior of the spaceship. Then, out of the shadows, steps a thick-set man with a big head who puts out his hand. As he does, the spaceship's side shuts.

The chief technician looks into the camera's lens. "Now, sir, we've done some very close analysis of what you've just seen. Let me show you, sir."

On the screen inside the boardroom screen the big head of the thick-set man has been frozen. The big head comes into even closer close-up. They all have a chance to examine the features. The big head *does* look familiar to all of them. The forehead is bulbous. The hairline receding. The smile is wide and lovable. The eyes crinkle with good feeling. The jowls are, perhaps, too large for the tight collar but the face is that of a very nice man.

"I'm relieved," says Chloris to Clive, "that it is not some sort of monster."

"Now," says the technician. "Some other studies." The face is shown from different angles under different lighting conditions. There is mounting excitement in the boardroom.

"We have now come to the unanimous conclusion," says the chief technician, "that the man who can be seen greeting our Mayor inside the spaceship—on the Fourth of July—is none other than our former United States Senator from Minnesota—"

"My God!" exclaims Bellamy, "it is Hubert Horatio Humphrey!"

50

Pablo, at the head of his Aztec Terrorists, moves like a shadow in the night through the deserted complex of skyscrapers that makes up McKinley Center at whose center is the tallest of all the skyscrapers, the Communications Center Tower, owned entirely through a series of trusts and shelters by Bellamy Craig II.

Guards outside the main door of the Center are swiftly overcome. When Pablo rings the front door bell, the night watchman comes to the door and asks through the security intercom what his business is. Pablo's thirty-one armed illegal aliens are hidden behind the jumbo-size Henry Moore statue that Chloris gave to Duluth as a tax deduction.

"I'm here for the *Rod Spencer Show*," says Pablo. This

is a popular late-night talk show where Rod talks to murderers who have written books and would-be suicides and even—he is nothing if not gutsy—social climbers. The viewers can then call in on the telephone and take part in the fun.

"O.K.," says the night watchman, who has seen a lot weirder guests than Pablo for the *Rod Spencer Show,* which he and a number of other born-again Christians are trying to get off the air.

After he unlocks the door, Pablo pulls a gun on him. The night watchman puts his hands up. He has seen this done, as has Pablo, on a million television programs. He also knows that a TV camera in the ceiling is recording everything that is happening. Pablo will not get far. Were he not wearing new dentures, the night watchman might have smiled at tight smile.

"You've got to sign in. Regulation," says the watchman, indicating an open book on a table.

With a sneer, Pablo writes "Benito Juárez," unaware that no one in the building or Duluth will ever figure out who this Benitó Juárez is or was as there is no FBI file on him.

"*And* the time," says the watchman, who is a stickler for detail.

With a look that could kill, Pablo writes the time, after which he ties up the watchman. Then he gives a whistle with two fingers in his mouth and the thirty-one loyal muchachos and Carmencita come around and through the Henry Moore statue and race into the lobby, which they then occupy.

Ignoring the stickler watchman's barked orders to sign in, they follow, pell mell, Pablo to the elevators.

For an hour they ride up and down, aimlessly, getting off first at one floor then at another. They don't know how to find the special elevator which goes to the boardroom. At last, exasperated, Pablo says, "We will now have to seize the television station, and ask where the boardroom is," which they proceed to do.

Rod Spencer is on the air, discussing the pros and cons of masturbation with three onanists and three dissenting Freudians when Pablo, gun in hand, joins the group at the round table that is the Rod Spencer trademark or logo.

"Hands up!" says Pablo. All hands go up—albeit the onanists are slow about this because of their "primal affliction," as Freud calls it.

"Good evening," says Rod, brightly. "I assume you're a terrorist from the barrios."

"Yes. I am Pablo. Chief of the Aztec Terrorists Society." Pablo has never been on television before and he finds that he likes it. Very much. He also senses that Rod likes him. An Aztec can always tell.

"It's wonderful having you like this on the show. Are you also an onanist?"

"What?" Pablo falls back on his first English word.

"He means," says one of the dissenting Freudians, "do you beat your meat?"

"Shit, no!" Pablo's macho pride is aroused. In the barrios there is no worse insult than to accuse a man of self-abuse. A true man with powerful *cojones* abuses others, only.

The Freudians are delighted. The onanists, hands now restored to their laps, look downcast.

"That's very interesting, Pablo," says Rod.

"Listen," says Pablo, aware that Calderón is waving urgently from behind the tied-up cameraman. "Where is the private elevator to the boardroom?"

"I don't know . . ." begins Rod but the pistol that is suddenly aimed between his eyes brings his always quick mind into sharp focus. "It's inside the broom closet at the end—on the left—of the bank of elevators in the outer foyer of station KDLM-TV in the heart of downtown Duluth. Why," asks Rod, an inveterate questioner, "do you want to know where the secret elevator is?"

"Because—and this is no secret as we are on national television—"

"Local," says Rod, sadly. "There's a *chance* of syndication. But I wouldn't count on it if I were you. Irv Kupcinet out of Chicago is going up in the ratings and . . .''

This is all over Pablo's head. He stares into the camera. "We're going to hold captive the civic leaders of Duluth who are in that boardroom. We'll want maybe a million dollars a head. And a plane to fly us to . . . uh . . .'' Since Pablo cannot think which of the many enemies of the United States he'll be going to for refuge, he simply jumps to his feet and shouts, "Follow me, muchachos!'' The studio is soon emptied of terrorists.

"I think,'' says Rod smoothly, "we'll take a few calls now. But . . .'' He cocks an ear mischievously. "Is that a vibrator I hear under the table, Glenda?''

The guilty onanist blushes, guiltily.

"Dr. Freud,'' says one of the Freudians, "regarded masturbation as worse than alcoholism. But then he regarded any form of sex that does not lead to procreation as—and I use *his* word—perversion.''

"He sounds like Moses,'' says one of the onanists.

"I think,'' says Rod, meaningfully, "that Freud is a lot bigger than Moses in the Greater Duluth area these days.''

51

Darlene turns off her set and vibrator at the same time—each is connected to the same switch beside her bed.

Darlene is thoughtful. She has never thought there was anything wrong with masturbation. *Cosmopolitan*, Masters and Johnson, *Good Housekeeping* have always encouraged her, egged her on, in fact, but now, on the *Rod Spencer*

Show, her favorite talk show, she is told by psychologists that it's all wrong—and a perversion to boot.

As for Pablo, she assumes that his appearance was simply a promotional stunt of some kind. On the other hand, she is surprised that a rapist and would-be sex killer—she recognized him immediately even with his clothes on because she has the trained policeperson's eye—would be allowed to appear on Rod Spencer. Of course, Rod probably does not know what happened at the abandoned warehouse.

Darlene decides to give Rod a call. She has talked to him many times before on the air. She dials his number. But there is a busy signal. She hangs up. Then *her* phone rings. "Drat!" she exclaims, looking at the clock. It is one in the A.M. She picks up the receiver.

"Darlene!" It is "Chico."

"Yes, 'Chico'?"

"You heard?"

"Heard what?"

"The Aztec Terrorists Society has seized the KDLM-TV boardroom at the Communications Center Tower. They've nabbed all the town's leaders."

"Good grief!" Since Darlene's pregnancy, she has been cleaning up her language. For one thing, she feels warm and maternal. She must also set a good example for baby. "Where are you?"

"The lobby of the McKinley Tower. Captain Eddie's here."

"I'll be right there." Darlene hangs up.

Quickly, she dresses, wondering what on earth that doctor—what's his name? Freud—could mean by "primal affliction."

154

52

There is both consternation and pandemonium when Pablo and his gang burst into the boardroom, guns and razors drawn.

Unfortunately for the very important people, Bellamy Craig II has never been able to abide his own employee Rod Spencer so instead of watching his own station, Bellamy has tuned in the local Petroleum Broadcasting System where the Robert Aldrich Film Retrospective is airing, courtesy of Exxon.

Robert Aldrich is related to the Rockefeller family, as Chloris was quick to point out when the second reel of *The Twilight's Last Gleaming* started—with Joseph Cotten, as always superb, as the secretary of state. "So," she had said, "it is highly fitting that his cousin David Rockefeller tell the family firm, Exxon, to sponsor this retrospective."

"Now, Chloris," Bellamy had chuckled, "that's not the way it works in programming. Remember that Mr. Aldrich is one of the all-time movie greats . . ."

At that exact moment Pablo appears in the doorway. In the course of the ensuing consternation and pandemonium, Clive decides that this is not his kind of scene. Like a wraith, he flits from the room. The fact that he is in riding togs helps. He looks like some sort of oppressed worker, thinks Calderón, as Clive with a polite "buenas noches" leaves the boardroom and heads down the emergency staircase, followed by the one-eared Wayne, for whom Calderón has compassion, having so recently lost his plume.

Meanwhile, Pablo is bringing order out of chaos. On one side of the room the thirty-one terrorists settle down comfortably on their haunches, sombreros over their eyes. On the other side, thirteen very important people stand stock-still with terror and amazement, as Pablo spells out what he wants. He has already upped the ante.

"For the lives of you fourteen gringos, I want one hundred million dollars. In cash. Then I want a plane to transport all of us to . . . our destination of choice. Then you will be set free."

"But suppose," says Bellamy, who has already seen *The Twilight's Last Gleaming* on Z channel and knows what an awful fate befalls the fictional though wonderfully rendered president of the United States who becomes a hostage, "you do not live up to your part of the bargain?"

"That," says Pablo, "is a chance that *you*—not I—will have to take." Pablo has not seen *The Twilight's Last Gleaming*. If he had, he would be less cocksure because if there is a lesson to be learned from that incredible film it is that no one—but no one! including any of the presidents—has a chance against those who control the boardrooms of the nation.

"Now make yourselves comfortable," says Pablo to the hostages. They are allowed to sit on the sofas at the far end of the room with a good view of the television screen.

"You," says Pablo to Rastus, the trembling black servitor. "Come here."

The black servitor obeys, without alacrity. "Yes, suh?"

"Although you are a nigger and carry a transistor and live only for the pleasures of sexual congress, you are still oppressed and our brother."

"Yes, suh. Can I make you a bullshot? Or, perhaps, a Campari and soda? A toothsome daiquiri? A Pink Lady, mayhap?"

"Margaritas for all my men—and Carmencita, who is Calderón's woman!" The Aztecs all burst into "olé's" when Pablo's English has been, laboriously, translated into Spanish by Calderón.

Rastus goes off to make the margaritas, hoping against hope that "these crazed spicks," his private characterization, will not know the difference between celery salt, of which he has an ample supply, and rock salt, which he is almost out of, for the rimming of the glasses' edges.

Pablo is staring at Chloris, who is staring at Pablo. Bellamy stares out the window. He recalls, a bit late in the game, that the open marriage was his, not her, idea.

Pablo feels a slight warming of what Darlene had so sneeringly referred to as his okra and prunes. He could have this beautiful gringa, exquisitely garbed in what he immediately recognizes as Givenchy's most expensive Mao-style model. Pablo thinks of the pleasure that he will have tearing to bits the Givenchy, as she screams. Then the rape, followed by the slow dismemberment with a knife—starting, as always, with the left titty. But knives remind him of Darlene's knife. He flushes at the memory. How can he rape this gringa—or any gringa—without pubic hair? How can he ever do anything to a woman after what Darlene did? He still does not know that his tormentor was Midge, the look-alike, and not Darlene. All desire drains from him. The plumed serpent's crest falls.

Chloris is thinking, he *is* cute, definitely cute. So virile. So masterful. She is somewhat put out when he turns from her to Bellamy. "We better get down to business, gringo."

"Very well. Your demands will be met." Bellamy trusts Pablo about as far as he can throw him, which, considering Pablo's slight wiry frame and Bellamy's powerful arms, would be a fair distance. "I shall speak to the president."

"Good. Which one?" Even Pablo knows about the confusion in the gringo capital.

Bellamy presses a button on the console. To everyone's horror the old television president is still talking. He has been on for more than an hour. "Right after that—no, maybe, *before* that happened. Yes. Don't want to spoil the

157

punch line.'' The old television president twinkles. ''I went into Jack L. Warner's office at Burbank, and I said, 'Mr. Warner . . .' I never dared call him Jack . . .''

Bellamy switches off this president.

''The wrong one?'' Pablo feels a moment of compassion.

''Yes,'' says Bellamy, slipping into a blue funk. ''And I don't know how to get through to the fat one.''

''Margaritas, gentlemen,'' announces Rastus. The illegal aliens—seventeen are barefoot now because their corns, mashed in by the Darlene look-alikes, have been hurting them—scramble for the margaritas. To Rastus's relief they like the celery salt that rims the glasses. ''Actually,'' says Calderón to Carmencita, ''there is less sodium in celery salt and so it is more healthy.''

For response, she embraces him passionately; causing him to wince.

''What a man!'' she whispers. ''I feel you like a bull even through those thick plaid trousers. Do I inflame you so much, my *toro?*''

''Yes.'' Calderón groans; flaccid, his *membrum virile* is now twice its usual size and very painful.

53

In the lobby of the McKinley Communications Center Tower, Captain Eddie is examining the ledger. '' 'Benito Juárez,' '' he murmurs, thoughtfully. ''Doesn't ring a bell.''

''Probably a pesudonym,'' says ''Chico.'' The lobby is filled with Duluth's finest. They have riot equipment.

Poison gas. Even a neutron bomb. Fortunately, no one knows how to set it off.

Darlene pushes her way through the crowd of colleagues. "Lieutenant Ecks, reporting for duty," she says, smartly.

"Hi, honey." Captain Eddie is stymied. There are no leads. Fortunately, Darlene has seen the *Rod Spencer Show*. Quickly, she fills in her chief.

Captain Eddie takes all this in with his usual swiftness of mind. "So it's not Benito, it's Pablo."

"Yes. And he means business, Chief."

"That's pretty plain. Somehow, we've got to get in touch with him. Find out his exact terms for releasing the hostages. But how?"

Captain Eddie and "Chico" are at a complete loss. It is Darlene who saves the day. "I know one way," she says, slowly, turning it over in her mind, "and it just might work."

"What?" Captain Eddie is edgy. He'll try anything.

"We can telephone the boardroom and ask to speak to Pablo."

"Why didn't I think of that?" "Chico" is filled with admiration. But it is Captain Eddie who throws cold water on the scheme.

"The number," says the Chief, "is unlisted. I know. I tried to ring Mr. Craig there once. And the operator wouldn't give me, *me*, the chief of police, the number. Only the FBI can get it without a court order, and we're not on speaking terms, obviously."

54

As Mayor Herridge set foot inside the spaceship, a man—thank God, a man and not a monster—comes forward to greet him. "Hi, Mayor, it's great to see you!" In the gloom Mayor Herridge cannot make out the man's features. But he allows the man to pump his hand vigorously. Plainly, he has met this creature from outer space somewhere before. The Mayors' Convention, maybe, the previous year at Tacoma?

"Welcome to Duluth," the Mayor croaks. "It's sure dark in here."

Suddenly, the door behind him shuts out Duluth and daylight and he finds himself aboard a Boeing 707, shaking hands with his late friend Hubert H. Humphrey. "Hubert!"

"Mayor!" Humphrey knew Mayor Herridge before he was mayor of Duluth—which was after Humphrey's death—so when Hubert calls the Mayor Mayor he is using his old first name and not his current title. "Come on back to my compartment. The airport says the reception committee isn't ready yet and we're a half hour *ahead* of schedule. For a change. I'm surprised they let you on."

The plane is filled with bored journalists as well as with Hubert's numerous aides. "Hey, fellas," says Hubert. "This is my old friend Mayor Herridge, who's from right here in Duluth where he's city judge. The two of us grew up together." This isn't true as Hubert grew up in South Dakota while Mayor Herridge really *is* from Minnesota to which Hubert later moved in order to become a senator and go to Washington.

There is much applause from the cynical newsmen. As Hubert leads Mayor to the front of the plane where he has a private compartment, Mayor has not only a sense of *déjà vu* but an actual memory of having come aboard Hubert's plane at the Duluth airport in September of 1968 when Hubert—at that time the vice president of the United States—was running for president of those very same states against Richard M. Nixon, who beat Hubert. This was in the old days when there was only the one president at a time.

Mayor Herridge is in a real quandary. He's already lived through this scene once before and he refuses to go through it all over again, as so much has happened in the intervening years—like Hubert's sad death of cancer. Should he mention this to Hubert?

But Mayor Herridge does not have much chance because Hubert, living or dead, is a real chatterbox. They are now seated in the vice president's personal compartment at the front of the plane. Through the windows Mayor Herridge can see the old Duluth airport the way it was that day in '68 when Hubert came to town. Mayor Herridge feels kind of nostalgic seeing the old Duluth that is no more, having given way, as all things must in an up-and-coming community, to progress.

Hubert is reading from the latest polls. "I've caught up with Tricky Dick everywhere but in the south, where I'm trailing by three percent. Not bad considering that disaster we had at Chicago."

He's obviously referring to the Democratic National Convention, thinks Mayor Herridge, where the police rioted. What a long time ago it seems, he broods, looking at Hubert—who looks very young to him now as he, who used to be younger than Hubert then, is now older than Hubert now. "I'm sure you'll beat the bejezus out of him."

"I've got to," says Hubert, very seriously. "For the sake of the country. Nixon's a crook."

"How did you know that even then?" asks Mayor Herridge, getting his tenses mixed.

"How do I know *now?*" Hubert corrects him. "Lyndon and I don't just sit around the White House singing 'Hail to the Chief' to each other. We got the CIA on Nixon's tail. Of course he's got the FBI on our tail. J. Edgar Hoover is Nixon's man. He's been dating Betty Grable, by the way. Hoover, that is."

"I thought Hoover was a fag."

"He is," says Hubert, irritably, "but that doesn't mean he can't use a beard from time to time. Clyde Tolson, his long-time live-in boyfriend, is fit to be tied. You know, I'm going to end the war in Viet Nam," Hubert adds. "Sooner or later, anyway. And that's a promise."

"Good," says Mayor Herridge, who was actually very gung-ho about the war in '68, as he was too old to be in it. Now, of course, he sees it for the tragedy that it was, the cause of all the inflation and unemployment, not to mention the highest interest rates since the Civil War. The city of Duluth has not been able to raise a bond issue for five years.

"Now, Hubert, let's get down to brass tacks." Mayor Herridge takes the bull by the horns. "What about the spaceship?"

"What're you talking about?" asks Hubert, putting down the latest Gallup poll but not before Mayor Herridge detects a somewhat sly expression in that usually guileless face.

"You know what I mean."

"You sure you're not flipping your lid on me? For a minute there you sounded just like Lyndon. He's bats, you know. Lyndon thinks he's being secretly poisoned, which is why his feet keep growing." Maybe, thinks Mayor Herridge, it's a good idea, after all, to have a whole batch of presidents the way we do now, instead of just one at a time who might then turn out to be a crook or bats, or even both at the same time.

"Are his feet really growing?"

"Well, he *thinks* they are. And I will say that this boot-maker from Austin says that Lyndon *does* need to wear one size larger than he used to wear. Hell, maybe he *is* being poisoned by the Communists. Or J. Edgar Hoover. After all, they got Kennedy.''

''Who killed Kennedy?''

''Which one?'' Hubert is now sparring with Mayor Herridge.

''Either one.''

''A lone crazed killer. In both cases,'' says Hubert promptly. ''Now what about the spaceship?''

''So you admit we're inside a spaceship?'' This is a breakthrough for Mayor Herridge.

''I'm on my campaign plane as you can plainly see. But I have a sort of offer to make you from—''

At that moment the entire plane begins to shake up and down and back and forth. Hubert Humphrey and Mayor Herridge are thrown about the compartment like dice in a cup because this is the exact moment when Captain Eddie moves the spaceship from the waterfront to the swamp in the Duluth Woods. But neither Hubert nor Mayor Herridge can know this. They just know that all hell is breaking loose.

55

Beryl, Marchioness of Skye, takes the heavy loaded matchlock and aims it at the footpad outside the left-hand window of her carriage, which is hurrying toward Paris. The driver wants to surrender but Beryl does not. ''I will die first,'' she says. ''For the Emperor!''

The driver mutters an expletive in French and continues to whip his horses as two footpads gallop on either side of the carriage, shouting, ''Halt! or we'll shoot!''

But little do they know the mettle of the Emperor's master-spy and mistress. Although the carriage is jiggling her arm, Beryl is a superb shot. She takes aim. She fires. There is a cry, as one of the two footpads hits the dust.

Beryl quickly darts to the other side of the carriage, reloading her matchlock as she does, pushing the bullets in with a long stick and arranging the white powder in the pan. Rosemary is one lousy novelist, Beryl thinks, irritably, having to do all this with an eighteenth-century matchlock when there are perfectly decent revolvers available in the Regency period, but Rosemary is too lazy to give an extra punch or two to the old word-processor and tap one of Georgette Heyer's gems for some much-needed verisimilitude. Fortunately, Beryl is not the sort of character to be confounded by a mere footpad—much less a Klein Kantor plot. Beryl is now fully aware that she is—or was—Beryl Hoover because Rosemary wrote this installment of *Rogue Duke after* Beryl's death in *Duluth.* Although Rosemary is conscious that what she took to be Beryl in *Countess Mara* was someone else, she is not yet conscious that Beryl Hoover has just surfaced midway through *Rogue Duke.* For one thing, Rosemary is hitting the old word-processor much too fast to pay attention to that sort of detail. For another, Rosemary is miffed that Clive has chosen to live not in the Crescent City but in Duluth with Chloris Craig. Although Beryl is fit to be tied to find herself in a piece of junk by Rosemary, she is grateful for this one last chance to help her son Clive, who is in mortal danger. The trick is, she wonders, aiming her matchlock out the window, how to get through to him back in *Duluth?*

Beryl fires a second time. "Take that!" she shouts.

The second footpad falls to the ground, with a terrible cry. The driver of the carriage shouts, "You're some shot, Milady!"

"Shut up and drive on!" Beryl wants no lip from an employee, Regency or not.

It is dawn when they arrive at the Tuileries. The clouds

are pink. The grass is green. There is a delicious scent of croissants in the air, always a sign, thinks Beryl as she crosses to the main door of the palace, that Rosemary, who is on a diet, is getting peckish.

The chamberlain receives Beryl with a low bow. He knows her of old. "Milady, welcome to the palace of the Emperor of all the French."

"Take me to him."

"He is not here, Milady. He has only just now left for Moscow."

"How long will he be gone?"

"He did not say, Milady."

"A working holiday?"

"I believe so, Milady."

"I see." Beryl is thinking hard. Then she writes in code—for Clive—the following number. 757-804-936. "Give this to M. Talleyrand, the foreign minister, sometimes called the Fox of Europe. He will know what it means."

"Your word is my command, Milady."

56

Thoughtfully, Clive puts down the copy of *Redbook* in which he has been reading, without much pleasure, the latest installment of *Rogue Duke* by Rosemary Klein Kantor. He knows that Beryl, Marchioness of Skye, is his late mother. But up until now he's been fairly certain that *she* has no idea that he is reading her. Now he realizes that she's clued in because she is sending him a message. Proof? The Duluth area-code number is 757.

Clive dials the number that Beryl has given the chamberlain to give Talleyrand, the Fox of Europe. Pablo answers the telephone from the boardroom high atop the McKinley Tower. "Who dat?" Pablo's voice is a bit slurred from all the margaritas that he has been drinking.

"This is Clive Hoover. Who are you?"

"The fagola?" Pablo sniggers.

"I beg your pardon." Clive mounts his high horse. "You must be a wetback, from your accent."

"Hey, weren't you here when we seized the boardroom?" Pablo is sobering up fast.

"Yes. But I escaped. Which is more than you're going to do. Put Mr. Craig on the line. And be quick about it, shinola!"

"Clive! God, boy, it's good to hear your voice." Bellamy does sound glad to hear his rival's voice.

"How are things going up there?"

"Well, everybody's watching *The Twilight's Last Gleaming* except me. I saw it on the Z channel."

"So did I. I couldn't believe that a president would talk so dirty in front of high government officials." Clive spars for time. *Why* does Beryl want him to talk to Bellamy?

"Well, the Nixon tapes *do* suggest that sometimes some of the presidents may talk *some*thing like that."

"Even so, I thought it was in very poor taste. Is Chloris enjoying the film?"

"I think so. The reason I'm glad that you called is that we've had no luck getting through to anybody. No one in authority is at police headquarters, while my special audiovisual line to the White House is engaged. The old TV president has been talking for more than two hours about what it was like when he was an actor in Hollywood."

"Has he told the story about Ida Lupino yet?"

"We refuse to listen. Anyway, now that you've got the unlisted telephone number of the boardroom, please contact the chief of police and have him call me so that we can come to terms with our captors."

"All right, Bellamy. I will. A big kiss for Chloris."

"You're a sweetheart, Clive."

Somewhat bemused, Clive hangs up. Then he rings police headquarters but there is no one there who knows where Captain Eddie is. So still dressed in riding togs, Clive leaves his fashionable apartment, gets into his Porsche, and varooms down the Heights to the lobby of the McKinley Tower, where, sure enough, Captain Eddie is still directing operations.

Captain Eddie is delighted to get the unlisted boardroom telephone number from Clive. "But how did you get the most secret unlisted number in Duluth, known only to a handful of initiates?"

"My mother, Beryl," says Clive, with a twinkle in his eye, "left it for me. In her will, you might say."

<h1 style="text-align:center">57</h1>

For five days the negotiations have been going on. The money is no problem. The plane is no problem. The departure of Pablo and the hostages to an as yet unnamed destination is a big problem. The president of the United States who is in charge of terrorism—not the old television president or the fat one but the bald one—is adamant. He has already said, on the *A.M. Show,* to David Hartman himself, "Never will we allow a gang of international terrorists, directed by the Kremlin, to leave the greatest nation in the world with a baker's dozen of the leading citizens of Duluth, the Venice of Minnesota."

"But," says Mr. Hartman, "the Aztec Terrorists, as they call themselves, are Mexicans, not Russians . . ."

"They are, Dave, dupes of Moscow. They are being used. But we will not let them use us."

"Suppose they kill the hostages, Mr. President in Charge of Terrorism?"

"Naturally, we'll review our options when that happens."

This was a very hard line indeed and it did not go down at all well in the boardroom.

With only one small bathroom, the forty-six occupants are becoming very seedy indeed. Naturally, food has been sent in regularly. Tacos and black beans for the terrorists, *fois gras des Landes, terrine de canard, chien mange chien* for the very important people. Rastus is worn out taking the drink orders.

Pablo is now beside himself with nerves. He is in over his head and he knows it. He is becoming whiny. "So what do we do now, gringo?" he asks Bellamy, as they watch the *Six O'Clock News* repeat of the president on the *A.M. Show*.

Bellamy frowns. He is not in over *his* head but he is in pretty deep. Chloris is literally, *on* her head, doing yoga. "There's only one thing we can do. And that's bring pressure to bear on this particular president."

"How?" Pablo has heard all of this before. He is streetwise, if nothing else.

"It's a long shot. Get me the chief of police."

"Yes, señor," says Pablo, suddenly polite.

When Captain Eddie comes on the line, Bellamy says, "You've got to get in touch with The Dude!"

"The Dude! You're joking!" says Captain Eddie. "Nobody gets in touch with The Dude. Nobody even knows who he is. He's a legend. A myth. A wraith. A will-o'-the-wisp."

"I know," says Bellamy. "Don't get carried away. But he's the only man alive who can force this particular president to change his mind. Because he is the only man now alive who understands all the details of Onyx.''

''Of what?''

''Onyx. O-n-y-x. That's all you need to know, Captain Eddie. And that's all that you need to tell The Dude, whoever he is. Just say the one word 'onyx.' Then say, Bellamy Craig II wants that plane to leave within twenty-four hours, or else.''

''I'll do my best, sir,'' says Captain Eddie.

Wayne Alexander is seated in the chair beside Captain Eddie's desk. While Captain Eddie has been talking to Bellamy, Wayne notices that the red thumbtack is stuck in the Duluth Woods. Frowning, Captain Eddie hangs up.

''Say, Chief, is that the missing spaceship?'' Wayne points to the red thumbtack.

''What? Oh, no. I just stuck the thumbtack there to get it out of the way. No, the ship's really missing.''

''Have you any statement to make about Mayor Herridge?''

''He was my opponent. But he was a worthy opponent. He was a statesman of the sort that comes along only once or twice in a decade—''

''Not so fast.'' Wayne has never learned shorthand. Captain Eddie picks up the telephone. ''Get me Lieutenant Darlene Ecks, Homicide.''

''What do you think that the late Hubert H. Humphrey was doing on the spacecraft?''

''Since Senator Humphrey—God rest his soul—has been dead for some years, what we saw was someone who *looks* like him. I have no further speculation.''

''Chico'' Jones enters the room. ''Darlene is on her way, Chief.''

''Good. How are the barrios?''

''Still in flames, Chief. Fact, it's now more of a holocaust than a conflagration.''

''Is that off the record?'' asks Wayne.

"No. You can *quote* me," says Captain Eddie. "Has he confessed yet?"

"No, Chief. But he's cracking."

"You're referring to Bill Toomey, aren't you?" Wayne is shrewd. He is also being sued by Rosemary Klein Kantor for ten million dollars. Luckily for him, when she sued the makers of *Hiroshima Mon Amour* for plagiarism, it was discovered in the course of her pretrial deposition that she had never been to Japan at all, much less to Hiroshima at A-bomb time. After the case was thrown out of court, Rosemary claimed a moral victory because "there is the Japan of the Mind and that is the sole truth." Rosemary picked up all the marbles with that one. But then, year in and year out, the more lies that Rosemary tells, the higher her stock on the celebrity exchange rises. Not for nothing is she the role model for every American pen person, as well as the word-processors' annual Processor of Choice.

"Yes, we caught Bill Toomey. He was directing the whole operation. In order to destroy the DPD."

"But why?"

"So that . . ." But Captain Eddie knows that the first rule of politics is never to knock your opponent if he happens to be caught inside a spaceship—particularly a spaceship that you yourself have moved on the QT. "We're not sure. But we do know he's been working closely with the FBI, the CIA, the DIA, the DEA, and all the rest."

Captain Eddie has a sudden inspiration. "It is also possible that the president—what's his name? in charge of terrorism?—may have wanted to destabilize Duluth. If that's what he wanted, he failed. The barrios are burning but they are under control. While the leader of the Aztec Terrorists is holed up in McKinley Tower."

Darlene is now at the door. She is wearing an auburn wig, dark glasses. Since the Darlene look-alikes inflamed the barrios, everyone has agreed that Darlene ought not to look like Darlene until things have cooled down a bit. "Gentlemen, excuse us, please."

Wayne and "Chico" go. Wayne is excited. He has got a big story at last.

Darlene sits down in the chair beside Captain Eddie's desk. She starts to cry. She always cries at about this time every day. Captain Eddie consoles her. Then he says, "I've got an assignment for you, Darlene. But it's one that will take guts. And imagination. And fearlessness."

Darlene dries her eyes. "I'm your man, Chief."

"Good girl. You've heard of The Dude?"

Darlene's eyes open very wide. "Who hasn't?"

"You're going underground, Darlene. You're going to vanish. I'll want you to wear a black bouffant wig. That means a darker make-up base. Wardrobe by de la Renta. Ilona Massey mole. The works."

But Darlene does not look as delighted as she should. "No one who has ever tried to nab The Dude has ever come back alive," she says. Basically, Darlene wants to be a mother first and a corpse second. Death is low on her list of priorities this season.

"That's why I'm sending *you*. We're not out to nab him. God forbid! We're out to get a message to him. He likes beautiful women, they say. Well, that's Darlene Ecks."

58

At the end of the brothel-lined Gilder Road, near Lincoln Groves, in a mock-Victorian mansion, ten times standard-size, is one of the largest gambling casinos in the world. It is known to gamblers the world over as The Dude Ranch. But who the anonymous Dude is or even *what* he or she is no one knows.

The Dude's original Silent Partner, Bellamy Craig II, put up the seed-money for the enterprise during the Nixon years when anything went in Duluth, yet Bellamy has never met The Dude. Bellamy always dealt with him through an intermediary, usually The Dude's Answering Service.

Shortly after the New Year, Beryl Hoover bought out Bellamy's interest in the casino. Although Bellamy had not wanted to sell, The Dude told him that he had no choice but to meet Beryl's terms. What The Dude wants you to do, you do. That is a law in Duluth that no one dreams of breaking. So Bellamy Craig II sold Beryl his interest, without ever knowing her identity. The Answering Service handled the entire transaction.

It is said that The Dude pays off, liberally, Mayor Herridge, Captain Eddie and the fire chief. Although everyone knows that the casino is a firetrap, once a year the fire examiners give the building an A for effort. The Dude is also involved in national politics. At election time, boxes of Political Action Committee money are shipped here, there and everywhere. He is a real powerhouse, there's no getting around that, thinks Darlene, as she crosses the main lobby of The Ranch.

To left and right, rows of one-armed bandits are being played by elderly women, many of them Daughters of the American Revolution out on the town and fancy-free. The employees of The Ranch are all dressed in cowboy outfits, a reminder of Duluth's original importance as a frontier outpost and cattle center. Darlene—incredibly beautiful as a brunette—makes her way, languorously, across the lobby to the chemin-de-fer room. Here wealthy gamblers from all over the world wear evening clothes. Fabulous jewels sparkle. Rows of miniature foreign orders adorn the odd lapel of this or that foreign nobleman. All eyes take in Darlene as she makes her entrance. The de la Renta ball gown is the envy of every woman while its contents arouse the passions of every real man in the room, of which there are several.

Darlene has also remembered, for once, to wear her diaphragm, even though it hardly matters now.

Darlene crosses to the table. A cowboy brings her the obligatory glass of Dom Perignon. Sipping daintily—and carefully, the bubbles always tickle her nose!—Darlene makes her bet.

Darlene is unaware that the rococo gold-framed mirror just opposite her is—for anyone on the other side of the glass—not a mirror but a window through which a pair of cold eyes are studying her every move.

Darlene wins a penny or two. Then she moves to the inner sanctum where anything goes. Bets are made on the population of Hong Kong. The exact arrival time of the P.M. shuttle from New Orleans. The result of a throw of I Ching yarrow sticks. Darlene radiates beauty and mystery. She makes a big impression in the inner sanctum, which is designed to resemble the interior of a chuck wagon, except that all the chairs are covered with red velvet.

An elderly cowboy—an important employee, perhaps even the manager—comes up to her. "Good evening, Miss." There are no last names at The Dude Ranch, a house rule until it is time to sign a check or transfer a mortgage.

"Good evening." Darlene smiles mysteriously.

"Anything special you might be liking?"

"Yes."

"What?"

"The Dude," she whispers in the tiniest of voices.

The elderly cowboy is startled. "You're not serious?"

"Yes."

"No one sees The Dude."

"I must. I have a message for him. From Bellamy Craig II."

The elderly cowboy is getting nervous. "I don't even know if he's on the premises. He comes and goes—like a shadow, they say. I wouldn't know. I've never seen him. But I'll see if The Silent Partner is available."

"The one who bought out Mr. Craig?"

"I've already said too much, Miss. Wait here." The elderly cowboy leaves the gilded chuck wagon. Darlene sips her champagne. So far, she is enjoying this assignment.

A moment later two mean-looking black cowboys approach Darlene. She is beginning, now, to like this assignment rather less than she had anticipated. For one thing, she is not up to another rape on the ground that it could be bad for baby.

But to the extent that rape is on the minds of the black cowboy duo, it has been sublimated. Even so, Darlene cannot fail to notice how, in small ways, each is highly attracted to her glorious blond—or, in this case, brunette—beauty. "This way," says one.

A black cowboy on either side, Darlene walks to the far end of the chuck wagon, head high, as if to the gallows. Is this the last mile? she wonders, a bit frantically. As she is, on orders from Captain Eddie, packing no rod, she feels naked, defenseless.

One of the black cowboys opens a door and motions for her to enter. Heart racing, Darlene enters a large dimly lit room—done in Art Deco with numerous Lalique glass works of art on pedestals and coffee tables. The black cowboys shut the door behind her—and lock it. She is alone. There is no sign of The Dude or of The Silent Partner.

As Darlene's eyes grow accustomed to the rich gloom of the Art Deco chamber, she notices the reverse side of the rococo mirror. She crosses to it and looks out into the chemin-de-fer room. She has heard of this sort of mirror-window before. At Duluth High the athletics director—male—had installed one in the girls' showers. He had been arrested, in due course, and charged with degeneracy.

"Good evening." A cultured male voice comes from behind her.

Darlene jumps a foot in the air. Then she turns. A young man in some sort of peculiar military kind of outfit is standing in front of a black lacquer desk on which rests a large Lalique bowl in which floats a single red camellia. He has exquisite taste, she cannot help thinking, even though her life may be in danger.

"Whom do I have the honor of greeting in my sanctum sanctorum?"

"I am—oh, does it matter? Mister . . . I didn't catch the name."

"It was not flung. Miss . . . ?"

"Darlene Ecks. You must be the . . . The Silent Partner?"

"Champagne?" asks The Silent Partner, acknowledging, in a sense, that he is whom she thinks he is. That "whom" has really got to Darlene. On the DPD a "whom" is about as rare as a four-leaf clover in the desert off ethnic Kennedy Avenue.

"I don't mind if I do." Darlene can be as refined as the greatest lady on Garfield Heights, if she puts her mind to it.

The Silent Partner pours two glasses of the bubbly. Silently, they toast one another. He is impressed by her put-on insouciance.

"Now," he says, "to business. You told the manager that you want to see The Dude. Why?"

"It is about the prisoners in the boardroom of KDLM-TV. You know what trouble they are in."

The handsome Silent Partner nods. "According to the *Six O'Clock News*, one of the presidents has refused to let any plane take them out of the United States. He plays fast and loose, that president."

"Mr. Craig . . . You know Bellamy . . . ?"

"Yes. Yes. I know him. He is one of the captives."

"At one time, he was The Silent Partner of The Dude."

"Until he was obliged to sell out, to me. As a result, The Dude Ranch is now a conglomerate. Oh, not as large as ITT . . . , yet. But we are *world*wide, Miss Ecks. May I call you Darlene?"

"Oh, please. And what shall I call you?"

But The Silent Partner is too busy talking about himself to give his name. "You see, The Dude and I have begun to diversify. We own coal mines. Sea beds. Cleaning establishments. We have just made a bid to buy Fiat in Italy. We think big. We are big. I see, Darlene, a whole world—the great globe itself in my hands—our hands, I should say."

"Mine, too?" Darlene smiles to show that she is serious.

"No, not yours. The Dude's and mine." Lines crinkle at the corners of his eyes.

"Well, I wish you luck, I really do in your . . . uh, ventures. Now about The Dude helping out with the hostages . . ."

"Why should he do that?"

Darlene takes the plunge. "Onyx," she says in a loud voice.

"And what," asks The Silent Partner, "does that mean?"

"The Dude will know. Mr. Craig says that if The Dude hears that word—whatever it means, some kind of code name for an old caper, I guess—the president in question will let the plane leave the US of A PDQ."

"I see."

There is a long moment while each studies the other. Then Darlene says, "Is that some kind of uniform you're wearing? It's awfully attractive. Sort of like what those Canadian Mounties wear only it's not red."

"No. No. These are just my riding togs. I'm sorry. I didn't have time to change."

"Funny. I've never actually seen togs before. I've heard of them, of course." He is masterful, she thinks. Bronzed visage. Intense blue eyes. Tiny but weak hands.

"God, you're a beautiful woman, Darlene," says Clive—yes, Clive Hoover is The Silent Partner of The Dude and he has been ever since Beryl passed on into *Rogue Duke*.

During the Nixon years, Beryl Hoover made a fortune—the story about taking Mr. Hoover to the cleaners was never more than a front—in a chain of Oklahoma massage parlors, adult book shops and hard-drug dispensaries.

176

Ever since Clive's voice changed—at twenty-one, a bit late—he had worked for his mother, a business genius. But when Beryl suddenly announced one day in their sumptuous Tulsa home that it was time for them to move on to Duluth, Clive was a little fearful. "Duluth is the big time, Mother," he reminded her.

"We're ready," she said. Then she told him about The Dude. It was her dream to join forces with this will-o'-the-wisp. She knew that The Dude was not happy with the silent partnership of Bellamy Craig II. She was now ready not only to buy out Craig but to cut in The Dude on some of her own operations, as a sweetener to the merger. So it was that Beryl Hoover, disguised as a wealthy social climber, came to Duluth, visited The Dude Ranch, bought out Bellamy through the Answering Service. Then shortly after her first and only meeting with The Dude himself, she died with Edna Herridge in a snow drift. Clive then took over as The Silent Partner.

The day after Beryl's funeral, Clive vowed to make his mother's dream come true. Posing as an idle playboy and lounge lizard, Clive insinuated himself into the innermost circle of Duluth's inner circle—which is, literally, Chloris Craig's circular bed. In the process, Clive has managed to deceive Bellamy, who never in a hundred pages would suspect that this social butterfly with whom his wife toys is the hard-nosed son of the hard-nosed woman who replaced him as The Dude's Silent Partner. Clive is now one of the most important criminals in the United States, which means the world. Yet even Clive does not know who The Dude is.

The de la Renta ball gown is now mixed with manly togs on the floor while on the sofa two gorgeous youthful bodies are joined together at a number of overheated moist points. Darlene is impressed by Clive's impetuousity—and ardor. Clive is so overwhelmed by her lustrous flesh that he finds himself worshipping at the shrine of the pink delta. All in all, this is so much more satisfying, thinks Darlene, than rape, always excepting those two hours—out of time now, out of sight—in the Lunar Bar at the Hyatt.

As they lie in one another's arms, sated passions for a moment slaked, Clive whispers in Darlene's ear. "I adore you."

"I adore you, too. Whoever you are." Even in a fit of passion, Darlene is always the alert policeperson. She must discover his name.

"Can I ask you something?" asks Clive. "Something very, *very* personal?"

"Anything, my beloved." Darlene suddenly slips back into the installment of *Rogue Duke* that she has been reading in the last *Redbook* but one. For a moment, she is again at the Prince Regent's country villa. She is making love to Lord O'Berners when her implacable enemy Beryl, Marchioness of Skye, throws open the bedroom door. If only Darlene could know that her nemesis in *Rogue Duke* was once Clive's mother in *Duluth!*

"Why," asks Clive, "are you wearing a wig? You're not bald, are you?"

"Oh, you are a . . . silly!" Ordinarily, Darlene's language would have been harsher. "I just wanted to be a brunette. For you." With that Darlene tears off her wig.

"A blonde," Clive says, with pleasure. Actually, Darlene's disguise is highly typical of Captain Eddie, who likes elaborate detail for its own pointless sake. Had Captain Eddie given the matter an instant's thought, he would have known that The Silent Partner could never have seen Darlene before and Darlene could never have seen him before—whoever he might be. As for The Dude, it is highly unlikely that *he* would be aware of a lowly lieutenant in Homicide, blond or brunette, since social circles in Duluth are concentric, not contiguous.

"Now, my darling," says Darlene, starting to tidy up. "You've got to get through to The Dude. 'Cause we gotta save those hostages."

Clive is of two minds about the hostages. Naturally, he

does not want Chloris to come to any harm but the rest—
including Bellamy—are, in Clive's rather puritanical view,
simply social parasites. Sometimes, after a really brilliant
performance as the effete playboy Clive Hoover, he is, literally, ill, and only the snorting of a half dozen grams of cocaine can get him out of his depression.

Behind Clive's back he is known, laughingly, to The
Dude—whom he has never met—as the man with the crystal
nose. Actually, Clive has begun to worry that the enormous
flat potato of a nose that mother nature has designed for him,
as if suspecting from the very beginning the uses that he
would put it to, is showing some inner signs of wear and
tear. "You will need a total inner restructuring," said Duluth's leading ears, nose and throat specialist and confidant
to the *crème de la crème,* Dr. Mengers. "If you continue
sniffing at your present rate."

Clive saunters, naked, to the telephone. Darlene admires
his dimpled rosy buns. Clive punches out a number on his
touch-dial system, unaware that Darlene can tell by the music of the numbers that he is pressing the telephone number
that he is calling. Darlene has perfect audio recall. Darlene
is the finest, Captain Eddie always says, of Duluth's finest.

"It's me," mumbles Clive. "Listen, there's a problem.
What does 'onyx' mean?" Clive frowns. "The Answering
Service? Well, where is he? I see. What? *You* know what
'onyx' means? Well, tell me. After all, I'm The Silent Partner."

Darlene cannot hear what the Answering Service is saying on the other end but whatever it is that the service is saying, Clive's eyes are growing round as circles. Finally, he
whistles. "The Dude actually paid off that particular president? But has he got proof? The president what? He signed a
receipt?"

Clive is delighted. Darlene is ecstatic. Mission accomplished! The only sour note in what otherwise has been a
perfect symphony of an evening is the rip in the shoulder of

her de la Renta ball gown. Passion, she muses, is often hard on fabric.

59

At dawn the next morning, Pablo and his Aztec Terrorists climb into a large school bus with the hostages and a trunk full of money and then, escorted by Captain Eddie's motorcycle squad, they barrel down McKinely Avenue at a hundred miles an hour.

Pablo says to Calderón, "Boy, this is some trip!"

Calderón nods, gloomily. He has decided that his *membrum virile* will have to be written off for good. He has not dared tell Carmencita yet. In the movies women are always compassionate when a man loses his *cojones* or *membrum* but this isn't a movie and, besides, those women in the movies are gringas who cannot properly appreciate the dark gods whose emblem the plumed serpent is. Calderón is now seriously thinking about joining his father in the priesthood at Guadalajara.

Chloris is feeling better. A suitcase of lovely clothes has been brought her and she looks quite fetching, thinks Bellamy. He wonders if—on the plane—there might not be some secluded aluminum nook where they could see what it might be like to make it after all these years of open marriage.

The plane is waiting for them at Duluth International Airport. Captors and captives hurry aboard. Pablo gives one last interview to the team from KDLM-TV.

"We're going to freedom," Pablo says to Leo Lookaloney.

"We're going to go to a place where the revolution of the third world is respected. We're going to go where the true Mexican revolution, which I represent, is honored."

"I assume, sir," says Leo respectfully, "that the city you go to will be in a country that is hostile to the United States?"

"That's right. I have already made the arrangements."

"Well, sir, now for the big sixty-four-thousand-peso question. Which is it going to be? Havana or Moscow?"

"Bonn, West Germany." Pablo scurries up the steps to the door to the aircraft where he stops, holds up a fist and shouts to the news team below, *"Auf Wiedersehen, Amerika!"*

60

When Hubert H. Humphrey's campaign plane finally stops shaking and rattling, Hubert looks very pale and Mayor Herridge is sick to his stomach again. They are lying side by side on the floor of Hubert's private compartment, covered with copies of the Gallup poll.

"I think that must've been a bomb," says Hubert, struggling to his feet.

"Who?" Mayor Herridge can barely talk.

"Nixon. Who else? I'm catching up in the polls." Hubert fishes in the debris at his feet and comes up with a printout from Gallup headquarters. "California!" Hubert is again the happy warrior of American folklore. "I'm going to take California away from him. So what can he do to stop me now? Nothing. Except . . ."

Secret Service men are now in the compartment, eager to see if the candidate is all right—and to get him off the plane. But Hubert is now the happy warrior and that is the way he behaves as the Secret Service accompany him and Mayor Herridge into the main part of the plane, which looks as if a tornado has just struck.

Hubert takes a speech from his pocket and says, "I better get out there and do my number." He waves out the window to a fair-sized crowd of Duluthians, mostly dead by now, thinks Mayor Herridge, in a somber mood.

The door opens. A band plays "Happy Days Are Here Again." Then Hubert says, "The politics of joy . . . ."

That's that.

The interior of the plane fills up with what looks like gray smoke.

"We're on fire!" Mayor Herridge screams, clawing his way toward the door. But there is no door. In fact, there is nothing at all to claw. There is no smoke even—just a total all-pervasive grayness. Hubert and the Secret Service agents and the journalists and the interior of the plane and the exterior of the old Duluth airport are obliterated.

Mayor Herridge is now at the center of—a space. That's the only word he can think of for where he is. He can see neither walls nor floor nor ceiling—just shimmering gray. Then a small figure approaches him. Electronic music sounds, eerily.

The figure is humanoid—with a bald head a third the size of the whole of him or her or it. Mayor Herridge has not seen *Close Encounters of the Third Kind* but he has seen enough publicity stills from that seminal film to know that this visitor from outer space closely resembles the most wondrous of all the special effects of a masterful film *auteur*.

"Welcome, Mayor Herridge, to our spaceship." The voice is gentle and incredibly wise.

"Where is . . . uh, Senator Humphrey? We are—well, we used to be—old friends."

"I fear that that projection was not quite satisfactory. So we dissolved it."

"You mean it was all a . . ." Mayor Herridge's vocabulary is not, at the best of times, rich in abstract nouns, much less conceptions. Now, of course, is the worst of times, for him.

"It was all a reconstruction. We found it in your head, actually. So we thought you'd be more at ease with an old friend in a familiar situation. Not until too late did we discover that your charming old friend is no longer what he was."

"What *is* he?" Mayor Herridge is a Lutheran but he is open to almost any news about the afterlife, from any source, no matter how weird.

"Something else. Yet always the same." The little man smiles at Mayor Herridge.

"Welcome to Duluth, the Venice of Minnesota," begins Mayor Herridge.

"Yes. Yes. You did that earlier. We heard you."

"Where were you?"

"We were all those people aboard Senator Humphrey's plane." For an instant, the interior of the 707 is again visible and Mayor Herridge is talking to the famous young journalist Murray Kempton. Then all things familiar and human fade away and he is again in the gray mist with the tiny extraterrestrial humanoid.

"That's quite a trick."

"Is it?"

"What can we do to make your stay in Duluth more comfortable? We have a baseball series going on. Then there's the symphony. And at the City Center José Ferrer is starring in a revival of *Man of La Mancha*. We also have the oldest dinner theater in the United States, the creation of Mrs. Bellamy Craig I, now totally paralyzed. Then if you like gambling, which is sort of illegal, but I can probably fix you guys up at The Dude Ranch Casino . . ."

"Please. Please." The little creature holds up a restraining paw. "I fear that we cannot leave the ship without wearing cumbersome space-suits. We are not of this earth," it giggles, rather appealingly, "earthy."

"Would you like me to put you in touch with Bishop O'Malley? He's very spiritual. So far this year he's raised twenty million dollars, just out of bingo."

"For what?"

"For what?"

"What will he spend these . . . *dollars* on?"

"Oh, good works, you know." Actually, this is the first time that Mayor Herridge has ever even wondered just what happens to all the money that O'Malley is constantly raising. It isn't as if the Bishop has a common-law wife and a bunch of little shavers stashed away like Cardinal what's-his-name.

"My friend, we wish you and your planet only good things."

"Thanks. A lot. No. I mean that."

"But," and soft eerie music hums in the background, "we have observed the flames in the barrios."

"Oh, that's just the illegal aliens. No sweat! Really. Duluth is still a great place to invest in. To live in. To do your own thing in."

"It is sad that you cannot live in peace with one another, as we do."

"You're a higher civilization, I guess?"

"Ah, yes. After all, we are here. And you are certainly not there."

"And just where might there be?"

"None of your fucking business, asshole," says the little man softly.

"I see," says Mayor Herridge, somewhat surprised at this abrupt change in tone.

"You can live in peace. If only you try." The little creature is now very, very wise. "Look—look into your innermost being. There you will find true peace. You will find

compassion for all things that live. You will find that ultimate harmony which *is* the universe."

"Well, I'll certainly give it a try. And that's a promise.
Now I better be moseying back to Duluth to spread your
. . . uh, message."

"Yes. You do that."

"I suppose you know how to open the door?"

"Yes. But, unfortunately, we were moved from the
waterfront by a Captain Eddie."

"How?"

"It's an obscure local—even parochial—principle called
Pynchon's false corollary. It seldom works outside a university literary lab, where we may well be. Anyway, we are
now partly submerged in a charming swamp at the heart of
the Duluth Woods."

"I'll take care of that bastard!" Mayor Herridge is really
angry now.

"We can always move someplace else but for the time
being we're perfectly happy in the swamp. It's rather like
home."

The little man makes a curious sound—all breath—and
there is a lot of clattering and scampering and then the side
of the ship opens, filling the spaceship with about two feet
of muddy water.

"What a mess," says Mayor Herridge, looking out at the
swamp, which is pretty sickening even as your average
swamp goes, with a lot of spiky rushes, water moccasins,
bullfrogs and God knows what else in the yellow mud of
what is, after all, a unique macrocosm of insect life, or so
the bug-lovers contend. "I'm going to have to wade
ashore." Cockroaches, spiders, centipedes—and worse—
start to converge on the spaceship.

"Remember my words," says the extraterrestrial

"Inner peace. Right. Ultimate harmony. Right." Mayor
Herridge does not like the look of those bugs.

"That is the key. Then, once you have achieved this harmony, with the help of the vibrations from our ship, once

the fires in the barrios are put out, we shall speak to you again, and unfold for you our Over-all Investment Plan.''

''Your *what?*'' Mayor Herridge is afraid that he has missed something or misunderstood something.

''Love one another,'' says the little man and now, just back of him in the gray fog of the interior, Mayor Herridge can see several dozen little men, all identical with the one he has been talking to. ''Love one another,'' they sing in unison, waving their tiny hands in the air to the sounds of unearthly music. ''Be supportive of one another,'' they hum. ''Only relate,'' says the one he has got to know.

''I will. I will. Thanks a lot. That's pretty heavy stuff. And I'll tell Bishop O'Malley . . .'' With that Mayor Herridge steps out of the spaceship and sinks up to his chin in mud. Fortunately, the bugs scurry away.

''Shit!'' says his Honor, as the spaceship door closes to the very same sound that the rings of Saturn make.

61

August is the month of Duluth's Coming Home parties, of which the most important, socially, is the lovely reception that is being held at The Eucalyptus Club for the Bellamy Craig IIs.

All things considered, both Bellamy and Chloris enjoyed the kidnapping, while their marriage, though by no means altogether shut, is a lot less open than it used to be as a result of the happiness each experienced during a week in Rome—preceded by a single uncomfortable night in Bonn—where they were able to attend the showing of Valentino's new line of evening wear.

At The Eucalyptus Club reception, Clive is very much a hero to the former hostages because it was he who, as if by magic, found the secret telephone number to the boardroom.

"You were wonderful," says Chloris, a vision of perfect happiness in her off-the-rack La Standa afternoon frock.

"That's all right, Chloris." Clive is modest. He is also stoned. He is in love with Darlene, who has vanished from his life. After the one encounter at The Dude Ranch—nothing. He cannot find her, anywhere. He is dressed from top to toe by Armani.

"Yes," Bellamy says, "you did a great job. I don't think we'd be here today if you hadn't got me through to Captain Eddie."

"It was the most I could do," says Clive, nose like a glacier. It amuses him to know about "onyx" in front of the unsuspecting Bellamy, who still thinks that he is just another lounge lizard in an Armani suit with Dunhill accessories.

"By the way," says Chloris, "I understand that that mean old president who wasn't going to let us have the plane to go to Bonn has resigned under a cloud."

"I don't keep up with politics," says Clive. "I am into tactile things. Rare fabrics. Jewels. Semiprecious stones. Jasper. Moonstone. Onyx."

Bellamy frowns when he hears the word "onyx" but then he thinks that it's only a coincidence. In his book, Clive is still very much a silly-billy.

62

The reunion of the mayor of Duluth with his people took place, naturally, on the *Six O'Clock News*—the full seventy-second slot; then, at midnight, his Honor got the full four hours on the *Rod Spencer Show*.

"I think we should be grateful to these . . . uh, superior beings from somewhere else for showing us the way to love one another. How by looking into ourselves we can see the basic harmony in all things. . . . That's a great message, folks."

"But are they Catholic?" asks Bishop O'Malley—this is on the *Rod Spencer Show*, where the bishop is a well-loved regular panelist.

"Well, I wouldn't know, your Eminence." Mayor Herridge is cautious. As he is a Lutheran, the bulk of his support in Duluth comes from the blue-collar Roman Catholics.

"You should've asked them, my son."

"Well, I will on my next visit to their spaceship."

"When will that be, your Honor?" asks Rod Spencer, still collecting kudos for his interview with Pablo just moments before the seizure of the hostages.

"They'll send for me, they said, when peace is restored to the barrios, and there is love in the hearts of all men."

"Are you sure they aren't Mormons or something funny?" Bishop O'Malley cannot abide other faiths and his outspoken bigotry packs Duluth's cathedral every Sunday to the rafters.

"Well, it's possible. None of them smoked or drank, as far as I could tell. That's like the Mormons."

"Well, we can always send them on to Salt Lake City," says Bishop O'Malley with a hearty laugh.

The party that night, welcoming the Mayor home, was just what the doctor ordered for a politician seeking reelection. Somewhat spoiled by the arrival of Captain Eddie and half the DPD riot squad to the firehouse which Mayor Herridge's followers have taken over.

"Glad you're safe and sound!" Captain Eddie shakes the Mayor's hand for the ever-present crew from KDLM-TV.

"I barely made it through that swamp you went and put us in."

"How about that?" chuckles Captain Eddie, not letting on a thing.

Then there is dancing and Mayor Herridge holds in his arms Mrs. Mayor Herridge and as they dance to "Your Eyes Are the Eyes of a Woman in Love," the song he courted her to, there are tears in all eyes. Everyone knows the warmth and maturity of their relationship—the essential wholesomeness of this model family, including the three shavers of whom only one, something of a record in Duluth, is on methadone.

63

The welcoming-home party for Pablo and Calderón is clandestine but no less festive for that. The barrios are mostly all ashes and embers now but new hovels have been erected and the Daridere Dance Hall is again in business despite the heavy smell of smoke.

Pablo is the hero of the barrios. Dark-eyed señoritas flirt with him from behind their fans. He has a great sense of power. The dark gods of the blood once more surge through him, and his plumed serpent is making a comeback even though the pubic hair is taking forever to grow back in.

Calderón is also recovered but he does not encourage Carmencita to take too good a look at his de-plumed serpent. But he is relieved that he will not have to join his father in the Jesuit seminary.

As the dancing to castanets sets every foot a-tapping, Pablo stares, thoughtfully, at the ruins of the barrios.

"What are you thinking, my leader?" asks Calderón.

"I am thinking that now we have the money, I can buy the barrios from the rich gringos for nothing. Since they had already got their insurance money, they will sell cheap."

"Then what?"

"We rebuild. A model community. With an esplanade. Colored lights. A Virgin that lights up."

"You are a dreamer, my leader." Although Calderón is touched by Pablo's passion to help his people, he feels obliged to point out that all this goes against his own sense of Thomistic-Darwinism. "You cannot do for others what they will not do for themselves."

"But they *will* do it, Calderón, with me to lead them. We lacked the money before. But now it is ours. And I will share it. All of it."

"Not *my* share," says Calderón, sharply, "you won't."

"You still want to go back to Mexico and introduce decadence?" Pablo is bitter at Calderón's defection.

"That," says Calderón, edgily, "is like bringing the trots to Yucatán."

"You have your dream. I have mine," says Pablo, brooding in the hot air of August, a lonely leader, alone with his thoughts—his dreams of a better world in which he will be able to dismember, at leisure, Lieutenant Darlene Ecks.

At the thought, the plumed serpent awakens and stirs. The dark gods are once again at the controls.

Although Darlene enjoyed her session with The Silent Partner enormously, she is not ready for seconds. After all, she is in her sixth month of pregnancy and she is feeling more and more like a mother every day. Not only does she have daily crying jags but when she starts to fret over who the father of the little stranger within might be, she breaks out in hives.

In the busy weeks after the simultaneous return of the hostages and the reemergence from the spaceship of Mayor Herridge, Darlene has not had much time to herself. For one thing, she was obliged to spend four days in court, confronting the Darlene look-alikes from the FBI. At first she made no headway at all until Captain Eddie, losing his usual paternal cool, said, "For Christ's sake, get out of that black wig!" She has taken to wearing the wig almost everywhere.

When she removes the wig in court, there is a gasp. She is indeed the real Darlene and it is now plain that the others have been made up to resemble her in order to inflame the barrios against the DPD.

"Why?" asks the judge.

But Bill Toomey just chuckles.

When the judge threatens him, on the fourth day, with contempt of court as well as with incitement to riot and rape, Bill Toomey's lawyer rises and gives the judge an envelope. When the judge reads the contents of that envelope, he becomes red in the face. "Case dismissed," he says.

Bill Toomey and the twenty-four Darlene look-alike government agents leave the courtroom in triumph.

"What happened?" asks Darlene, turning to Captain Eddie.

The Chief is in a very bad mood. "You remember the president in charge of terrorism, the one who just resigned? Well, he gave Bill Toomey and the other agents a blanket pardon before he himself went off to Lewisburg Federal

Penitentiary, where *he* is about to be pardoned by one of the other presidents, the thin one."

"But that is . . . illegal," says Darlene. But she is a true-blue policeperson and she knows that the word illegal means nothing in Duluth, where only law and order reign.

64

In the Camellia Room of the Duluth Hyatt, the *Duluth Blade's* annual Book and Author Lunch is underway. Wayne Alexander presides. On his left is Rosemary Klein Kantor—it is a very delicate situation because of the libel suit but, so far, each has carried it off quite well. Wayne did try to disinvite her but Rosemary has never missed a book and author lunch anywhere within a thousand miles of the Crescent City and she never will until age and illness take their inevitable toll.

On Craig's left sits Chloris, in her capacity not as Mrs. Bellamy Craig II but as "Chloris Craig." She is behaving very well with Wayne because she wants him to go on writing her life of Betty Grable for her. She is also dying to know who really killed Betty, something Wayne knows but is not telling—what an old meanie! she thinks, smiling at him over the cherries jubilee.

The women at the luncheon are thrilled, as always, to see Rosemary in the flesh and they are also curious to see what Mrs. Craig, their social leader, is wearing. They are dazzled by her organdy pleated skirt whose eight hundred pleats had left Carmencita exhausted and revolutionary.

"Inspiration," announced Rosemary in the course of her

extensive remarks on the art of true fiction, "is all in the mind. I myself have no idea what's up here," she taps her brow with a long red enameled nail, "until it flows forth upon the page. I'm now struggling with the next installment of *Rogue Duke* for serialization in *Redbook* to be followed by regular hard-cover publication and then reprint rights as a Romance Jumbo!" There are ladylike cheers from the audience. To a woman, they have been reading with delight Beryl, Marchioness of Skye's adventures in Regency England and Napoleonic France, and they are as frustrated as Beryl to find that her lover Napoleon Bonaparte has left for Moscow for what sounds like an extended working holiday.

"Will Beryl follow her beloved to Moscow—in the cold winter—with the wolves howling as her samovar hurtles across the frozen wastes of—uh, inner Europe? Truth to tell, I don't know," says Rosemary in a hoarse conspiratorial whisper. "But I do know that when, finally, Napoleon and she are together again in one another's arms, this will be a Napoleon never before revealed in a true fiction. Picture a tall muscular man, with flashing gray-blue eyes beneath black brows . . ." There is a lot more in this vein and the women are very happy—and privileged—to hear in advance what is in store for them and for Beryl in the pages of the next issue of *Redbook,* whose editors will also be relieved since Rosemary is notoriously late with her copy, made no easier to set in type by her ignorance of spelling and grammar. Rosemary's plots, of course, spring not from her mind but from the word-processor's memory bank, where ten thousand novels are available to her, as she hunts and pecks on the old processor, taking a thrilling courtroom scene from Daphne du Maurier or a comical character from the pages of Edgar Rice or William Burroughs—of business-machine fame.

"And now a few memories of my early career," says Rosemary, with a challenging look at the one-eared Wayne. "As you know, I was in Hiroshima—as a secret agent— when the atomic bomb fell. Perhaps some of you have seen the marvelous film—in French, I'm afraid—of my love affair with this Japanese man. It is called *Hiroshima Mon Amour.* Anyway, I won the Wurlitzer for *Dateline Hiroshima.*'' Rosemary gives Wayne a challenging look. No matter how anyone pronounces the word Wurlitzer it always comes out Nobel Prize. You can't win with Klein Kantor, thinks Wayne, glumly.

Then Chloris gets up to speak. She speaks haltingly, but from the heart. ''I cannot tell you what Betty Grable means to me. In death she is even more alive than she was in life. At least to those of us who loved her image on the screen. As for the woman *off*screen, I intend to tell all—absolutely all—about her passionate love affair with—Herbert Hoover!''

There is a gasp from the women. This is really *inside* information of a sort that mere readers seldom get. ''No relation, let me quickly say, to one of our social leaders from Tulsa, Mr. Clive Hoover.'' That name, thinks Chloris, losing her train of thought. She has not been to bed with Clive since she returned from the kidnapping. There is something about being a hostage that changes a woman. You grow, Chloris thinks, thoughtfully. You see the world from a different perspective. You look into your own heart of hearts . . .

Suddenly, Chloris is aware that Wayne is hissing, ''Say something, Chloris. They're waiting.''

''Oh, I'm sorry, ladies and gentlemen.'' Chloris flashes her loveliest smile. ''And I was reliving, in my mind, what it was like to be what I was until very recently, something that few women ever are, no matter how privileged their social position, a hostage.''

The women are ecstatic as Chloris tells them all about *The Twilight's Last Gleaming,* Pablo, the flight to Bonn. Rome. The women are particularly keen on her description of Valentino's latest collection.

As Chloris sits down, applause ringing in her ears, and daggers from Rosemary's eyes winging toward her, she murmurs to Wayne, ''Tonight we finish Betty Grable.''

65

Pablo is suiting action to word. He sends a trusted accomplice, Jesús Gonzales, to Bellamy Craig II. Jesús has been well rehearsed by Pablo.

Bellamy Craig II receives Jesús at the edge of the polo field on Garfield Heights. Bellamy has just finished scoring a number of goals and he is in an excellent mood as he strides into the polo clubhouse, Jesús beside him. There is a bit of a nip in the autumnal air and Jack Frost has begun to use his paint-box on the leaves.

Jesús Gonzales is a tall young man in a three-piece ice-cream—vanilla—suit. He does not look entirely at home in the polo clubhouse snack bar—even though polo fans, as Bellamy likes to say, know no class or season.

"Mr. Craig, I am Jesús Gonzales. My card." He gives Bellamy a card, which Bellamy gives right back to him, without looking at it.

"What can I do for you?" Bellamy is always polite with inferiors. Then Bellamy sits in a straight-backed chair and holds up a boot. "Pull!" he orders.

Jesús tries to pull the boot straight off, but Bellamy shows him how to do it properly. Jesús is obliged to turn his back on Bellamy and straddle the boot that Jesús is now holding firmly in his two hands as Bellamy, with his other booted foot, kicks him hard in the buttocks, sending Jesús—and the boot—halfway across the room.

"There!" Bellamy is genuinely pleased with Jesús, who now has a large muddy bootmark on his vanilla trouser seat.

"Good boy, Jesús. Now take the other one . . ." And again Jesús and a boot fly across the snack bar to the amusement of the other polo players, snacking with their groupies.

"Now then let's hear your beef. Sit down, boy. Man to man. Or *mano* to *mano!*" Bellamy laughs at this ingenious play on words.

Jesús's butt hurts from the two hard kicks but he knows that one day the barrios will rise again and he personally will detach the *cojones* of this gringo bastard. For now, grin and bear it is his policy.

Jesús makes Pablo's pitch for him, only Bellamy does not know that it is Pablo, the Aztec Terrorist, who now wants to buy what's left of the barrios with Bellamy's own ransom money.

"A hundred million, you say. That's a lot of *frijoles* for you muchachos."

"We have the money, Mr. Craig. What we want is to buy as much of the burnt-out area between McKinely and ethnic Kennedy Avenue as we can, and then rebuild."

"I see. Well, I own a few parcels. Maybe eighty, ninety blocks or so. I *could* be interested. I'll take it up with my lawyers."

"And the other owners? Will they sell?"

"Why not?" Bellamy is struck by that figure, one hundred million dollars. He has heard it before. Luckily, he does not put two and two together. "I suggest you also have a pow-wow with Mayor Herridge. He's got quite a bit of wampum tied up in the barrios." Bellany looks at his watch. "He should be in his teepee right now. And then there's The Dude . . ."

"But he is never to be found," says Jesús, inadvertently trembling. "He is an enigma. A wraith. A will-o'-the-wisp . . ."

"But he likes a sweet deal. Keep in touch, Jesús." Bellamy waves Jesús from the room. When he and the other polo players and their groupies see the bootmarks on Jesús's vanilla trousers, they hoot with laughter. Jesús vows vengeance on them all.

Pablo congratulates Jesús on a job well done. They are in the basement of the Daridere, where Pablo rules the barrios like some chieftain of yore.

"I think I'll deal with Mayor Herridge myself," says Pablo, cuddling a dark-eyed señorita on his lap.

"You!" Jesús is astonished. "There is a price on your head. Your face is known to everyone in Duluth through the exposure you got on the *Rod Spencer Show* . . ."

"*And* the *Six O'Clock News.* At the airport, remember?" Pablo has all of his television appearances on cassettes. He often plays them for the dark-eyed señorita of his choice. " '*Auf Wiedersehen, Amerika!*' " Pablo quotes himself with gusto. "No. I have a thick moustache now. My hair is combed different. I wear glasses. No one will recognize me. After all, if they all look alike to us what do you think we look like to them?"

"Shit," says Jesús.

"Exactly," says Pablo.

66

Mayor Herridge is having a bad morning at City Hall. Bill Toomey has brought him the latest polls and even after all the media exposure as a result of his return from inside the spaceship, he is still trailing Captain Eddie by eleven percent—and this is October first. He has only one month to turn the numbers around. "Otherwise, I'm a dead duck in Duluth."

"And after all you've done for this burg!" Bill Toomey worships the ground Mayor Herridge walks on. No one knows why, not even Bill. It's just that some men need someone whose ground is worshipable and Mayor Herridge has provided just that bit of special earth for Bill.

"What happens if we actually count the black vote?" muses Mayor Herridge.

"No one ever has. So no one knows."

"True. But if there's one thing a nigger hates it's a police chief . . ."

"And if there's another thing a nigger hates it's a white racist mayor."

"So you're trying to tell me, Bill, that Captain Eddie and I would pretty much split the waterfront vote?"

"That's about the size of it."

"I see."

The intercom box on the Mayor's desk announces, "A wetback to see your Honor."

"Haven't I told you . . . !" begins the Mayor, seized by a burning choler that lights up his face like neon.

"He wants to buy the barrios."

"Send him in, honey!" The familiar warm rich tone has returned to Mayor Herridge's voice. Not even Bishop O'Malley can outcharm Mayor Herridge, tone- and volume-wise.

Pablo's hunch was right. Neither Mayor Herridge nor Bill Toomey even begins to recognize—or even to look at—him. As Pablo approaches the huge teakwood desk beneath the marble twice-life-size statue of Chloris's ancestor the founder of Duluth, Jean-Pierre Duluth, the famous *coureur de bois* from France, Mayor Herridge comes around from behind the desk to greet Pablo.

"Buenos dias, señor," says Mayor Herridge, shaking Pablo's hand.

"My card," says Pablo, giving him the card that Jesús gave Bellamy who gave it back to Jesús who returned it to

Pablo who receives it back from Mayor Herridge who leads him to a comfortable leather chair.

Between the American flag and the municipal flag of Duluth, a tall picture window looks out on Lincoln Groves—miles and miles of beautifully landscaped cemetery. My sister Edna is there, thinks Mayor Herridge, every time he looks out the window, or sees her on "Duluth," a series that he has got to like more and more. Lately, Edna has been so much in character that she has not been in touch with him. He wonders, idly, if she ever had an affair with Captain Eddie. Mrs. Herridge is positive that they did, years ago, in high school. But Mayor Herridge thinks not, aware of Edna's tragic Sapphic bias.

Pablo goes into his rap. He is inspired. He paces the room, making impassioned gestures. He describes a new barrios, emerging like a phoenix from the ashes of the old but without hovels. This barrios would be made of the best cinder-block with roofs of corrugated tin so that when the Minnesota monsoons blow, the sound of the rain on the roofs will be like millions of castanets. Then Pablo shows Mayor Herridge the bank balance of the Luxembourg Holding Company. The Mayor takes in the big figures with a practiced glance.

"I think the kid—I mean Señor Gonzales—has got something there," says the Mayor to Bill Toomey, who has been watching Pablo intently, with cold eyes.

"I think, maybe, we can do business," says the Mayor to Pablo. "You know, I own a parcel or two out there. Nothing much. I'm a poor man. But my wife owns a bit more—maybe a square mile or so just off Kennedy. You see, after she won that church raffle, there was no looking back. God, what a head that girl has for business! Real estate. Broadcasting. The stock market." It is an open secret that Mayor Herridge has put all the money that he has either stolen or taken in the form of bribes into his wife's name. They are now a very rich as well as a very warm family, far richer—and certainly far warmer—than many of the members of The

Eucalyptus Club who disdain them because they are common as dirt.

"When do we begin?" asks Pablo—the dream, ever the dream before him!

"When this damned election is out of the way." Mayor Herridge frowns. He knows that in a month's time he may have to give up his huge round office with the tile floor and teakwood desk, the banners and the statue of the frog Duluth . . . Oh, the memories! he thinks, eyes moistening.

Pablo is back in his chair. Bill Toomey is now on his feet. He tiptoes over to where Pablo is sitting. Although Pablo is aware that Bill is now standing beside his chair, Pablo thinks nothing of it because his eyes are on Mayor Herridge, the one man who can make the dream a reality.

The Mayor is poring over the last election returns. Of the two million legal and illegal aliens in the barrios, forty-two thousand voted for his opponent and eleven hundred voted for him. Unlike the black vote, which no one has ever bothered to count, the Mexican vote is always counted as it is so small and, usually, susceptible to Bishop O'Malley's divine guidance. Since Bishop and Mayor seldom see eye-to-eye, the vote has always gone against the Mayor. But now . . .

"If you—and your friends—can deliver the votes of the barrios, your dream will become a reality. You'll get that land. I'll even give you a special rate when I fix the zoning laws for you and all the rest of the crap. Is it a deal?"

"A deal it is, your Honor!"

Bill Toomey is now swinging a gold watch on a chain in front of Pablo's eyes. At first, Pablo is slightly annoyed. Is he being tempted to steal the watch? What do these gringos take him for? Then—presto—he is hypnotized.

"Stand up!" commands Bill Toomey. Pablo stands up, mouth ajar, lustrous Latin Lover's eyes out-of-focus.

"What in the name of all that's holy . . . ?" begins his Honor.

"Dance the colorful native tarantella of your people,"

commands Bill Toomey. Pablo dances like an alien pos-
sessed. Snapping his fingers. Swaying this way and that.

"I've hypnotized him." Bill is well pleased with himself. "I could tell the second that he came into your office
that he is a natural subject."

"Where did you learn this, Bill?" The Mayor can never
get over all the things Bill Toomey knows.

"When I was on leave at Langley."

"The Central Intelligence Agency?"

Bill nods. "They have a course in hypnotism and if you're
any good at it, you can then go on to graduate work in autosug-
gestion and political assassination, which is what I did."

"Well, ain't you a ring-tailed wonder!" The Mayor is
staring at Pablo, who is now sailing about the room like a
dervish. "Get that little spick to stop, will you? It's getting
to my stomach."

"You will sit down, Pablo," says Bill Toomey in a soft
voice. Pablo sits down, shirt soaked with sweat. "You are
now a one-year-old baby." Pablo puts his thumb in his
mouth and goes to sleep.

"That's quite a trick, Bill."

"Now, Mayor, I know that the Darlene look-alike operation was not all that we'd hoped for . . ."

"No, Bill, it was not." The Mayor has tried to put the
whole mess out of his mind. He has been counting on the
media coverage of his bravery inside the spaceship to make
the folks of Duluth forget Bill's plot to discredit the DPD but
they haven't forgotten because Captain Eddie won't let them
forget. Although the Mayor has never been directly linked
to the caper—Bill Toomey and the FBI are the official
culprits—the Mayor is known to be the one and only beneficiary should the barrios ever, due to police brutality, become inflamed, as indeed they did—and so he was the one
and only beneficiary in the eyes of all Duluth.

"Well, I think I've got something that might just work
this time, your Honor."

"I'm all ears, Bill."

67

Unaware of the machinations of Mayor Herridge, Captain Eddie, "Chico" and Darlene are studying the latest polls with as much pleasure as those same polls are being studied at City Hall with dismay.

"I'm certainly looking forward to that limo," says Captain Eddie.

"But surely," says "Chico," an idealist of sorts, "you must have some conception of what the future of the Greater Duluth area should be once you are the mayor."

"Huh?" No one has ever suggested such a thing to Captain Eddie.

Darlene takes the Chief's side. "Come on, 'Chico'!" she says. "One day at a time. Isn't that our motto here at the DPD?" She runs her fingers over the dark aubergine patina of the witness chair. "Once the Chief is in that big round office at City Hall, *then* you'll see things really buzz."

"That's right, Darlene." Captain Eddie likes the way she always gets him off the hook. He opens a folder on his desk. "That telephone number you memorized—you know, to the place where The Dude's Answering Service was speaking from to The Silent Partner that night at The Dude Ranch? Well, we've traced the Service. Acme Cleaners."

"Which one?" asks Darlene.

The Chief studies the folder. "The one off McKinley Avenue . . ."

"That's the one I use! Big John owns that chain. You don't think he . . . ?"

Captain Eddie nods. "I think he's working with The Dude. After all, next to gambling, car rentals and software, drugs are the biggest single item in The Dude's empire. Well, what better partner—or employee, more like it—to have than Big John?"

"I hate thinking of a colored man, pushing junk in the playgrounds." "Chico" cannot bear the way the world is. Even so, Captain Eddie has a permanent soft spot in his heart for "Chico."

"Don't take it so hard, 'Chico.' Anyway, Darlene. I know that you're interested in the case. So I'm transferring you from Homicide—where you'll be sorely missed—to Narcotics."

"Great, Chief!" Darlene is really excited.

68

Chloris and Wayne have not taken up where they had left off because once a woman has been a hostage she simply cannot, thinks Chloris, as they lie side by side in her round bed, the Porthault sheets a mess, remain unchanged in her relationships, no matter how deep—or even shallow they might have been to begin with.

For Wayne's part, now that he knows that he has been putting the horns on what turns out to be his employer, the affair has lost a lot of its zest. But then he knows that he might, any day now, lose his job as he cannot for the life of him learn how to use the word-processors on which all

Blade stories, except his, are currently being written. He has decided that his only hope is to score big with the new "Chloris Craig" book and then leave Duluth for points west.

"I hear that *Rogue Duke* is not attracting as many new readers for *Redbook* as they had hoped." Chloris has taken against Rosemary, her one-time literary idol, not so much because of the suit against Wayne as because of the very uncalled-for behavior at the party that Chloris had given in Rosemary's honor the previous spring.

"I wouldn't be surprised," says Wayne, "if Rosemary's had it with *Redbook*. People are tired of her old formula. You know, she can only hunt and peck on her word-processor." Wayne is haunted by this infernal machine and what it will mean for the Friends of Gutenberg.

"She needs a *new* old formula," says Chloris, absently grasping Wayne's turgid powers and comparing them, mentally, with Clive's, whose turgidity she has not even had in the house much less the round bed since her spiritual rebirth as a hostage.

"I've finished the next-to-last part of your Betty Grable book."

This is what Chloris wants to hear. She is radiant. "I'm so glad! When will we know?"

"About who killed Betty?"

"Yes."

But unknown to our high-born authoress and her faithful ghost, Rosemary Klein Kantor, seated at her rosewood desk in fashionable Audubon Park, is at work on what promises to be her most audacious true fiction—"My Secret Conversations with Betty Grable." *Cosmopolitan* has made an irresistible offer. Also, as a sop to Rosemary's real passion, megabucks to one side, a composite photo of Betty Grable and Rosemary will adorn the cover, making it look to all the world as if the two girls are letting down their hair with one another.

Although Rosemary never actually met Betty Grable, she was often in Hollywood at exactly the same time that Betty was also there, making movies. Best of all, in the memory bank of Rosemary's word-processor are complete sets of *Silver Screen* and *Photoplay* as well as the *Collected Columns of Louella Parsons*. Rosemary can hunt and peck this corker in her sleep. Finally, Rosemary knows that she alone has the requisite daring—or art—to re-create a far more exciting and plausible Betty Grable than anyone who might actually have met and got to know the poor frightened kid would be able to because Betty's *secret love—and now it can be told*, hunts Rosemary, then pecks with a triumphant thin-lipped smile—*was General Douglas MacArthur, the former husband of Lionel Atwill's wife.*

"Rosemary," says Betty to me, in that soft hushed voice of hers. We are seated at Romanoff's chic restaurant in Beverly Hills, and Prince Michael himself has taken the order, corned beef hash for two. Egg on top for me, none for her. "Doug gives head like there was no tomorrow!"

Little did I suspect that day at Romanoff's that miles away, across the Atlantic, the Inchon landing is taking place . . .

Rosemary has never been so wound-up as she is now, inventing what really and truly happened—with a bit of Parsons here, a *Photoplay* paragraph there. She also knows that she will beat "Chloris Craig" and her faithful ghost Wayne Alexander to the punch.

69

Pablo has taken an office in the McKinley Tower. Jesús works closely with him. Together they are buying up bits and pieces of the barrios but the biggest piece of all, Mrs. Mayor Herridge's, will not be theirs until Pablo has delivered the Chicano vote for the Mayor on the first Tuesday in November.

After the attack of the Darlene look-alikes in DPD uniforms, the delivery of the barrios' vote is no problem at all. Pablo is amazed how easy it is. Even though the illegal aliens all know that Mayor Herridge had something or other to do with the assault, what they actually recall, with rage, are the police uniforms, the probing red fingers, the brutal smashing of masculine corns. Mayor Herridge Clubs are blossoming like cacti in Little Yucatán.

In the office next to Pablo's office, Bill Toomey is at work on *his* plan to reelect Mayor Herridge. He has developed a fine working relationship with Pablo, who has at last decided that here, maybe, is a gringo who can be trusted. They work together, registering as voters the illegal aliens, which is, of course, illegal but easily manageable in Duluth, where the election commissioner just happens to be Mayor Herridge's old mother.

At the end of each day, Bill Toomey invites Pablo into his office—just the two of them. "Put your feet up, son, and relax. Loosen your tie. That's a boy." Then while Pablo is relaxing and shooting the breeze, the gold watch starts to swing, idly, back and forth. Pablo is so used by now to this trick of Bill's that he hardly notices it. But he does notice that there are times when time passes a lot faster than he remembers it should have passed—particularly, when some dark-eyed señorita complains that he has kept her waiting for more than an hour. "Obviously, you have found someone more interesting than I," she pouts. Fortunately, the uncoiling of the plumed serpent always assuages temporary anger. Never before has Pablo been so potent, so in touch with the dark gods of the blood.

What Pablo does *not* know is that while he is in Bill Toomey's office, hypnotized out of his skull, he is taking dictation from Bill into a high school composition-class notebook.

Bill Toomey is well pleased with the way things are working out. But then not for nothing did Bill make the highest score in the Kozinski Communal Effect Class at Langley, Virginia, where half the modern classics now being taught were assembled by a team of word-processors with access to the largest memory bank in literary history assembled—the truth can now be told—by Roland Barthes, a French CIA mole, now dead—of what looked to be a street accident! Another feather in Bill Toomey's Indian chief's war bonnet.

70

Thanks to the smoldering resentment in the barrios against Darlene, she now wears her dark wig even on the waterfront, where she has taken to hanging about in various rib joints, looking for Big John.

As always, Darlene dresses fashionably—the little Hattie Carnegie black dress has been revived just for her—but discreetly. She does not want to go through any more rapes now that she is into her eighth month of pregnancy. She has never been so huge—so dolphin-plump. Yet Darlene doesn't care. As she feels the new life stirring inside her, she prays that she can find the father of this new life, assuming that the father is who she hopes it is.

But Big John is still underground. Casual inquiries in the black—or colored, as "Chico" calls it—section lead only to blank stares. No one knows nothing. No one's talking to this mysterious, somewhat overweight, white woman in the black wig and Hattie Carnegie suit.

Svelte black women in fashionable dresses snigger as Darlene waddles up and down the waterfront, looking for her man. "She lookin' for her man," says one to another. "She sure got it bad," says the other. "Yeah, she got about eight months of bad!" They giggle with delight at what one of their dudes has gone and done to Darlene. Woman is woman, no matter what her color or economic status. Woman always knows.

Darlene steps out onto the silky sand of the beach. Although it is mid-October, the night is warm and there is a huge golden moon above the palm trees. Of all Duluth's many seasons, Darlene most likes Indian summer. There is even, her sensitive nose tells her, a smell of curry in the air. How joyous and natural these people are! thinks Darlene, listening to the pounding of drums from the transistors, to the giggling of couples mating amid the dunes, to the odd death-rattle in the oleanders.

Darlene walks, barefoot, on the sand, exulting in the velvet warmth of the night, pistol at the ready, as this is a tough part of town.

Up ahead, a cabin cruiser is tied to a wooden wharf. It is the sort of cabin cruiser that is often used to get heroin from the Crescent City down the Colorado River and into Lake Erie and then over to Canada. Languorous Indian summer or not, Darlene is always a policeperson, assigned now to Narcotics, the deluxe squad of the DPD.

Holding her tiny shoes in one hand, Darlene, on tiptoe, slips behind a palm tree that is just a yard from the cabin cruiser's prow. Two men are sitting in deck chairs on deck. Although the golden moon makes a beautiful night of the night, it is still pretty dark.

Darlene strains to hear their conversation.

One says, "The market's soft for snow."

The other says, "Then we push the residue of angels. We'll make it kiddy-special time."

Darlene starts to tremble. Snow is the aficionados' word for cocaine while the residue of angels can only be angel dust—the most terrible, the most addictive of all drugs, and the most popular with the children of Duluth.

Darlene draws her revolver. She will take these two snakes alive or dead. She does rather wish that she had remembered to bring her walkie-talkie as well as the unmarked police car with her trusty partner. Darlene has always had a tendency to forgetfulness, thanks to her tendency to daydream. Even so, she is more than a match for any pair of unsuspecting drug pushers, assuming that there are only the two of them.

As Darlene cranes her neck around the bole of the palm tree, a powerful arm wraps itself like a boa constrictor of steel about her throat. She gasps. Tries to call for help. Is mute. Tries to breathe. Chokes. Starts to faint. Then a gun is shoved in her back and she is propelled, barefoot, aboard the cabin cruiser. Fortunately, her wig is not askew and the black frock only slightly crushed. A huge mulatto thug has captured her.

"Look what I found, ears flappin' behind that old palm tree there," says the mulatto thug.

The two men remain seated. Now that she is close to them she can make out their features in the moonlight.

"My God!" Darlene's legs give away.

"Darlene!" Clive leaps to his feet and catches her before she falls. "Here," he says to his confederate. "Give me a hand, Big John."

71

Mayor Herridge is also aboard a boat—not a cabin cruiser, just a rowboat. He has received an urgent telephone call from the spaceship. He is now, glumly, being rowed by two state troopers across the bug-ridden marsh to the spaceship, whose round door is uninvitingly open. If it wasn't for the damned election, thinks the Mayor, I'd have the Defense Department take this thing off my hands because from the beginning this has been a federal and not a municipal problem. But when the Mayor tried out that number on Washington, the old television president promptly went on the air and said, "As all you folks know, we're turning everything back to the states 'n' the cites 'n' the small towns like . . . uh, like that one that I grew up in. Friendly sort of place it was. Oh, we were rich, sure. But we didn't know it. Which is what made America great. And that's what's going to make America great again. 'Cause we're taking the government off your backs. This means that from now on each town can go out 'n' print its own money 'n' have its own army, navy, customs—even space program, if it wants. Like they got out there in Duluth. The sky's the limit for the little guy! 'Cause just as soon as Nicaragua says uncle, we're shutting down Washington. Oh, 'n' by the way, I can now like reveal to you that Disney has made us a very attractive offer for the whole city of Washington, D.C. Fact, even as I speak, we're in negotiations to sell it. Just think! Another Disney World right here on the Merrimac—or whatever that river over there is. You know, I can remember Walt tellin'

210

me—this was years ago, of course, before he died, a great American—that *family* entertainment is the secret to big grosses. Sure, we laughed at Walt then. He was a dreamer, we thought. But he was right. Look at *The Absent-Minded Professor.* He knew that the family is the secret to the greatness of our Christian-Jewish . . . Moslem . . . and Scientological, too—society, menaced by monolithic atheistic 'n' godless Communism. Well, anyway, I said to Walt, how do you explain the grosses of *Last Tango in Paris?* I've never seen it, of course. But I don't have to see a porno film to be able to define one. Well, Walt said . . .'' And so on.

The old television president has got to go, says Mayor Herridge to himself, getting out of the rowboat and stepping inside the spaceship, which, thank God, is now above marsh level and so there is no yellow slime to wade through.

Inside the spaceship, all is gray and eerie. Has anything changed, he wonders. And if it has, how can a mayor tell? Then the large-headed humanoid comes forward to greet him. "Welcome. Welcome, dear friend."

"Welcome to Duluth," says Mayor Herridge, automatically.

"Have you searched inside yourself? Have you found that basic harmony which is in all things?" The eerie music begins.

"Well, I've been working on it, yes. But, you see, there's this election next month, and . . .''

"We'll be rooting for you."

"Well, thanks. But I thought you'd be gone by then."

The little creature looks up at him, sadly. "I'm afraid not. There's been . . . an accident."

"What kind?"

"We don't know yet. As you see, we were able to raise the spaceship to the same level as the swamp—a very attractive swamp, by the way. We like it tremendously."

"We don't, actually. So then what happened?"

"The spaceship has—broken down, I guess you'd call it."

"You mean you're stuck here? In an *election* year?"
Mayor Herridge would have slumped into a chair except that
there is no furniture of any kind in what he can see of the
ship through all the gray haze.

"Well, not permanently, no. We've rung home and they
are sending us a repair ship . . ."

"So in a week or two, you'll be on your way?"

"Well, yes. One of our weeks, that is. But for you one of
our weeks will be . . ." The little alien blinks its eyes
twice. "One thousand twelve years. In round numbers."

"Jesus!"

"I know it's a nuisance for you, having us here, spoiling
the view of your wonderful swamp, which is a macrocosm
of higher life forms . . ."

"No. No. It's our pleasure, of course—"

"So," the alien interrupts him. "I thought we might
make a sort of amusement park out of the ship."

"You mean have people *pay* to come in here and look
around?"

"Yes. Naturally, we'd sell the tickets and license the con-
cessions but the city would also benefit because of the tour-
ists that would come here from all over your planet. You'd
have overflowing hotels, motels, snack bars . . ."

"I like it—off the top of my head," says the Mayor, cautiously. "Naturally, I'll have to rezone the swamp but that
shouldn't set you back too much. On the other hand," the
Mayor looks around at the gray nothingness, "you don't
really have a lot to offer, you know. I mean, there's not a lot
to see—or do in here. With all this fog. Now don't get me
wrong. I'm not knocking the fog. Or your message, which is
heart-warming, only . . ."

The alien claps its tiny hands.

Mayor Herridge cannot believe his eyes. The film *2001*
plus *Star Wars* plus every other Hollywood version of a science fiction spaceship interior has been surpassed. Flashing
lights. Marvelous sounds. Cute little robots, quacking
away. Beauteous girls in leather. Astonishing-looking mon-

sters from truly alien life-cycles. Huge glass windows with views of galaxies unseen before by man.

"How did you do that?"

"Do you think your people would pay to see this?"

"Pay! Duluth is going to do more business than both Disneylands combined. We'll build new hotels. A convention center . . ." Mayor Herridge is beside himself with excitement.

"Naturally, we'll incorporate under the laws of the state . . ."

"No sweat!" Mayor Herridge is all atingle with greed. "But I do think we natives should be allowed to put up a few taco stands, on a concession basis, naturally. And I'll personally lease you the city's portable chemical toilets cheap . . ."

"We'll discuss that later." The alien gestures for Mayor Herridge to sit beside him in what looks to be the control room of the spaceship. Through curved glass, galaxies spiral whitely against the black intensity of the multiverse.

"Is . . . is that the way things really look, when you're out there?" Mayor Herridge is feeling queasy. He's not into science fiction.

"Of course not. But we don't want to disappoint the customers. So we've cooked all of this up extra-special for you dummies."

"But how? I mean how do you *do* all this?"

"The same way that we produced and directed Senator Hubert H. Humphrey aboard his campaign plane in 1968."

"I see."

"No. You don't. And it's not important. Now I want you to meet some of my colleagues."

The dazed and bemused mayor of Duluth is led into an exotic greenhouse, filled with plants that no earthly eye has ever seen before outside a movie.

A half dozen godlike men and women in strange costumes bow low to the Mayor. He is introduced to them by the tiny alien who suddenly becomes, in the twinkling of an eye, a magnificent raven-haired beauty, with plunging cleavage. "You're a girl!" says the Mayor dumbly.

"For *you*, anyway," says the gorgeous creature. "Call me Tricia."

"Tricia! My favorite girl's name!" Mayor Herridge is now positive that he is dreaming. He has no desire to wake up. Tricia motions: a conference table and chairs rise from the floor.

"Take your seats," says Tricia.

Everyone sits. Mayor Herridge has never seen such beautiful women and men anywhere, even on television.

"Since we are probably going to be stuck here longer than the city of Duluth is going to be here we will want to invest mostly in short-term bond issues." Tricia is very business-like. "Also, at current interest rates, month-to-month certificates of deposit are attractive to us, as well as Treasury bills—short-term, of course. Naturally, one fourth of our total portfolio will be in gold. A traditional store of value. Silver futures are interesting, as are Louisiana oil leases. And, of course, foreign exchange speculation will be the keystone to my financial wizardry. Now then." Tricia frowns. She is simply gorgeous, thinks Mayor Herridge. "Since Duluth's real estate will be exceptionally good during the better part of our first century of operation—"

"I can sell you the entire barrios!" shouts Mayor Herridge, selling Pablo down the river.

"We're in the market, your Honor," says Tricia. She makes a note on a yellow legal pad. "Bought, one entire barrios."

"What about a couple of Savings and Loan companies . . . ?"

"Herridge!" Tricia is suddenly stern. "Try and pull a fast one like that on us and there will be a great big hole in the ground where Duluth used to be."

"I was just kidding, Tricia. Honest. I mean it's sort of an old joke around here. Want to be safe as the grave? Invest in an S and L. You see, my sister Edna was in real estate . . ."

214

But Tricia is now on the telephone to the president of Duluth's First National Bank, where she is about to open an account: "In the name of—Visitors from the Friendly Skies!" she sings. Mayor Herridge applauds this inspired name for the Spaceship Amusement Park.

72

Edna has finished the wedding segment, which took two whole days of shooting with no overtime, as Universal is not into overtime.

Edna's final scene has had all the grips applauding. Even Rosemary was so moved that she came rushing down onto the floor from the control room to give Edna a big kiss. "That's Emmy-time again!"

"Oh, you're just saying that to make me feel good because I left out eight dots in three sentences."

"To hell with the dots!" This is a very rare thing for the strict Rosemary to say: no one ever ad-libs or paraphrases in a Klein Kantor series.

Edna is now in her trailer, removing her makeup and changing into her own clothes. There are telegrams all over the dressing table mirror. Most of them are good-luck messages from out-of-work stars.

Edna has a sense of real accomplishment. The part was difficult. The director hopeless. The other actors were all from television, which means that they never look at you in your big scenes. Even so, she has once again pulled off a prize-winning performance.

Humming softly, Edna removes her makeup all by herself. She doesn't like to disturb the makeup man, who is usually placing bets at this hour. The monitor in the trailer is still turned on. Since they are striking the set, there is not much to see. But from force of habit, Edna keeps an eye on the monitor, just in case.

What Edna sees in the monitor gives her instant migraine. When she is at work on "Duluth" or back at the Montecito or on the telephone to her children, she is entirely herself—this particular self which is Joanna Witt—Emmy Award-winner. But whenever the camera lens connects, somehow, with *Duluth*, she is Edna Herridge again.

False eyelashes clutched in one hand, she is again Edna as a scene from *Duluth* replaces the "Duluth" wedding reception set.

Bill Toomey—whom she has always mistrusted, his eyes are too far apart—is out on a rifle range that Edna recognizes as part of an amusement park, next to Lincoln Groves, where she is buried in the Herridge vault.

It's a cold autumn day. She can tell this by the brown leaves that fall from the trees. Bill and a young Mexican are firing at targets.

"Good shot," says Bill.

The young Mexican seems to be on drugs. He pays no attention to Bill. He keeps on firing at his target, bull's-eye after bull's-eye. He is a much better shot than Bill Toomey.

Edna puts down the eyelashes. The headache is now excruciating. She switches off the monitor. Immediately, she feels better. What, she wonders, is that all about?

As Edna makes her way to the parking lot at Universal City, she does her best to put *Duluth* out of her mind—or herself out of *Duluth's* mind because she is slowly being torn to pieces by a fictive law that she cannot begin to fathom. But then she has never played in any of the classics other than Archibald MacLeish's *J.B.* A season of Aeschylus and she might have been able to cope with the demands of conflicting gods, otherwise known as opposing fictive laws of the sort that once upon a time drove right up the wall a Greek named Orestes.

Edna adjusts her bifocals and starts up her Budget rental car. Then she pulls out into Barham. As she comes to the first red light, a light switches on in her head. She understands what she just saw. She is appalled. She must get through to *Duluth* just one more time. The television set in her room at the Montecito is on the blink but she knows that she can stop off at Rosemary's house on Mulholland Drive and ask the housekeeper to let her use Rosemary's set.

I'll stop him! says Edna grimly to herself, turning into Mulholland Drive, where she collides head-on with the Santini moving van that is coming around the mountain.

There is a crash. Then—no more Joanna Witt. No more Hilda Ransome. No more Edna Herridge. She is now, mercifully, free of all past fictive identities, and so able to appear, over and over again, in countless true as well as false fictions, in television miniseries and feature films. Wherever there is a need for a character that is warm and giving, mature and loving, there we shall find her just so long—and no longer—as mimesis rides herd in the wide empty spaces of the human heart.

73

Things are not going entirely Darlene's way aboard the cabin cruiser. Her left arm is handcuffed to a chair in the salon of the boat. The mulatto thug stands guard on deck. Clive offers her a glass of champagne, which she drinks, thirstily.

Big John cannot take his eyes off her. He knows that he knows her from somewhere but the black wig has him fooled—also, the added weight.

Clive is both delighted and perturbed. Delighted to find Darlene again and yet perturbed by her behavior. What is the goddess of the de la Renta ball gown doing, skulking about the waterfront, and overweight?

"I waited," says Clive, "but you never rang. You treated me like a one-night stand." He turns to Big John. "I am in love with her, I think. We met only once—yet those passion-charged minutes changed my life."

"How about that?" says Big John.

"Have you never had that experience?" Clive turns again, as if in appeal, to Big John.

"Me? No, hump 'em and dump 'em is more my bag."

Darlene starts to cry, softly.

Neither man pays the slightest attention to her.

"I can't be that indifferent," says Clive. "A woman is always something more to me than just a . . . a receptacle for my lust. I need the *whole* relationship."

"Not me. Oh, I got them three foxes and the kids. I pay for the kids. I mean a man's got to do that. You know what I mean? You owe it to the kids. But the foxes—shee-it, there's more poon-tang where that come from."

Darlene, through her tears, thinks that if they don't stop all this boy-talk and pay attention to her—rape, dismemberment, no matter—she will scream the siren-scream.

"I could never regard women as anything but people first. Mothers second. Mind you," says Clive, thoughtfully, "I've had a vasectomy."

Big John shudders. "I wouldn't let no knife anywheres near my whang."

As Darlene starts to think of that huge source of life that she once so thoroughly tapped in the Lunar Bar, her tears begin to dry. He *must*, she says to herself fiercely, be the father!

"With a vasectomy—and it couldn't be easier, Big

John—no, really, there's no change at all—you are then able to have a real one-on-one relationship with a woman in a way that you can't when there's always that nagging fear in the back of your mind of an unwanted pregnancy or, horror of horrors, an abortion. Naturally,'' Clive pours himself more champagne, ''as a Catholic convert, I'm against abortion all the way down the line.''

''My mother made herself a fortune out of abortion,'' says Big John, dreamily. He is puffing some very good pot. Darlene can tell, by the smell. ''I can remember how those knocked-up foxes used to line up all the way 'round Bourbon Street—we're from the Crescent City, you know, and there would be Mammy with her trusty coat-hanger. Push it in, twist, and out. All over in a jiffy. And she never lost a customer,'' he adds. ''You see, the coat-hanger was always clean from the lye.''

''I felt something different with Darlene. I don't know what.'' Darlene does not like the use of the past tense. Well, if worse comes to worse, her siren-scream will bring out the whole waterfront squad of the DPD. ''It was like my first time, in a way. She was so . . . genuine, somehow. Not like those brittle Duluth society hostesses I've had to bang ever since I left Tulsa. Why,'' finally, Clive turns to Darlene—and about time, she thinks, ''did you never come back into my life after what happened between us?''

''Because,'' says Darlene in her softest little-girl voice, ''I'm pregnant.''

Clive almost drops his champagne glass. ''You can't be! My vasectomy . . .''

''It wasn't you, Clive. May I call you Clive?''

''Oh, yes. Of course. Who is the father?''

''You'll hate me if I tell you.'' Darlene is getting a bit sweaty now. Things could get seriously out of hand. ''You'll *both* hate me.''

''Huh?'' Big John looks at her, rather sleepily. He is stoned and she is, admittedly, pregnant and a bit on the large side. He's into the more svelte foxes.

Darlene, slowly, dramatically, with her one free hand, removes the wig.

Clive says, "Oh, yes! I remember. I was afraid you might be bald. So many women are in Duluth. Because of the chemical effluents in the drinking water. I like you blond. But then I like you brunette, too."

But Darlene does not even look at Clive, much less listen to his palaver. She stares at Big John, her moist lips invitingly ajar, her large blue eyes luminous with soon-to-be-maternal tears. Big John stares back with a stirring of lust and then—recognition. *"You,"* he says, finally.

"Me," she says.

"The fox who try bus' me im pantry Lunar Bar?" Big John occasionally lapses into nigger talk for effect.

"The fox *you* raped in the pantry of the Lunar Bar."

"The fox who got two whole hours' worth of Big John's best."

"The fox who now, eight months later, is about to bear *your* child."

There would have been a long almost reverent silence in the salon of the cabin cruiser were it not for the slapping of waves against the sturdy bulkhead.

It is Clive who speaks first. Darlene is quick to note that he has now dropped all the shit. "Police?"

"Yes," says Darlene. "Lieutenant Ecks, formerly Homicide. Now Narcotics."

"Prepare," says Clive, coldly, to Big John, "the cement negligée." He turns to Darlene. "You are headed for the bottom of Lake Erie where all enemies of The Dude and The Silent Partner end up. And to think I thought I loved you."

"Now, let's not go so fast," says Big John, beginning to emerge from his drug-induced lethargy. "It's true that the fox here did set out to bust me but then after she had me shuck down and saw what I got—"

"Stop!" Clive is icy in his anger. "No more of this black chauvinism. Keep your tool out of this."

"Well, I can't really, 'cause that's what went and got into

her, with that gun at my head, for two whole hours, with me pumping like—''

''Stop!'' Clive claps his hands over his ears.

''O.K., O.K.'' Big John is amiable. ''Anyways, when I'm finished, she says, no prison will ever hold you if I can help it, and she let me tie her up and escape. You devil, you!'' Big John gives Darlene a big kiss. She nearly dies right then, from happiness. He loves her, maybe. She hopes that he will just hold her in his arms for six or seven hours. That is all that she wants in this world. But then that is all that any woman ever wants.

Clive is pacing up and down, thinking slowly but carefully. ''You say she let you go even though she had actually caught you—''

''Peddling coke at the bar.''

''Why do you do that?'' Clive explodes. ''Here you are the richest nigger in Duluth, owner of Acme Cleaners and I don't know what else, and yet you go risk everything by pretending to be a barroom waiter, a small-time hustler, a penny-ante peddler?''

Big John shrugs. *''Nostalgie de la boue,''* he says in French—he is from nearby New Orleans, after all.

Darlene shudders with delight—she loves French more than any of the other languages that she does not know.

''And so because of this passion to wallow in the mud you put yourself at risk *and* me *and* The Dude himself.''

''I don't do it no mo'.'' says Big John, contritely. He is now eying Darlene with something like real interest. ''Honey, how I know that's my kid you got in there?''

''You'll know by the color,'' says Darlene, praying that when baby does come out he won't look like a taco.

''So how I know you're not into us black stallions? With our big, long, powerful—''

''Shut up!'' screams Clive.

''O.K., boss man. Don't get all hot and bothered. I just want to know for sure that the kid's mine.''

"It is yours because I have never before," says Darlene, solemnly, "committed miscegenation."

Both men are shamed into silence by this announcement. Darlene takes advantage of their guilt. "That is why I asked Captain Eddie to assign me to Narcotics. That is why I came down to the waterfront tonight. Alone. I wanted you to know about our child, Big John, because," Darlene takes a deep breath, "I want to be your lawful wife and the mother of all your future children."

Big John is stunned. Clive is moist-eyed—he has loved and lost to a bigger if not better man.

"How can I marry a police lieutenant when I am in this line of business?" Big John has never been the marrying kind. Lover, yes. Father, yes. Husband, no. Darlene is something special, of course, but even so . . .

"There are two ways of handling that small item," says Darlene. "But, first, remove the handcuffs." The two men rush to free her. Big John is the lucky man—the first with the key.

"More champagne," she says to Clive, who fills her glass to the brim. Fascinated, they watch as she sips, wrinkles her nose, sneezes. "I always do that," she says lightly. Then she is all business. "As you know, the DPD is rife with corruption. I could remain on the force and protect you in your illegal activities. That is no problem. And if it is what . . ." She pauses, swallowing hard. ". . . the man I love wants, then that is what I will do."

"Great!" says Clive.

"No," says Big John, cannily, "there's something more."

"Yes," says Darlene, "there is. I want you to go straight. You own Acme Cleaners—by the way, the one just off McKinley Avenue ruined my silk Pucci gown and now refuses to reimburse me . . ."

"Asses will burn," says Big John grandly. "Go on."

"If you go straight. Give up your life of crime, we could be *the* couple in Duluth."

"Me? A nigger?"

"Trust me, Big John. We can go all the way, you and I. To the top!"

"But what about me?" says Clive, feeling excluded. "What about The Dude and The Dude Ranch?"

"Well, you all was doing O.K. before I come along . . ." Big John is wavering.

"Who is The Dude, by the way?" asks Darlene, who, even in love, is always a policeperson.

"I wouldn't," says Clive sharply, "tell you even if I knew. And I don't."

"He's got a key to every Acme Cleaners and every night he breaks in to take calls," says Big John, "but we never see him or if we do we don't know whether it's him or just his Answering Service."

"A man of mystery," muses Darlene.

"Only one person ever knew his identity and that was my mother, Beryl Hoover, who took the secret with her to the grave."

74

Beryl, Marchioness of Skye, clothed in a heavy sable mantle, drives in her carriage across the steppes of Asia. In her jewel box—which she never lets out of her sight—is the one-page plan of the Prince Regent for the invasion of France. She must give it to her beloved Emperor Napoleon, who is now looking for digs in Moscow.

Beryl gazes out the window at the monotonous snow-covered steppes as they ascend toward Moscow. Suddenly, two crazed mounted Cossacks order her carriage to stop. Beryl shouts, "Drive on!"

The reluctant driver cracks his whip. One Cossack rides to the left of her and one to the right of her. As Beryl grimly loads her matchlock, she cannot help but curse—that part of her which is still, from time to time, Beryl Hoover, queen of crime—the inept Rosemary Klein Kantor, who, because she works in monthly installments for *Redbook,* assumes that the readers forget from one installment to another what she has written, making it possible for her to repeat herself, endlessly punching out the same old bits from Baroness Orczy's oeuvre.

"Take that!" Beryl fires into the Cossack's open mouth. He falls onto the icy steppe. Wearily, Beryl reloads her matchlock and then kills the other Cossack. Thank God, there is only one more installment—Moscow and then a wrap-up that she can only guess at, never having been in a woman's serial before—as far as she knows, which is not far at all since everything pre-*Duluth* is a blank; a good thing, all in all, as Beryl has played a million parts in her time, including Tess of the d'Urbervilles—the Polanski movie, not the original book.

I wonder, wonders Beryl Hoover, how Clive is doing at The Dude Ranch?

75

Negotiations aboard the spaceship have had their ups and downs but, finally, Mayor Herridge and Tricia have pretty much ironed out all the wrinkles. Meanwhile, Tricia has already had a considerable effect on the world's money markets. Singlehandedly, she has doubled the value of Mexico's government bonds. Since she has invested so heavily in them, the world banking system has followed suit, aware of her financial wizardry as a Vistor from the Friendly Skies.

"I'll have the lawyers over tomorrow with the final contract. I can do the notarizing myself." Proudly, Mayor Herridge shows his notary public stamp which he always carries with him.

"Nice to do business with you, your Honor." Tricia could not be more gracious, he thinks, as they walk together through the dazzling spaceship with its vistas of galaxies being born and dying, of black holes opening and shutting, of weird creatures crawling and flying, appearing and disappearing. This is beyond anything ever dreamed of at Anaheim, he thinks, or even at Orlando, Florida.

"We'll start on the causeway from the mainland first thing Monday. I'll put the contract up for bids, as I always do."

"I'm sure the lowest bid will get the contract!" Tricia winks at him.

"You slyboots!" Mayor Herridge has taken a shine to Tricia, but then she is extraterrestrial. The secret of Mayor Herridge's political success is that—outside of the warmth of his own family—he has never met a man or woman that he has ever liked. As a result, he is the biggest vote-getter in Minnesota—or was. With sinking heart, he suddenly recalls the latest polls. Well, this will turn the election around. He is certain of that. He'll be a local—no, a national—no, an international—no, an intergalactic—hero!

At the door to the spaceship, Mayor Herridge says, "What do you really look like? You know when you're in here all alone with each other."

"Oh, you wouldn't want to see *that!*" Tricia shakes her head.

"Oh, sure, I would. Come on. I won't tell anyone."

"Well," says Tricia, "you asked for it."

Tricia claps her hands. The brilliant *2001* spaceship interior vanishes. In its place there is a dull unpleasant glow, rather like too many fireflies jammed together in a milk bottle. There is, also, an overpowering odor of bugs in the spaceship because . . .

Where Tricia was standing now stands, on its hind legs, a six-foot-tall centipedelike creature. In the background Mayor Herridge sees what look to be a thousand huge bugs, all waving their mandibles at him. He screams. He can't help it. He hates bugs.

"Well," says the Tricia-bug in a voice like a wheezing accordion, "you asked to see us as we really are."

Then, at that exact moment, from above and below the viscous surface of the marsh, millions of bugs of every variety begin to converge on the spaceship. Before Mayor Herridge can scream a second time—he has a total horror of insect life—Tricia, the beautiful woman, is standing beside him and all is as it was before in the *2001* interior.

"Goodness, how embarrassing!" says Tricia, apologetically. "About all those bugs out there. You see, they're so keen to get to know us that whenever we open the door, looking as we really do, they come from miles around because of this ancient legend among the cockroaches—the oldest form of life on your planet, by the way—that their gods will one day reappear and destroy the human race with some sort of radiation—or erasure lever—to which cockroaches are immune and then the Golden Age of the Bug will begin!" Tricia laughs a musical laugh. "Such a silly story, don't you think?"

Mayor Herridge can only nod, speechless, as the rowboat comes to get him, through a sea of disappointed bugs.

76

Mayor Herridge's press conference dominates not only the *Six O'Clock News* but the front page of the *Duluth Blade* as well. By the time that the wire services pick up the story, people from all over the world are making reservations at the Hyatt and at all the other hostelries and moteleries in the Greater Duluth area. Everyone wants to see the inside of the spaceship.

The old television president welcomes the strangers from another world to the United States, telling them that "the latch string always hangs outside," a sentence no one has been able to figure out. At least one pundit thinks that this is a message in code to the Russians, who are still the enemy of every single peace-loving United Statesperson.

The day after the spaceship amusement park announcement, Pablo is at City Hall waiting to see Mayor Herridge about the finalization of the deal to buy Mrs. Mayor Herridge's square mile of land in the barrios. Pablo is obliged to wait for over an hour while all sorts of contractors and builders and architects come and go both in and out of the round office.

As Pablo waits, he flirts with the blond receptionist. Since he has become a man of power in all Duluth as well as in the barrios, he has overcome his lingering fear of blondes—the result of what Darlene and then the Darlene look-alike did to him. Also, his pubic hair has finally grown back, thick and glossy, and the plumed serpent has never been so potent—or so busy.

Finally, the cute blonde says, "You can go in now, Mr. Gonzales."

He gives her a smoldering look from Latin Lover eyes. Then he goes into the round office. Mayor Herridge does not get up to greet him. This is a bad sign, thinks Pablo.

"I have the papers," says Pablo, opening his attaché case.

"Mr. Gonzales," says Mayor Herridge in his richest, most organlike tone. "I'm afraid that the deal is off. Mrs. Herridge has developed a great fondness for those parcels of land in the barrios and, try as I might, I am unable to get her to sell them to you."

Pablo is stunned. "Mayor Herridge, we agreed . . ."

"You and I agreed, son. That's true. And I'm a man of my word. But the deal has always been contingent on Mrs. Herridge's willingness to sell. She has turned us down cold."

"But my dream . . ." Pablo cannot continue.

"There will be other dreams, my boy."

Bill Toomey enters the round office, carrying a stack of polls. "Hi, buddy," he says to Pablo.

"What?" Pablo is reverting to his original inarticulate self.

"Mr. Gonzales understands," says Mayor Herridge to Bill Toomey. "He's been a real brick about all this. So long, son. And remember, the latch string always hangs outside." Mayor Herridge has a fondness for the old television president's stories and sayings, even when he doesn't know exactly what they mean.

Glumly, Pablo goes. He is shattered. On the other hand, if he had known that only that morning Mrs. Herridge had sold her square mile to a developer for the largest sum in the history of Duluth realty, Pablo's rage would have set the barrios—what is left of them—ablaze yet again. But Pablo has no way of knowing that Mayor Herridge has double-crossed him by reneging on a deal that each party had agreed to.

"Well, what's the bad news?" asks Mayor Herridge, with a big smile. He is on top of the world since his total media exposure, not to mention the fortune that he has just made that morning from the sale of the better part of the barrios to the developer.

"Bad," says Bill Toomey, to the Mayor's amazement. "You're trailing Captain Eddie in every part of the town except the barrios, where the kid has made you the frontrunner."

"Jesus!" Mayor Herridge is appalled.

"And I expect that now you've sold that land out from under him, you'll be a dead pigeon in the barrios come the first Tuesday in November, which is next week."

"O.K." Mayor Herridge swings into action. He picks up the intercom. "Get me my mother, the election commissioner."

"What're you going to do?" Bill Toomey really empathizes with Mayor Herridge. But then he will never case to worship the earth the Mayor treads.

"You'll see!" There is a buzz from the intercom. "Hello? Mother? This is your son, Mayor Herridge. Of course I'm all right. Well, *I* didn't think I looked sickly on the *Six O'Clock News*. O.K. Next Tuesday we *don't* count the votes from the barrios . . . What? I know I said to count them but now I'm saying don't count them. Burn them . . . What? I don't care what Bishop O'Malley will say. I've got enough on him with that bingo scam of his to send him up the river. Now. Get this. Got your hearing-aid screwed in? O.K. We're going to count the black vote for the first time. Yoo. I know it's a break with tradition but, God damn it, Mother, we're living in a democracy! You just can't pick and choose who you're going to let vote. So the whole waterfront—all six wards—are going to be counted. Got that? O.K." Mayor Herridge slams down the receiver.

"Why?" asks Bill Toomey.

"It's the last chance I got. I'm in with most of the ministers and I'm also in with you-know-who."

"Big John?"

The Mayor nods. "He can swing three wards all by himself."

"What's the deal?"

"My collaboration in the future," says the Mayor, smooth as silk.

"You think of everything," says Bill, really impressed. "They say he's been working with The Dude lately."

"Who knows?" Mayor Herridge is studying the polls again. "Who cares?"

"I think sometimes The Dude doesn't exist," says Bill, thoughtfully.

"Oh, he exists all right. We'll nail him one of these days."

The intercom sounds. "A Mr. Big John to see your Honor."

"Send him in." Mayor Herridge turns to Bill Toomey. "I better handle this one alone."

"O.K., boss. Now about Project Hot Tamale . . . ?"

"All systems go!"

"Yes, boss." Bill Toomey is gone before Big John, resplendent in a mauve velvet suit and frilled shirt front, sashays into the round office.

"Gimme some skin," says Mayor Herridge, as adept at black talk as he is at white or at brown.

Nonchalantly, Big John flicks his huge mahogany hand across the Mayor's stubby red one. "What's up, my man?" Big John settles into the biggest arm chair, as befits the biggest buck on the waterfront.

"Oh, nothing much." Mayor Herridge pushes the box of good cigars at Big John, who helps himself, liberally. "How was life underground?"

"Kind of lazy. Spent a lot of time out on my cabin cruiser."

"In Canadian waters, I'll bet." They both laugh at this hyperbole. "Now, Big John, I guess you know why I sent for you."

"Election?"

"Bull's eye! Big John, I want you to deliver me the black, the colored *and* the Negro vote."

"But you never count our votes."

"I've told Mother—I called her just now, you can call her if you don't believe me—I told her, 'Mother,' I said, 'we are counting every last nigger vote this year.' "

"How come?"

"Because you're Mr. Big on the waterfront. They'll do what you tell 'em."

"So why should I tell 'em to vote for you?" Big John is enjoying watching The Man sweat.

"Eight dope charges will be dropped and there will no longer be, what there is now, a price on your head."

"Well!" says Big John. "That's mighty tempting. Yes, siree. You'd make me legal?"

"Until you do something illegal again, of course, which you will."

"I could," muses Big John, "start a new slate."

"A new what?"

"That's what Darlene says."

"Darlene who?"

"I don't know what it means either except, I suppose, it means to start all over again. You know? Clean." Big John is in a brown study now. He and Darlene have been dating steadily ever since the night on the cabin cruiser. He feels that he has matured in many, many ways since she has come into his life. He has given up the other foxes. He has even been *considering* going straight, if that is possible. And now it suddenly looks highly possible, as the Mayor, in exchange for a ton or two of votes, is willing to launder his record for him.

"We don't have much time." Mayor Herridge is jumpy.

"O.K." Big John shakes the Mayor's hand firmly. "The fix is in?"

"The fix is in. Go to it, Big John! Get out the vote!"

77

While Big John canvasses the wards along the waterfront, exhorting, pleading, commanding his people to vote for Mayor Herridge, Captain Eddie is out speaking from one end of Greater Duluth to the other. He is running scared, even though he is ahead in the polls. Since Bellamy Craig II is secretly supporting him, the *Six O'Clock News* has entirely reversed themselves—so much so that Leo is no longer allowed to ask him questions in prime time.

"I think we're going to make it, Chief," says "Chico," who goes everywhere Captain Eddie goes in the big trailer with the "Vote for Captain Eddie" stickers all over it and a public address system.

"I don't know." They are now on the waterfront. Captain Eddie is getting ready to speak when he sees another sound truck under the palms. A huge crowd of darkies are all cheering a tall handsome black dude who is telling them to vote for Mayor Herridge.

"Who the hell is that?" booms Captain Eddie over the public address system, which "Chico" quickly switches off.

"It's Big John."

"What the hell is he doing down here? I thought he'd gone underground."

"Well, he's overground now. Captain Eddie, I've been meaning to tell you that Big John's gone and made a deal with the Mayor. All charges against him are being dropped if he delivers the waterfront vote."

"But the Mayor *can't* drop those charges. Only City Court . . ."

"The judge, he's dropped all of them."

"You mean I can't arrest that black bastard and beat the daylights out of him in the suspect's chair in my office?"

"Afraid not, Chief."

Captain Eddie is thinking hard. "The fix is in, I guess. So . . ."

"What do we do, Chief?"

"Why does the Mayor want the black—sorry, 'Chico,' the *colored* vote when we never count it?"

"His mother's going to count it this year. That's all I know."

"I have never realized," says Captain Eddie, slowly, grievously, "until this very moment, the extent to which the city that I was born and grew up in, has become so entirely and irreversibly—amoral."

"Well, Chief, it didn't happen overnight."

"That's for sure. Get me Bellamy Craig II. I want to see him. Pronto."

78

Bellamy and Chloris are seated side by side on the suede sofa of their spacious living room, holding hands and listening to Wayne Alexander read the last pages of "Chloris Craig's" life of Betty Grable.

The beautiful time was at an end. Betty sensed that something was wrong. At her last meeting with Herbert Hoover he had said, "Our platonic love must end. I cannot see you again." As Betty wept, she blamed herself for having lost his platonic love.

Chloris feels a tear beginning to form at the corner of her left eye. She is touched. She is also excited. She will soon know who killed Betty.

Little did Betty suspect that the man she had loved platonically for so many years was not the former President Herbert Hoover but J. Edgar Hoover, the Director of the Federal Bureau of Investigation. Apparently, Betty had not really been listening when they were first introduced on the set of Mother Wore Tights. *She just knew that the famous man's name was Hoover—a name that was sheer magic to her, as everything connected with this forceful bulldog-faced man was magical. J. Edgar, in turn, realizing that she thought he was* Herbert *Hoover, deliberately maintained the imposture. He charmed her, as he charmed all women. She fell so deeply in love with him that she accepted the platonic nature of that love which he insisted on. She never dreamed that the man she saw clandestinely—and even openly where they could be photographed together, something he seemed mysteriously to want—was J. Edgar Hoover, whose long-time live-in lover Clyde Tolson, finally, in a fit of jealous passion, took out that contract on her life which . . .*

"I knew it!" says Chloris. "It was Clyde all along!"

"Betty Grable died," says Wayne, gravely, "because she knew too little."

At that moment, Captain Eddie strides forcefully into the room. "Mr. Craig, I'm going to lose the election. Good afternoon, Mrs. Craig. Mr. Alexander," he adds, remembering his manners.

"Don't fret, Captain Eddie." Bellamy pours the police chief a bullshot. "I know you're disturbed by the decision to count the black vote for the first time . . ."

"Something unheard of in Duluth!" splutters Captain Eddie.

"True. But I have already had the old computer at work on the problem. Without any illegal alien votes and with *all* the black vote—a statistical impossibility—you will win by eleven thousand four hundred twelve votes.''

''Are you sure, Mr. Craig?''

''Yes, I am sure. I think you know me well enough to know that if there is one thing Bellamy Craig II plays, it is hardball and,'' he pauses for dramatic emphasis, ''in the fast lane.''

79

Clive Hoover is seated in his office at The Dude Ranch, skimming the latest installment of *Redbook*.

Beryl, Marchioness of Skye, is waiting, impatiently, in the palace of the Kremlin, for her lover the Emperor Napoleon.

''He will be here any minute now, Milady,'' says one of the loyal guardsmen who travel with Napoleon wherever he goes.

''I smell smoke,'' says Beryl.

''The chimney does not draw properly like everything else in this God-forsaken country.''

''A pity that my late husband, the March of Skye, isn't here. He could fix a chimney in a jiffy.''

The loyal guardsman excuses himself.

Now where, wonders Beryl, did I place the Prince Regent's invasion plan? Of course Beryl knows where it is but this is one of Rosemary's ways of creating suspense. Thinking of Rosemary, Beryl recalls *Duluth*. As she stares out over the golden onionlike domes of the Kremlin, she recalls that she has always meant for Clive to know who The Dude is so that he will know just where, as The Silent Partner, he stands in relation to that alleged wraith or will-o'-the-wisp. But just how, wonders Beryl, noticing that Moscow has caught on fire, am I going to help Clive to find the message that I left for him in my office at The Dude Ranch?

Then Beryl is inspired. "I am certain," she declares in her best Rosemary-ese, "that I left the information that Clive will need in a copy of Thornton Bloom's *Cabala* on the console beneath the two-way mirror in The Silent Partner's office at The Dude Ranch."

This does not come out in *Redbook* quite the way that Beryl would have wanted it to but there is enough meaning left, by the time Rosemary and her hard-pressed copy-editor get through with Beryl's instructions to Clive, to cause him to leap up from his chair, rush to the two-way mirror through which he can see—but not be seen by—the chemin-de-fer players. On the console is a copy of Bloom's *Cabala,* half-hidden by a much-thumbed copy of the *Duluth Social Register.* How Beryl had loved society!

With trembling hand, Clive opens the book. A single sheet of paper falls out. Across the top is written "The Prince Regent's Plan for the Invasion of France." But Beryl has drawn a line through this. Below the line she has written:

"My dearest son, I have a presentiment that I may be withdrawn from this turbulent human drama where I have done my best to play a part—mostly offstage, I confess, in Tulsa, except for the one interlude in the snowdrift—that has been, in many ways, a fulcrum to *Duluth*. Without the empire that I, Beryl Hoover, created in Oklahoma, I would not now be The Silent Partner of The Dude, sitting here in my Art Deco office at The Dude Ranch so recently—and so ungraciously, rumor has it—vacated by Bellamy Craig II. I will not bore you with the details of how I was able to buy him out without ever meeting him, but I did. To this day, he does not know that it was I, Beryl Hoover, who put the arm on him and made him sell. I am now planning to buy a mansion on Garfield Heights within a stone's throw of the Craig mansion or home and I have made up my mind that ere summer ends I will be an intimate of Chloris's and Bellamy's with my own—*our* own, dear boy—box at the opera, where we shall be the cynosure of all eyes on Patrons' Night.

"I have always tried to impress upon you since you were a small large-nosed child that although it is a lot roomier and more comfortable at the bottom, the view is a lot better up here at the top."

Mother is—or was—awfully long-winded, thinks Clive. He hopes that she is enjoying her new situation as mistress of Napoleon. Of course Moscow is burning down, but even so.

"I have now spent a week in The Silent Partner's office—*my* office—going over the books. The Ranch is doing marvelously well. The Casino's take is ninety-nine percent—something I would not have thought possible. But The Dude is a fascinating character. Incidentally, I am the only person in the world who knows his identity. This is one of the reasons, for safety's sake, that I am writing you this note, since my presentiment might very well presage a swift departure from our on-going narrative—not to mention my own entirely happy life, once I was rid of your father, a cousin of J. Edgar Hoover, by the way, who was, and I tell you this in strictest confidence, part-Negro, which explains, somewhat, your nose, which must be restructured once we have settled down on the Garfield Heights."

Part Negro! Clive is stunned. In a sense, his whole life has been, inadvertently, a lie. He flushes when he remembers how rude he has been to the black servitors at The Eucalyptus Club—my brothers, he thinks, sentimentally. On the other hand, there has been no condescension on his part in the various business and social relations that he has had with Dig John, who is threatening to go straight—thereby, cutting off my right arm, broods Clive, returning to Beryl's missive.

"The gambling operations of our far-flung empire are in

A-number-one crackerjack condition and need no altering. But I am concerned about our drug traffic. Good pushers are hard to find since in the end what gets pushed is themselves. The Dude says a darky named Big John is worth cultivating, as he has his own network. I recommend him to you. The massage parlors are doing just average because of our laundry and dry-cleaning bills. I am trying, without much luck, to cut back on the use of towels and sheets, as I believe we are being gouged by Acme Cleaners. It might be worthwhile acquiring a cleaning establishment of our own. The adult bookstores are losing money, as no one can read anymore. So cut back on all books except kiddie-porn—and remember: cassettes and software are the wave of the future.

"I don't know why I am telling you all this, my darling boy, but, as I said, I have this presentiment. By the way, my gun collection—including the matchlocks on loan to the Norton Simon Museum—should be reinsured with Lloyd's. Meanwhile, I have a date tomorrow morning to go with a Sapphic realtor named Edna Herridge to look at a number of palatial homes on Garfield Heights."

Get to the fucking point, Mother, Clive snarls at the letter. And Beryl does. "In the event that you should, suddenly, take my place as The Silent Partner, I think that you should know the identity of The Dude. It is . . ."

Clive gasps when he reads the name. Never in a million years would he have guessed! Also, never in a life that has been almost entirely of Riley, has Clive Hooper been so frightened—or so endangered!

80

The Saturday before the election is a cold crisp bright autumn day. All Duluth is gathered in the Sports Palace, watching the Duluth lacrosse team play the Manitoba Avengers. Duluth is lacrosse-mad.

At the center of one side of the auditorium is the distinguished visitors' section. Opposite the distinguished visitors, the United Greater Duluth High School Band is playing "You Can Win Winsockie," a name that means nothing to anyone but a tune that sets every gorge to rising.

Seated in the front row of the distinguished visitors' section are Mr. and Mrs. Bellamy Craig II and Clive Hoover. As Wayne Alexander is only a newspaperman, he cannot sit down but he is able to walk about the enclosure, a notebook in one hand and a card that says "Press" in the ribbon above the brim of his fedora from Borsalino that sags jauntily to the right where there is no ear to hold it up.

Just outside the distinguished visitors' section Darlene and Big John sit side by side, his arm folded about her very large body. "I want only to be held," she whispers. "That's all a woman ever wants, you know."

"That's all a mature man wants, too," says Big John. Actually, he is bored shitless by all this holding but he does care deeply for Darlene and as soon as the baby is born—tacitly, each wants to make sure that it is black—they will be married and she will quit the police force and he will quit pushing in order to settle down as the wealthy sole proprietor of Acme Cleaners.

Then the band plays "California, Here I Come" and
Captain Eddie makes his big entrance. There is pandemonium. There is also some applause. Captain Eddie is the
frontrunner and, as Leo Lookaloney, who is covering the lacrosse match live, says, "Here comes our popular police
chief, the frontrunner in the contest for mayor of Duluth this
year. The crowd's gone mad for Captain Eddie Thurow."
There are long shots of the auditorium. And then a zoom-
shot of Captain Eddie taking his place in the front row center
seat of the distinguished visitors' enclosure. Captain Eddie
waves to the folks. Three short days from now, he thinks,
and I'm the mayor.

Then the incumbent mayor, Mayor Herridge, makes *his*
entrance, to the strains of Elgar's *Pomp and Circumstance*.
Everyone rises. There are tears in many eyes. A thousand
gorges rise unbidden in a thousand throats. This is *their*
mayor. This is *the* mayor. This is, for better or worse, Duluth personified.

In the hush—broken only by an occasional sob—Mayor
Herridge sits in the throne that has been prepared for him.
Just back of him Mrs. Herridge and the three shavers radiate
mature warmth and supportiveness.

Suddenly, there is the sound of a rifle being fired. Once.
Twice. Three times the rifle is fired.

Captain Eddie leaps out of his seat. Then he falls forward,
with a crash, onto the lacrosse field, where, in a welter of
blood, he lies, dead.

There is pandemonium yet again. Leo Lookaloney is out
of his mind with excitement. He remembers how Dan
Rather was made a television network star for *his* reporting
of what befell an entire nation that fateful day in Dallas.

"Captain Eddie has been shot! You can see the people
going crazy up there! Mayor Herridge is now hiding behind
his throne. Will the killer shoot him next? Is this an illegal
alien plot to destroy the leadership of Duluth?" With that
lucky rhetorical question—or shot in the dark—Leo
Lookaloney gets his secret wish. The very next season he

will go national because at the exact moment that Leo says "illegal alien," Pablo is being arrested, smoking rifle in his hand.

Pablo seems to be in a daze. While he is being beaten up, the standard order of procedure of the Duluth Police Department when making any arrest, the smiling Bill Toomey slips, anonymously, like a ghost or a wraith, into the million crowd. Operation Hot Tamale has been executed.

Finally, the lacrosse match gets underway, and the Manitoba Avengers win. During the booing and general excitement at the end of this exciting game, Darlene screams as labor pains commence. Then she squats, and the waters break.

In less than a trice, right then and there, Big John delivers a healthy baby boy—black as the ace of spades, his son. "My son!" he says to Darlene, handing her the scrumptious yelling package.

"Hold me," Darlene whispers, weakly.

81

Saturday night and Sunday morning prove to be as memorable in the annals of Duluth as any weekend since the last of the wars.

Pablo is interrogated for six hours by "Chico" Jones, the FBI and Mayor Herridge. He swears he can remember nothing. He thinks he must have been hypnotized. But no one is buying that. Then, at dawn, the FBI produces from Pablo's office in the McKinley Tower the composition-class notebook in which Pablo has been writing for the last few weeks but, most damning of all, the clincher in fact, in a locked secret drawer of his desk there is a photograph of the youthful actress Jodie Foster.

The notebook establishes, once and for all, that Pablo is a lone crazed killer who, first, wants to kill Mayor Herridge because he is the symbol of White Anglo oppression in Duluth but then decides to kill Captain Eddie instead so that Jodie Foster will love him in New Haven or wherever it is she is going to school.

Every word of this tragic crazed document was dictated to Pablo, under hypnosis, by Bill Toomey, who has done his work so well that Pablo never once associates Bill in any way with what has happened. For Pablo, everything is a blank. He thinks he must be crazy, that's all.

Needless to say, the world believes that he is what Bill Toomey has set him up to be. The world knows that anyone who keeps both a diary *and* a photograph of Jodie Foster is a lone, crazed killer, eager to kill a television president or mayor or even a chief of police on television.

As the sun begins to touch with roseate tints the black towers of McKinley Tower, Pablo is allowed to see a lawyer.

Pablo can barely keep his eyes open, as both are severely swollen, due to the pounding of the DPD. He has also lost a few teeth. He does not really feel too good.

The lawyer is the best in the business. He is taking on the case because of the publicity. "We're going to have major coverage, kid! Here. Eat this." The lawyer gives Pablo a chocolate bar.

"I don't eat sweets," mumbles Pablo, through broken teeth. "They give you cavities."

"Start eating, kiddo. Because that's our defense."

"What?" Pablo is growing stupid again. But he dutifully gums the chocolate.

"The Twinkie defense never fails. It is well known that too great an ingestion of sugar in the form of Twinkies, Eskimo Pies, bon-bons and cola drinks can derange a person to such a degree that he no longer knows his ass from someone else's. Also, the Twinkie syndrome makes the victim—and you're a victim if I ever saw one—hyperactive as well as hostile and paraonid. Here, start in on these.'' The lawyer gives Pablo a sack of Hershey Kisses. Pablo is feeling really sick now.

''When the mayor of nearby San Francisco was shot to death the former cop who did him in was able to establish that he was so packed with Twinkies and other sugary confections at the time that he could not keep himself from gunning down, repeatedly, the mayor and this fag supervisor. Yet because the court was sympathetic to the tragic fact of his diminished moral sense as well as overweight due to Twinkies, he'll be out on parole in no time at all, munching all the doughnuts and candy floss he wants. Twinkies saved that killer's life and Twinkies will save yours!''

Pablo throws up all over the lawyer. But the lawyer is right. Pablo will get a nine-year term in the Fond du Lac Penitentiary, which means, with good behavior, he'll be out in no time at all.

Duluth will be outraged at the lightness of the sentence but in America the law is the law and that is that, unlike Russia.

82

Clive is holding a plenary session in The Silent Partner's office at The Dude Ranch. Big John is thoughtful. Clive is dynamic. ''You want to go straight. O.K. You *will* go straight—to the top in Duluth. I am authorized to tell you that the Citizens Party is ready to nominate you to take Captain Eddie's place. This means that you will be the next mayor of Duluth.''

"Shit, man, Duluth ain't gonna vote for no nigger," whines Big John, reverting to his Stepin Fetchit number as he sometimes does when he's thoughtful or dubious.

"You'll inherit all of Captain Eddie's votes . . ."

"Clive, I'm a dealer." Big John is now cold and hard as steel. "When Mayor Herridge starts in on my record, I won't be elected nothin'."

"Don't be so sure. In fact . . ." Clive crosses, like a panther or stoat, to the intercom. He presses a button. "Send him in."

Pale and distraught, Mayor Herridge enters the opulent Art Deco office. "Why have I been kidnapped, Mr. Hoover? What is the meaning of this, Mr. John?"

Clive laughs unpleasantly. "You are here, Mayor Herridge, because those of us who care for Duluth—and though I am from Tulsa I feel that I have lived on Garfield Heights all my life—would like to see Big John carry the torch that has just slipped from the nerveless fingers of Captain Eddie . . ."

"May he rest in peace," all three men murmur in unison.

83

But Captain Eddie is not even beginning to rest in peace. One minute he is waving to his people and the next minute a bullet lands in his face like a fist with a ton of solid steel behind it. Captain Eddie sees stars.

Then when the stars go, he finds himself in a strange beautiful room with a marble floor, bejewelled icons on the walls, and a view through a mullioned window of gilded onion-shaped domes set against a sky of flame. The barrios have gone up again, he thinks, in his bewilderment, which is increased by the beautiful woman who throws herself at his feet.

"My Emperor. My beloved! My Napoleon!" She grasps Captain Eddie's knees. Is this a blow job? he wonders in his total confusion.

"Who are you?" he asks, amazed to hear himself talking Spanish—or maybe French. He can never tell the difference.

"Beryl, sire. Beryl, Marchioness of Skye . . ."

But Captain Eddie chuckles. "No, you're Beryl Hoover, the Tulsa crime queen who was all set to move in on Duluth until . . ."

Needless to say, Rosemary will eliminate most of this on her word-processor. She is now in a great hurry to polish off *Rogue Duke* in order to go off on a publicity tour for the Betty Grable revelations that *Cosmo* has dipped deep into its piggybank to pay her for, ruining the "Chloris Craig" book's chances for the big time.

Rosemary Klein Kantor has done it again, the authoress thinks, as she now puts Beryl and Napoleon through their paces in the burning city of Moscow. She even makes a quick raid on *War and Peace*, which has, somehow, found its way into the memory bank. "I knew that piece of junk would come in useful one day," she mutters. "Particularly the fire effects."

Although Rosemary is bound to have the last word, having so many words in her bank, Beryl is able to whisper to Captain Eddie, "How is Clive doing?"

And the Emperor Napoleon, a muscular godlike man, six feet tall, whispers into her ear, "On top of Duluth! A hero . . ."

"He's his mother's son." Beryl is proud.

"What the fuck do we do now?" asks Captain Eddie, who is now two characters at the same time.

"Just relax. We're almost at the end."

The doors are flung open. Five marshals of France enter the room and Captain Eddie is no more. Instead, it is Napoleon Bonaparte who announces in the voice of one born to command, "We shall leave Moscow ere night falls."

"Yes, sire!" they exclaim in unison.

"Here, sire." Beryl gives Napoleon the single sheet of paper that she has risked life and limb to bring him from one end of Europe to the other.

"You stole it?"

"Yes. For you. For France. For love."

Rosemary has a feeling she may be stretching this story out a little thin. She pecks in some more fire effects. Then she is inspired. As Napoleon and Beryl flee the burning city in his carriage, two crazed Russian priests—could one of them be Rasputin?—attack the carriage with flaming torches. As Napoleon stares with admiration and lust, Beryl grabs her trusty matchlock . . .

84

"Go to hell," says Mayor Herridge. He is succinct, as always. "You can't run this nigger for mayor. One word from me and the eight drug or drug-related charges against him will be back on the books and he'll be spending the rest of his life in Fond du Lac Federal Pen."

"Didn't I tell you?" Big John says to Clive. "It's a lousy idea."

"I'm running," says Mayor Herridge. "And I am going to win because this is my town, Mr. Hoover, and if you don't like it you can go back to Tulsa where you belong."

Clive is now at his sumptuous Art Deco Louis XVIII-style desk on which are arranged a number of papers. "Please step over here, your Honor."

With that ill grace which so becomes him, Mayor Herridge crosses to the desk. "What's all this?" he asks.

"Just look," says Clive, feeding his massive flat nose with a toot of cocaine. He likes being part-Negro. In fact, until now, he has never dared go to an Arthur Murray Dance Studio for fear that he might cut a poor figure on the glistening parquet but now he is more than ready to give the ever-elusive but always exciting Terpsichore a whirl, thanks to the jungle beat that he has inherited.

Mayor Herridge is making a series of small noises as if he is having respiratory trouble of an asthmatic or psychosomatic nature.

"You see?" says Clive.

Mayor Herridge nods. He turns to Big John. "I shall withdraw from the race on Monday. On the *Six O'Clock News*. The prime spot, of course. I suggest you announce your candidacy Monday morning at seven o'clock on the *A.M. Show*. There are fewer viewers at that hour but you will get the headline in the second edition of the *Blade*."

With dignity, Mayor Herridge crosses the office and shakes the hand of the stunned Big John. "I wish you all the luck in the world in the round office. But remember this. That's where all the bucks stop—and stay—in Duluth. Gentlemen, I have done my best, according to my lights. I have served Duluth lo! these many years. I have no regrets. I do have one final request."

"Yes, boss?" Big John is a bit too Stepin Fetchit, thinks Clive, irritably. First thing after the election, Clive plans to get him a speech therapist.

"I would like—as would, I believe, my friends in the spaceship, particularly Tricia, a wonderful human being

—or bug, I suppose, is the correct terminology—for you to rename the swamp in the Duluth Woods the Mayor Herridge Swamp.''

''Yes, siree, boss!''

''Thank you, gentlemen. Have a nice evening now.''

With the dignity that ever marked his long and useful public life, Mayor Herridge leaves the office of The Silent Partner.

''Shee-it!'' says Big John.

Clive rounds on him. ''I have just made you mayor of Duluth and I'm damned if I am going to let you talk nigger. You hear me?''

''Yes, Clive. I do. And of course, you're right. I talk like that only when I want to mask my true emotions.''

''Which are?''

''First, profound emotion at his Honor's behavior. I never dreamed that he was such a . . . such a . . . what is the *off-white* word?''

''Mensch.''

''Exactly.'' Big John is now pacing the thickly carpeted floor. ''He made me see that there was another side to him, an unsuspected depth and . . . well, a basic patriotism.'' Big John pauses at the one-way mirror. He looks out at the chemin-de-fer players. ''How the fuck did you get him to quit?''

''Because, Mayor John . . .''

''I'll always be just plain Big to you.''

''Because Mayor Herridge is The Dude.''

''Shee-it!'' Big John's eyes are now all white.

''What emotion are you trying to mask now?'' Clive picks up the telephone book and riffles the yellow pages, trying to find the Ss for speech therapist.

''I was giving way to emotion, I guess. I'm sorry.''

''You're going to a speech therapist, Big John.'' Clive writes down the names and numbers of several plausible-sounding specialists.

''Anything you say. Only how . . .''

"As you know, The Dude wanted to expand to Tulsa and Mother wanted to get her foot in the door here in Duluth. So Mother became The Silent Partner here and The Dude became The Silent Partner in Tulsa. Now, usually, Mayor Herridge works entirely through Bill Toomey—by the way, I think it was Bill who set up that Mexican kid to shoot Captain Eddie."

"How?"

"Hypnotism. And the dumb diary. That was the giveaway. Bill Toomey is CIA. And you can always tell if the CIA is involved in a political murder if the police are able to find a diary that shows just how lone and crazed the patsy of choice is."

"I'll buy that, Clive. But what about the photo of Jodie Foster?"

"Bill likes to keep up with the latest wrinkles, that's all. Personally, I thought it overdone. But it worked. Anyway, during Mother's negotiations with The Dude, she discovered his true identity. Since she had a presentiment that the Mayor was going to do her in because she knew too much—"

"Did he?"

"We shall never know." Clive frowns. "My mother died in a snowdrift with Edna Herridge, a realtor, a Sapphic *and* Mayor Herridge's sister. You see the pattern?"

"I didn't know Edna was a dyke."

"She concealed it, of course. But Beryl—my mother—could always tell. You know, she gave a fortune to the Save Our Children movement . . ."

"Save them from what?"

"Degenerates in the schools, the playgrounds, the bus stations."

"She must've been quite a lady." All in all, Big John is rather glad that he never got to know this particular mother of Clive's.

"She was. But now I am her heir. I am The Dude of Duluth." Clive stands, commandingly, beside his desk. Big John is deeply impressed.

"I guess you're about the biggest crime lord in the country not of Italian extraction, that is."

"Yes," says Clive. "I am."

85

The day of the inaugural of the new mayor of Duluth is bright and sunny. There is a grandstand in front of City Hall, covered with red, white and blue bunting. The Duluth Police Department, the national guard and several units from the nearby secret missile sites march in front of the grandstand where Mayor and Mrs. Darlene Ecks John sit, proudly, surveying the people of their city.

Former Mayor Mayor Herridge sits, with poker-face, in the second row, just behind the new mayor. Mrs. Herridge and the three shavers are supportive, of course, but they cannot control their weeping.

Bellamy and Chloris and Clive sit to the right of his Honor while Wayne Alexander, wearing the card with the word "Press" on it in the band of his Borsalino hat, takes notes; and the KDLM-TV crew records for posterity every moment of this historic occasion.

Although not a single illegal alien has turned out for the occasion, the entire black population is on hand, singing "We Shall Overcome" over and over again to Big John's annoyance. "At least," whispers Darlene in his ear, "they left their transistors home."

"I said I'd break ass if they brought 'em," says his

Honor, who has just fired the speech therapist that Clive engaged for him. Sooner or later, the now totally reformed mayor and the crime lord will be in conflict for the hearts, minds and money of Duluth. But for now all is serene between these two powerhouses.

Clive is pleased with his creation. Also, unknown to Big John, Clive has an extensive file on the new mayor and until the various statutes of limitations run out, he can send Big John to prison whenever he likes. Meanwhile, the bijou house on Garfield Heights is rising in all its multimarbled splendor. Under the sable coat that Chloris holds in her lap, she holds Clive's hand. The Craig marriage has split wide open again.

Mayor Herridge's thoughts are gloomy. Clive has bought him out, at a fraction of what their joint empire is worth. But Clive has the upper hand. To expose Mayor Herridge as The Dude would, simply, destroy the image of Duluth for a generation. Also, Clive moved so quickly that the Mayor was not able to call in Bill Toomey for a problem-solving session.

Easily, Bill's masterpiece of problem-solving was not the shooting of Captain Eddie—standard CIA boilerplate—but the elimination of Beryl Hoover and his own sister Edna, with whom he had never got on. Just how Bill arranged for the car to go out of control in front of the snowbank on Garfield Heights "is my secret" is all that Bill will say, with a chuckle and a wink. Bill is now traveling in West Germany, and Mayor Herridge, good American that he is, hopes that Bill will be able to stop that country from opting out of the only free world we have.

Of all those present at the inaugural, the proudest and the happiest is Darlene. She is now slender, blond, glowing. She is a wife and a mother. She is fulfilled, totally—she is also suffused with that warmth which only maturity can bring. Best of all, as she whispers to her man, her husband, her master yet perfect equal, as he holds her tight during the four-hour parade, "I am the First Lady of Duluth!" This means that the light which shines all round her now will be forever lime.

86

At first Tricia was upset to learn that Mayor Herridge was mayor no longer, but then, as she said to Wayne Alexander, "We can always do business with City Hall no matter what peg they put in the round office." So at least for the bugs from outer space, the changeover proves to be no big deal.

But all is not well in the spaceship—or the world, for that matter. Thanks to Tricia's demented speculations in the international currency markets, the Visitors from the Friendly Skies Corporation is bankrupt. Worse, the world's fragile monetary system is collapsing, while current box-office receipts at the spaceship barely cover the nut, as they say in show business.

The night of Mayor Herridge's dramatic abdication, there is a top-level board meeting in the newly named Mayor Herridge Swamp. Tricia is taking a lot of flak from the other bugs, who have now reverted to their original state, as they tend to do when no human beings are about.

Tricia tries to defend her investment policies. "All in all," she says, "with even the slightest upturn in the world economy—take housing, for instance, already up .01 percent in California—our portfolio will only be half a trillion dollars in the red, a mere third of the Pentagon budget—"

"Stop!" A senior bug raises its mandibles. "You know and we know and even the idiots on this planet know that there will be no economic upturn in this century. Since these fleshy dumb-dumbs are post-industrial and pre-apocalypse, this means—''

''I admit that I made a boo-boo when I put half our portfolio in Mexican pesos as a result of the enticing—even yummy—interest rates on their short-range bond issues, but—''

At that, Tricia is silenced by a furious clattering of mandibles. The senior bug speaks for them all. ''You have failed us. You have bought every pig in a poke that was offered you. We must now fulfill, prematurely, thanks to you, our mission.''

''You're really leaning on me,'' says Tricia, sadly.

''You have given us no choice. What *is* must now be what *was*.''

''So be it,'' whispers Tricia, a broken bug.

87

While Duluth is celebrating, some miles away, in Fond du Lac General Hospital, Pablo is undergoing a series of psychiatric studies to determine to what extent his system has been ravaged by sugar.

Returning, under guard, to his cell after his daily hour with the resident psychologist, Pablo sees a nurse coming down the corridor toward him.

It is Midge. But he does not recognize her, as the only time that they ever met she was a Darlene look-alike who did to him something that no one had ever done or would do again. Thus he had sworn at the time, to the dark gods of his blood.

Midge recognizes Pablo. Midge has often told the other nurses about her encounter with Pablo. Many find that encounter even more hilarious than the circumcision of Calderón.

After Midge sees Pablo in the corridor, she goes straight to the supervisor of the student nurses. Midge is now a full-fledged nurse as well as part-time teacher at the Fond du Lac Training Center for Practical Nurses. After a good deal of telephoning to the resident psychiatrist as well as the warden at the Federal Penitentiary, Midge is given the green light.

The next morning Pablo is delivered by his guards to a small room containing not his boring psychiatrist but a handsome young woman.

"Hello, Pablo," she says, smiling sweetly.

"Hello," he says, feeling for the first time in weeks a stirring of the plumed serpent. How he would like to throw her to the floor! Fantasies of rape and dismemberment flash through his brain.

"As you may know, Pablo, we're training nurses here at Fond du Lac General. Future Florence Nightingales to alleviate human suffering."

Pablo does not understand any of this. He is staring at her breasts, pressed in by the white overstarched uniform. She continues to babble. He continues to stare. He is, again, in contact with the dark gods of the blood.

Then he hears her say, "So put your clothes in this closet."

"What?"

"I said put your clothes in here. For the examination."

"What examination?"

"This one," she says, testily. "Hurry up."

"No way." Pablo opens the door to the corridor. The guard is standing there.

"He's not being cooperative," says Midge to the guard.

Pablo is hurled a number of times against the wall until he promises to be cooperative. Then the guard goes.

Mystified and nervous, Pablo undresses. Is it possible that she wants the plumed serpent as much as it wants her?

As he pulls off his socks, she givea a tinkling laugh. "Look at those corns! Tight shoes, Latin Lover," she says. This strikes a very slight warning bell. But no more. He is still the Aztec Terrorist, the macho symbol of the barrios, more admired than ever because of his murder of Captain Eddie, who is still given credit for the attack of the Darlene look-alikes. Pablo T-shirts are now worn from one end of the barrios to the other.

Pablo is down to his shorts. He is not at all happy about what is going on. He is aware—was made aware for the first time by the original Darlene—that the plumed serpent has a habit of vanishing when nervous. He stalls.

"Come on, big boy," says Midge, a glint in her eye that Pablo does not like.

Slowly, reluctantly, he pulls off the shorts.

Midge is delighted. Originally, some of the nurses questioned her veracity. How could it be so small as to not be visible through the pubic hair? But Pablo does not disappoint her. Nothing is visible except the thick glossy inverted triangle of black pubic hair. Pablo blushes when he sees what she is looking at—or not looking at.

"Good boy," she says, taking him by his wrist. "Come with me."

"What?" Pablo is verging on shock.

Midge opens a door and leads Pablo into a small auditorium with a stage on which there is an examining table. In the audience a dozen student nurses are waiting.

When Pablo sees the girls, he tries to bolt. But Midge holds him by the wrist with a practiced hand. Not for naught has she done time in the violent wards. As she leads the naked Pablo up onto the stage, he desperately tries to cover his manhood with his free hand.

The girls are fascinated. For one thing, they find him cute—also, young! Most demonstrations are performed on the elderly and unattractive.

"Midge has done it again," says one student to another.

"Latin Lover eyes, definitely," says the other.

"Nice muscles, good thighs," says another.

"What's he trying to hide?" asks the most predatory.

Pablo, released from Midge's grasp, stands facing the girls, both hands over his crotch, head down, eyes closed.

"Now, girls, this is Pablo. A murderer. From the Federal Penitentiary. The warden has agreed to lend him to us three times a week indefinitely.

"Hurray!" shout the girls.

Midge picks a razor from a tray of instruments on a table next to the examining table. "Now then, I am going to demonstrate dry hair removal. This takes great patience. And of course, the sharpest of razors."

The girls lean forward. Pablo has understood none of this. "Now, Pablo," says Midge, "put your hands on your head."

"What?"

Midge does not take "what" for an answer. She tears Pablo's hands from his crotch and puts them on top of his head.

There is a roar of laughter. And some concern. "Where is *it?*" "Where are *they?*" "Is he . . . complete?" Pablo is scarlet with shame.

"Oh, it's hiding in there all right," says Midge. "Now watch me, carefully. See how, with my left hand, I grasp the genitals." Pablo leaps a foot in the air as the icy powerful hand collects his hidden manhood. "See how, with the razor in my right hand—if any of you are left-handed, of course, razor and genitals will be reversed—I cut away the pubic hair."

There is a gasp of delight and admiration as Midge, in three strokes, removes Pablo's thick bush—which had taken six months to grow back after her earlier deforestation. Then she steps back so that the girls can get a good look. There is a lot of good-natured raillery.

"Miniature equipment," agrees Midge. "But in good

working order." Then she pushes the tip of Pablo's *membrum virile* back inside of him. He screams. The girls have never seen anything quite like this. Pablo is near collapse.

"Now for the demonstration." She half lifts, half shoves Pablo onto the examining table so that his knees rest on the edge in such a way that the tawny buttocks face the audience.

As Midge lubricates Pablo, he realizes with horror that what the Darlene look-alike did to him in the barrios is going to be done yet again. But he has sworn that he will die rather than submit to this fate worse than any life or even death known to the barrios.

In the end, it takes four guards a half hour to tie down the screaming and struggling Pablo. After the guards have left the auditorium, Midge says, "I feared that he might have this response because I was the nurse who was obliged, last spring, to give him something he had never had before but something he will have to get used to if I am to train you girls properly. This means that, in the weeks ahead, each and every one of you will have a crack at him!"

With fascination the girls watch as Midge gives Pablo the second enema of his life.

Pablo whimpers softly as the warm sudsy water slowly fills him up, drowning for all time the dark gods of the blood and shattering the plumed serpent. The one-time hero of the barrios is now simply a receptacle to be filled up with water by giggling student nurses—then emptied, a dozen times three days a week.

Thus, the dream ends for Pablo. Duluth has prevailed—yet again.

88

Despite a boycott by the Bellamy Craig IIs and the subsequent news blackout, Rosemary Klein Kantor is addressing the Penpersons Club of Duluth at The Eucalyptus Club. As always, she has drawn a good crowd. *Rogue Duke*'s last installment has been much admired while the revelations about Betty Grable are on everyone's lips. *Cosmo* is sold out on every newsstand in Duluth.

Briskly, Rosemary begins with a few of those canards about literature which are always sure-fire in Duluth. "I want us to think and feel for ourselves again. I want educated citizens to start reading what they like, instead of what they are told they must like." There are muffled cheers at this. "Give it to 'em, Rosemary!" exclaims a muffled voice. Rosemary does just that. "I want to see moral, aesthetic, spiritual and intellectual splendor enthroned as the criteria by which we identify true art . . ."

A single "Hallelujah!" sounds like a trumpet blast through the room. There is appreciative applause. Rosemary has caught fire again.

"I want to see the increase of the sum of human happiness, goodness and compassion . . ." Rosemary pauses; she is aware that she is the embodiment of these qualities. So is the audience, as more and more muffled cheers indicate.

". . . re-established as the objective of popular entertainment." How do you do it? wonders Rosemary, with some awe, aware that if a pin dropped in that crowded room, all ears would be deafened, as if Gabriel had let fly on his heavenly horn with a riff.

"A civilization that cannot identify and honor its purposes through its art and its philosophy is a civilization that has forgotten why it exists." Rosemary has now, unfortunately, forgotten what point she was about to make—or remember what the point was that someone else made. To her mill, nothing is not grist. But this doesn't really matter in Duluth, where Tone is all. Anyway, she has lifted the whole thing from a critic of genius.

"A civilization that has mislaid its own justification can never hope to summon the moral energy to grapple—scientifically, intellectually or spiritually . . ." The triad makes Rosemary feel secure. But then she is always excited—preorgasmic—whenever she is about to repeat a metaphor . . . "Grapple with the multitudinous nights that are so rapidly descending." A roar of applause. Who cares that even in Duluth only one night can descend at a time—to be grappled with.

After a few revelations about her long affair with Albert Einstein, the genius, Rosemary tells the penpersons, "You know, it was I who gave Bert the idea for the 'unified field theory,' which, of course, he could never prove mathematically because the old silly never learned to do long division—a secret that we were able to keep from the public all his life and a secret that the estate is still trying desperately to keep you from knowing."

Rosemary pauses to enjoy the look of excited awe on the faces in the audience. There is no lie so great that it will not be taken at face value in Duluth.

Then Rosemary waxes philosophic. "The reason why Bert could not get it all together was not due, as he thought, to his inefficiency as a mathematician. No, it was due to his inability to grasp those fictive laws which control our words and deeds."

There are a number of blank stares. Rosemary knows that this moment is crucial. She must explain to them once and for all what's what and why what's what is what it is. "We are simply formulations of words. We do not live. We are interchangeable. We go on, and we go on. From narrative to narrative, whether in serial form or in those abstract verbal constructions so admired by the French and boola-boola Yale! It is all the same. That was what I told Bert but I could never prove it to him in those days because the word-processor with its memory bank had not yet been invented. But I am now able to *prove* it to you with a hunt and peck, as it were, of my digit."

Rosemary raises her right arm, forefinger pointed toward the south windows through which Garfield Heights can be seen. "I shall now erase Garfield Heights, where so many of my enemies are." Rosemary makes a pecking gesture with her forefinger in the air.

A number of penpersons rush to the south windows of The Eucalyptus Club. There are horrified gasps. Garfield Heights—with all its mansions and houses, its bitter homes and gardens—is gone. There is now nothing at all where once the Heights were.

"I have erased the Heights from *Duluth*," says Rosemary. "Such is the power of fictive law when totally executed by a practiced word-processor. But, of course, Chloris and Bellamy and Clive and all the rest of my enemies are forever a part of that mimetic art which has produced, among so many other wonders, this race that calls itself human, which exists only because I dream it does.

"But should I ever *wake* . . . Well, watch as, one by one, the great eraser that is my finger crosses my imaginary console. There go the woods, the river, the desert, the lake! There goes Darlene, Big John, 'Chico.' There goes poor Pablo, his suffering is at an end. But without that suffering, *Duluth* could never have flourished. Now all are gone. Except for you, penpersons at The Eucalyptus Club . . ."

With a wave of her hand, Rosemary eliminates the last vestige of *Duluth*. Penpersons and club are now replaced by perfect blankness—as far as Rosemary goes.

But Rosemary goes only so far. She has only removed one *Duluth*, the fictional one that *she* knows, a mere drop in the bucket.

Darlene and Big John are standing in their mansion on the Heights, looking out the picture window, when they see what looks to be a huge claw with scarlet nails sweep across the sky.

"That looks like a hand," says Darlene, her trained policeperson's eye noticing that the polish on the nails is from Elizabeth Arden.

"Where's my city?" asks Big John, the mayor, somewhat anxiously. For an instant they are in limbo, erased by Rosemary. But then their *Duluth* is as it was—and is—and will always be, with a minor change or two as the tense goes from present to past to future, a terrifying future that is almost upon them.

Darlene smiles at Big John. "Duluth," she says, "Love it or loathe it, you can never leave it or lose it."

"I always wondered what that meant," says Big John, drawing her voluptuous body close to his own whipcord body.

"It means us, among other things," says Darlene. "It is what it is—forever." Then she whispers, "Hold me."

And Big John, warm and mature at last, says, of his own accord, with absolute sincerity and trust—and no prodding from Darlene—"I will. Because I know now that that is all that a woman wants."

Entangled in one another's arms, neither notices the millions and millions and millions of bugs that are now streaming across the Heights, devouring everything in their path.

The macrocosm of insect life at the heart of the Mayor Herridge Swamp has suddenly metastasized. Secretly egged on by the bankrupt centipedes from outer space, the bugs have taken over Duluth through a mere shift in tense, replacing those temporary interlopers, the human race.

Now Tricia sits at the late Rosemary Klein Kantor's word-processor and with her mandibles she proceeds to tap out a Duluth totally unlike *Duluth* or even ''Duluth.'' Mandibles clacking with glee, Tricia describes the metamorphosis from present-day human *Duluth* to the myriapodal one, simultaneous with the other, yes, but equally immutable and autonomous.

89

Duluth! Tricia taps, love it or loathe it, you can never leave it or lose it because no matter how blunt with insectivorous time your mandibles become those myriad eggs that you cannot help but lay cannot help but hatch new vermiforous and myriapodal generations, forever lively in *this* present tense where you—all of you—are now at large, even though, simultaneously, you are elsewhere, too, rooted in that centripetal darkness where all this was, and where all this will be, once the bright inflorescence that is, or—now for that terminal shift, Tricia; press the lever!—*was* present-day human Duluth has come to its predestined articulated and paginated end. Yes. *Duluth!* Loved. Loathed. Left. Lost.

About the Author

Gore Vidal was born in 1925 at the United States Military Academy, West Point, where his father was the first instructor in Aeronautics. After graduating at seventeen from Phillips Exeter Academy, he enlisted in the Army and served in World War II from 1943 to 1946. At nineteen, while stationed in the Pacific, he wrote his first novel, WILLIWAW. His other novels include IN A YELLOW WOOD; THE CITY AND THE PILLAR; THE SEASON OF COMFORT; A SEARCH FOR THE KING; DARK GREEN, BRIGHT RED; THE JUDGMENT OF PARIS; MESSIAH; JULIAN; WASHINGTON, D.C.; MYRA BRECKENRIDGE; TWO SISTERS; BURR; MYRON; 1876; KALKI; and CREATION. In the fifties Vidal wrote plays for live television and films for Metro-Goldwyn-Mayer. One of the television plays became the successful Broadway play VISIT TO A SMALL PLANET. He has written four other plays: AN EVENING WITH RICHARD NIXON; WEEKEND; ROMULUS; and THE BEST MAN, which ran for two seasons on Broadway. His books of essays include ROCKING THE BOAT; REFLECTIONS UPON A SINKING SHIP; HOMAGE TO DANIEL SHAYS; MATTERS OF FACT AND OF FICTION; and THE SECOND AMERICAN REVOLUTION. Vidal wrote one volume of short stories, called A THIRSTY EVIL.